WELCOME
TO THE ZOO

WELCOME TO THE ZOO

Robert Beane

Library of Congress Control Number:		2016913667
ISBN:	Hardcover	978-1-5245-3596-4
	Softcover	978-1-5245-3595-7
	eBook	978-1-5245-3594-0

Print information available on the last page.

Rev. date: 08/17/2016

To order additional copies of this book, contact:
Xlibris
1-888-795-4274
www.Xlibris.com
Orders@Xlibris.com
746811

MEMORIES

Welcome to the Zoo

Firefighting in an old New England city during the '60s, '70s, and '80s

ACKNOWLEDGMENTS

To Bill Yates

We looked at each other over the destruction and debris of many fire scenes and years later you pushed me to "get your stories down on paper, before you die and they are lost forever."

To all of those Old Guys
You taught me well. Thank you all.

To my Mary
Having you in my life has been the best gift that I have
ever been given by the Great Spirit.

To Joey
I will always remember you, man!

To Dennis Smith
Reading your books inspired me to write mine.

Please accept my heartfelt acknowledgment and deep admiration for the past and present members of the United States Marine Corps. Please know that this following statement is a salute of honor to you all and not a belittlement of you at all.

To paraphrase one stanza of the Marine Corps Hymn:

And when he gets to heaven
To Saint Peter he will tell,
One more firefighter reporting, sir
I've served my time in hell.

To every one of you firefighters all around this world, now and in the past, I salute you all, my brothers. And I leave to you all this quote from my mentors when I went on the job:

"Ya done good, kid."

The well-known radio commentator Paul Harvey recorded a short video about firefighters, which sometimes asked the question, Why do people become firefighters?

When I was interviewed for a job as a firefighter, I was cautioned that the interview would be about thirty minutes long. It was a Thursday afternoon. I entered the office and sat down at the table facing four Fire Department officers.

The first officer to speak asked me, "Why do you want to be a fireman?"

Without stopping to think about it. I immediately responded, "I want to save people's lives and property."

The officer folded up his paper, turned to the others, and said, "He's hired."

Turning back to me, he said, "Can you start next Monday morning?"

I told him, "No. I need to work out a notice at my present job. It will take me two weeks."

He spoke again, "Can you start on Monday after next?"

I answered, "Yes, sir."

My interview took less than five minutes. That's why I became a fireman.

I have received many well-worded compliments in my lifetime, and a few of them stay in my mind. On duty at a fire station one day, I was nursing an injured wrist. I had been favoring this injury for about three weeks. I finally went to see a doctor for the discomfort. He examined my wrist and ordered X-rays. When they were read, he told me that my wrist was broken. I replied, "No, it's not."

He responded, "I'm the doctor and yes, it is. It has three broken bones in it."

We went back and forth like this three more times. Finally, I said, "Okay, what do we do now?"

He said, "We splint it."

I replied, "Okay."

At this moment, he gave me a great backhanded compliment when he turned away from me and headed out the door of the examining room. He muttered, "Goddamned firemen."

We are a unique bunch of people, all of us. When normal people are running away from burning buildings or emergency scenes, we are those people who run toward them, to reach out to help others in need.

"A zoo is where the animals hang out."

This was on a two-inch round pin that I kept
attached to my leather fire helmet.

Chapter One

One of my heroes is the author Samuel Clemens (Mark Twain). In my reading his works, I have found that he considered himself to have the gift of being an observer of humanity and a storyteller. Some of his stories were dark, and some were humorous. Some of his stories disturbed people because they told of what people do to each other (man's inhumanity to man). I consider myself to have those same gifts. I observe what goes on around me, and I tell stories. Some of the stories are dark, and some of them are humorous, but they are all about people and what they do with each other, for each other, and to each other.

The chapters in this book are all short chapters for a simple reason. If a fireman is reading this book, in the fire station, then short chapters are a good read because you only have time to read just a couple of pages before you're headed out the door again.

This story is about a city fire department. A city fire department is an entity. It has a life of its own. When firemen speak of the FDNY, the Fire Department of New York; the Boston Fire Department; the Los Angeles Fire Department; the Chicago Fire Department; the London Fire Department; the Singapore Fire Department; or the Moscow Fire Department, these departments have evolved to the point where they are their own entity. This story will speak of the evisceration of the Portland Fire Department, the cutting out of its heart and soul. Today the Portland Fire Department, Portland, Maine, is a city fire department, but it is no longer an entity. It no longer stands on its own, as a being. Today it is just another city department.

At a reunion of Portland firemen a few years ago, one of the men said that we, those of us who worked from 1960 to 1990, "We were the generation that burned the city." We were the generation that experienced multiple building fires weekly and sometimes daily. Some of these times would later be nicknamed "urban renewal." We experienced a time when we had working fires almost every day of the week.

In talking to guys who work today in the Portland Fire Department, I have found that fires today are way down. I have been told that today they receive maybe twenty-five working fires per year. One man told me that his last working fire was eighteen months previous from where we were talking. We used to have an average of twenty-five working fires a month.

For those of us who were there, a working fire is any fire that involved one room or more. For any fire of one room or smaller, the Officer on the first truck on the scene would frequently call the dispatcher on the radio and say, "This is Engine _____, to Fire Alarm. We can handle this. Send everyone else back." In the event that the volume of fire was larger, for instance, in the case of more than one room, i.e., two rooms, an entire apartment, an entire floor, an entire house, or an entire building, the officer on the truck would start the stepping-up process of alarms. "This is Engine___, to Fire Alarm. Strike me a second alarm on this fire." We also had dozens of small fires during the average week: dumpsters, car fires, false alarms, grass fires, mattress fires, appliance fires, any small fire, or any emergency medical call, in any given month. Depending on the time of the year, this could mean twenty to forty or up to more than one hundred calls per truck per month. We used to have mattress fires, in "roach hotels," where we would get the call, arrive, get in, put it out, clean it up, and be back at the station cleaning up the truck in less than an hour. Sometimes, because we had a meal on the stove or because something good was coming up on television (*Gomer Pyle, Bonanza, Star Trek*), we wanted to get back quick to watch it. At that time. Engine Four and Engine Five were experiencing four thousand to five thousand calls a year. Rescue One had more than five thousand. Ladder Six had more than 3,500 calls a year. Engine Four and Ladder Six would later earn spots on the United States Fire Service's list of busiest fire trucks in the United States during these demanding years.

These stories are about the Portland Fire Department in Portland, Maine; the fires; and the men. Some of these men were the very best; some of them very, very good; some were moderate; and some should have been doing some other kind of work somewhere else—maybe mowing lawns or flipping burgers in a fast-food store.

Firefighting is so very akin to combat. This battlefield, though, is indoors, inside an enclosed structure, with firefighters doing battle with a raging beast, "The Orange Demon." This demon consumes everything in its path. Living or not. And it moves in predictable ways. Everything known to man will burn, if it gets hot enough.

The film director Ron Howard came very close to showing us what firefighting is like in his film *Backdraft*. But no film can truly show you what it's like inside a burning building. That film would just show a dark gray or black view. It cannot show the heat. This heat can range in temperature from two hundred degrees at the close floor level to four hundred degrees at waist height to seven hundred degrees at head height and upward of twelve hundred degrees at ceiling height. A film cannot show the lack of orientation because of the heavy smoke, an atmosphere in which you cannot see your hand if you hold it up in front of your face. An environment in which the firefighter is trying to move quickly but are burdened by carrying an extra sixty-three pounds of equipment and protective clothing on their bodies. You are in an environment where the enemy can be all around you at the same time—below you under the floor and above you in the ceiling, running upward through the walls. You are in an atmosphere where you cannot see the doors or the windows because of the smoke unless you place your face down onto the floor and look around to find the doorsills. You cannot see the furniture. And you may be desperately trying to find out if there is a victim someplace on the floor or on a piece of furniture. And they can be almost anywhere. Children may be found near a water source or where they instinctively feel safest. Adults can be anywhere.

I have been asked many times, "Would you do it again if you had a choice?" My answer is always an immediate *yes*. There are only a very few fields of endeavor that match the fire service. Those are law enforcement, the military, and those who work in emergency medical care.

These are the people who work the streets. The term *camaraderie* is sometimes overly used and abused by people who are not in these lines of work. And they don't have a clue what it really means. But to those of us who work in these fields of endeavor, it means so much. When you repeatedly go into life-threatening situations, where there is a good chance that you may lose your life, you learn to depend upon and trust that person beside you to be there for you, to watch your back. And that person knows that you are there for them. This bond, this love for each other, develops into a brotherhood, and it sometimes lasts for a lifetime. Even today, when I have been retired for more than twenty-seven years, there are men out there who, if they called me today for anything, I would drop whatever I'm doing and go to help them. The only question asked would be "Where are you right now, and what do you want me to bring with me?"

For those of us in the fire service, we have a truly unique reputation. Firefighting is the only profession where you are allowed to go into someone's home, and the people don't question that you should go there. If a cop knocks on the door, people will ask, "What do *you* want here?" If someone in a suit knocks on the door, people ask, "What do you want?" If a fireman knocks on the door, people open the door and let them in. Firefighting is the only profession that, if you are anywhere in the world, in any city in the world, and you walk up a street to a fire station and introduce yourself as a fireman from somewhere else, you will be immediately welcomed in and invited to sit down and talk. And the questions will most likely include these: "What kind of trucks do you have? How many firemen do you have? What kinds of fires do you have? Do you want some coffee? Do you want to eat lunch/dinner with us here?" Anywhere in the world! This is the brotherhood of firefighters that exists everywhere! During the days of the Iron Curtain, there were American firemen who visited fire stations that were located in cities behind that Iron Curtain, and they were welcomed into the station as brothers. I know a few Portland firemen who have visited fire stations in Havana, Cuba, and in Russia, at the height of the Cold War. Their only comment was that "they're just like us and the food wasn't bad."

When I was teaching firefighting classes, I would remind my students (volunteer firefighters, career firefighters, fire brigades, and those who were trying to become firefighters, men and women) that when they committed themselves to crawling down some smoky hallway to try to rescue someone's child or someone's relative, that they were doing the same thing that firefighters everywhere did. And that act, that willingness and action, made them a member of this brotherhood.

You never know what impact your words or actions have on other people around you. But once in a while, you are reminded that some actions that you take do affect other people. One of my fondest memories from teaching firefighting classes was the day that a fireman approached me on the Southern Maine Technical College Campus and said, "Hi, Bob. Do you remember me?"

I replied, "No. I'm sorry, but I don't."

He then said, "I was in your class here at Southern Maine Technical College last year."

I replied, "Yes, I remember that class. We had a good time."

He then said, "I want to thank you. A few months ago, I was fighting a fire in a building in my hometown, and I got disoriented and trapped inside the burning building, and I remembered what you taught me in your class, the part about how to get out, if you become disoriented inside a fire building. I got out of the building okay. I just want to thank you for what you do with these classes."

That's one of my favorite memories from teaching firefighting classes.

I also taught my students this basic rule in firefighting: The fire is a living thing that eats fuel and breathes air to survive. It consumes everything in its path, and for the fire, there is no difference between a wooden building, a car, a dumpster, or a human being. The fire will consume it all. If anyone ever tells you that there are some things that can't burn, remind them that they can watch any film, anywhere, about volcanoes. That dark red burning liquid that they see flowing in streams down sides of the hills away from a volcano is melted rock. Everything burns. All you have to do is to get it hot enough. Don't ever turn your back on the fire. If you give it a chance, it will reach out and kill you. Within the fire service, the fire is called the "Demon" for a reason. Those of us who have been up close and personal with the "Demon" know this to the depths of our heart. I have scars on my body because the fire reached out and touched me. But it didn't get me.

CHAPTER TWO

Portland, Maine

The City of Portland (not one of the other Portland) is located on the southeast coast of Maine. It is perhaps the most beautiful city in the United States that I have ever been in. It is located on a north latitude that places it about sixty miles north of the meridian (forty-four degrees, forty minutes, north latitude), that is the boundary between America and Canada. If that meridian continued in a straight line to the Atlantic Coast, then most of Maine and about one quarter of New Hampshire and Vermont would be located in New Brunswick Province, or Quebec Province, Canada.

Portland is situated on a peninsula, and on three-fourths of the area around the city are two bays. The city is surrounded on three sides by saltwater. There are four bridges over the water and three more bridges over railroads. Portland is also the location for the junction of three railroad lines and an international railroad connection: the old Maine Central Railroad, the Mountain Railroad to North Conway NH, and the old Canadian National Railroad that connects to Quebec Province and to New Brunswick Province, Canada.

Portland's working waterfront is three and one-half miles long and periodically floods out from extreme high storm tides. (This has already become a concern because of global warming and the rise in tidal levels.) There are two highway systems that pass through the city. Portland's main street is Congress Street. This street starts at the eastern end of the city (the Eastern Prom area overlooking Casco Bay). Congress Street then heads southwest, passing through the city and continuing past the Portland International Jetport for total of about eight miles to the southwestern end of the city at the city limits with Westbrook and South Portland. The major avenues in and out of the city are (1) Washington Avenue starting at Munjoy Hill and ending at the city limits with Falmouth; (2) Forest Avenue (starting at Congress Street near Congress Square and ending at the city limits with Westbrook); (3) Brighton Avenue, starting at the University of Southern Maine Campus and ending at the city limits with Westbrook; and (4) Congress Street. It is possible, on a clear day, to stand on either the Eastern Prom or the Western Prom, look at the saltwater harbor of Portland, turn completely around, and see Mount Washington (the highest mountain peak in New England at approximately 6,288 feet), located eighty miles away. Portland covers an area of approximately thirty-five square miles.

Portland is one of the oldest cities in New England. The city was first settled as a fishing community almost 350 years ago. These old New England cities are all patterned after European cities, and they don't really have any grid pattern to the street layout. Many of the streets are narrow (they were originally cobblestone paved). The streets are laid out in no particular pattern. Streets were added as they were needed, where they were needed. Portland currently has approximately eight hundred streets, avenues, boulevards, alleys, courts, and circles. This makes for a major factor in the firefighter's learning curve. He has to memorize the streets in the response area where he is stationed, depending upon which truck he is assigned to. Frequently, the firefighter has to listen especially carefully to how the name of the street is pronounced to him by the Fire Dispatcher. We have State Street and Tate Street; these two streets run parallel to each other. We have Park Street and Clark Street; these two streets are parallel to each other and four blocks from each other. We have Tyng Street and King Street; these two streets are five miles from each other. One man died one night because the ambulance driver went to Tyng Street instead of King Street on a call for a heart attack. Mistakes have been made, and these have caused delays in response time. Our average fire response time in Portland, Maine, is three minutes. I was driving for a lieutenant one night, and I headed for Bay Street when I should have been headed for Ray Street. These two streets are one mile from each other. (At 2:00 a.m., from a sound sleep, it's easy to get confused.) The lieutenant just turned to me and quietly, but bluntly, asked me, "Where in the f—k are you going?" I quickly turned the truck around and headed to the correct location.

Some streets are no longer in existence. When I was a child, in the neighborhood that I grew up in, the lower West End neighborhood, there was a dirt street named Horseshit Alley, which originally led to a horse stable. This street no longer exists. It is now part of a low-income housing project. Franklin Street is now Franklin Arterial. Lower Paris Street is now a parking lot. Hampshire Street is now gone.

These narrow streets become really interesting in the winter months. Portland, like all New England cities, has snow accumulation problems, with an average annual snowfall of more than eighty inches of that white, frozen stuff. These narrow streets quickly become narrow to the point where getting trucks through is a challenge. Add to this the problem of parked vehicles; during the day, they're parked on both sides of the streets. I've had some really close encounters. I drove Engine Four through a tight area one afternoon, on an emergency response (Granite Street near the University of Southern Maine campus), with parked cars and snow banks on both sides, and as I looked over at the lieutenant, he had his eyes scrunched shut so that he couldn't see me if I hit anything. The guys on the jump seats later told me that I had less than two inches of clearance on each side. But, hey, I got through, and I didn't hit anything. It becomes a learned skill.

The narrow streets become worse with the buildup of snow and ice on the street surface. Things get really slippery, really fast. During the winter, the dispatchers would be instructed, as soon as it starts to snow, to call all the trucks and tell them to put the chains on. One dispatcher did this task one night, and he must have been having a brain cramp. He called all the trucks to put on the chains. His calls included Engine Seven. When he called Engine Seven and told them to put on their tire chains, well, it became a little bit of a problem and the talk of the entire Fire Department. In the Portland Fire Department, Engine Seven is the Fireboat. The only way they could put on tire chains, would be to go into a dry dock and then try to find the tires on the bottom of that fifty-two-foot steel boat hull.

CHAPTER THREE

Memorable friends
Phil R.

Phil R. was the best engine driver (chauffeur/wheelman) I ever knew. He drove Engine Six and later Engine Three. Phil was a wiry guy, about five foot ten, with a cigarette smoking habit (two packs a day) that would eventually kill him. He had a great sense of humor, and he had a flattop haircut, a leftover from the sixties. He was a good man at a fire scene. He was driving Engine Six out of Bramhall Station one winter day. There were four of us on the truck. At that time, we still rode two firefighters on the tailgate of the truck. It was a snowy day. As we responded to a call, Phil turned left onto Congress Street, two blocks down to Weymouth Street, and then a right turn down Weymouth Street. From Congress Street to Park Avenue, Weymouth Street is only three blocks long. But it's a steep downhill street, from Congress Street down to Park Avenue, and on this particular day, it had a covering of about six inches of fresh snow over frozen slush. As he turned onto Weymouth Street and started down that hill, Phil looked ahead of the truck and saw a passenger car stopped at the bottom of the street, at the intersection with Park Avenue. As he tried to slow down, the truck went into a slide. The truck was sliding partially sideways down this steep hill toward a stopped car full of people. Those of us on the tailgate were getting ready to jump from the truck and hoping to land in a snowbank. As I said, Phil is the best that I have ever met, and he proved it once again as he played the brakes, the throttle, and the steering and brought Engine Six around, straightened it out, and passed that car with inches to spare and proceeded on toward the alarm call. All of us on the truck let out a whoosh of breath and started to breathe normally again.

Phil did have one habit that drove me up a wall, and sometimes this habit caused me to call him and tell him to do some things to himself that are physically impossible. Dozens of times when I was driving an engine company to a fire that Phil was already at, he would call me on the radio and tell me, "You have a hydrant at (such and such location). Lay in a feeder line to me."

And this was usually five, six, or seven hundred feet or up to one thousand feet of large-diameter (3½" canvas or, later, 4" plastic) water hose. After I had done so, I would look up the street past his truck and see another hydrant fifty feet beyond him. And then he would just laugh and say, "Well, now. Look at how much hose that you have to pick up." But he was the best, and I learned so much from him. And he became a good friend. I became a chauffeur myself, and I had the reputation of being really good at what I did. Thank you, Phil, for showing me how to do it well.

We all had to get creative to deal with the winter weather here in Portland. Iced-up fire scenes, frozen hose lines, frozen ladders. I have been on more than one fire scene where the frozen hose lines were brought back to the station in frozen solid fifty-foot lengths and thawed out before they could be hung up to dry. Or standing under a hot water shower nozzle, with your fire gear on, and waiting for the ice to melt off your gear and to thaw it out enough to be able to unsnap the buckles and take it off. Or being soaked to the skin from a fire scene and riding back to the station in an open cab truck and watching your gear turn to ice and freeze to the seat, as you're sitting on it.

I was the first man on the Portland Fire Department to grow and keep a mustache. This would become an almost universal symbol of firefighters. And I have watched it ice up at a lot of fire scenes. And sometimes I watched and waited and hoped that the mustache hairs wouldn't break off from the ice buildup on them.

CHAPTER FOUR

These old cities

Those of us in the New England cities have to deal with some unique conditions because of both the design of these cities and the conditions that we encounter within them. The son of a good friend of mine went to school at the University of Oklahoma, in their fire engineering degree program. On one of his trips back home, he commented, "The West Coast is progressive, the East Coast in aggressive, and in the middle, it's a sandbox."

Portland, Maine, has a city water system that is the envy of most fire departments in the eastern half of the United States. Our water system is gravity-fed from the second-largest lake in the state of Maine, which is filled with lakes and rivers. It comes to us through two forty-eight-inch main lines and one thousand miles on branch piping. These pipes are both steel and concrete construction. There are reports of a very small self-propelled scooter that every few years is used to inspect these pipelines from the inside.

We have fire hydrant static pressures that range in scale from 140 pounds per inch on the lower streets, near the water front, to twenty pounds per inch on the highest streets, the tops of the hills. We have hydrant pressures that have to be gate-valved down to be pumped through fire attack hose lines. We have hydrants that are plugged into water mains (four feet in diameter) that cannot be pumped dry. These hydrants have very low static pressures, but the available water supply is in the hundreds of thousands of gallons. I have also seen, during a water system replacement program, the removal of sections of wooden water pipes from beneath the city's streets. And in one area of the city, when I was first on the job, we were pumping at a fire scene and collapsed residential water heaters in some apartments that were nearby.

Portland is home to two major hospitals (there used to be three) and to one of the campuses of the University of New England. It is home to the University of Southern Maine; the Portland School of Art; the Casco Bay High School and MECA, the Maine College of Arts; and more than a dozen other specialty schools.

The city also has the dubious distinction of having more bars and restaurants per capita than any other city in America, except San Francisco, at last count more than four hundred in the Greater Portland area.

The city's buildings range in age from those built before the 1866 Great Portland Fire to those that have been built as recently as the last few months.

In the July 4, 1866, Great Portland Fire, the peninsula area of Portland lost more than 75 percent of its buildings totaling more than 1,500 residential and commercial buildings. This fire was the subject of a recent book by Don Whitney and Mike Daicey, both retired Portland firemen. The Portland Fire Department as a full-time career fire department dates from the after effects of this fire.

The city's buildings range in architectural style from stick-built, wood-framed, balloon-constructed, slate-roofed, Victorian-era homes, with all the little hidden nooks and crannies, including hidden rooms for escaped slaves, to multi-storey masonry-constructed buildings, to heavy-timber commercial buildings with forty-foot-high interior ceilings, to contemporary high-rise office or residential buildings.

One area of the city is all brownstone-style buildings (left over from the great age of sailing ships of shipping companies) that have been renovated into dozens of small businesses, restaurants, and bars, the kind of area that has a rapid turnover of businesses and is in a kind of constant flux of change. These buildings sometimes have interconnected cock lofts or cellars. These buildings also include a lot of small residential occupancies, mostly on the top floors. Today this is called "the Old Port area" and is the scene of a lot of controversy within the city administration because of problems with thirty or forty bars crammed into an eight-city-block area. The Portland Police Department is kept very busy here in the evenings and on the weekends.

Portland experiences a true four-season climate. It has a mountainous boundary to the west, the White Mountains (the northern extension of the Appalachian mountain chain). To the east, it has the North Atlantic Ocean. Saltwater temps in this ocean area range between twenty-five degrees Fahrenheit in the winter, to about sixty-five degrees Fahrenheit in the Summer. Portland's weather varies from summertime high temps of eighty to one hundred degrees Fahrenheit and wintertime low temps between zero to minus twenty degrees. Portland experiences the occasional hurricane and the regular northeast blizzards, and in the summer months, the occasional northeast gales, with winds in excess of sixty miles per hour. (Just a side comment: there is *no*, and there never has been, a word spelled *noreaster*. In Down East Maine, the word is *north easter,* pronounced "nawth easta.") This term indicates the presence of very strong winds that are coming from the northeast, from out over the Gulf of Maine. The only people here in Maine who say "nor easter" are people who are not from Maine. They are imports from somewhere else. Portland has an average annual snowfall of about eighty inches. We experience below-freezing temps from mid-November through mid-April. Our spring season is beautiful, and our fall season is a time of such gorgeous colors that people travel to Maine from hundreds of miles away just to see the trees in their fall foliage colors.

Portland was famous for many years as the northernmost, ice-free seaport on the Atlantic Coast of the North American continent. For about 150 years, Portland saw material unloaded from or loaded onto ships and then transported, by barge and by rail, throughout most of Northeastern North America, including much of Eastern Canada and as far west as the Great Lakes area. Portland has a fascinating history including being a major destination of the underground railroad during that period leading up to the American Civil War.

CHAPTER FIVE

The Portland Fire Department

When I first went on the job on the Portland Fire Department on May 15, 1967, we had 320 men. This was twenty-two years after the end of World War II. Most of these men had joined the fire department directly after coming home from the war. These men were military vets, and I was accepted by them because I am also one. There were a very few of them who had used the excuse of being firemen to dodge the military draft during WWII. The former military guys hated them and were frequently heard to say some comments about "those fucking draft dodgers."

We had eight fire stations. We had the following engines and ladder trucks: Engine One, a Howe with a 1,000-gpm pump (Munjoy Hill Station); Engine Eleven, a Maxim with a 750-gpm pump; Ladder Three, a 75-foot Seagrave aerial ladder (Ocean Avenue Station); Engine Eight, a Mack, and Ladder Four, a 75-foot Seagrave aerial ladder (Allen Avenue Station); Engine Nine (Arbor Street Station); Engine Three (Stevens Avenue Station); Engine Four, an American LaFrance; Engine Six, a Seagrave pumper; Ladder Six, a 100-foot Seagrave aerial ladder (tractor-trailer with a tiller) (Bramhall Station); Engine Five, an American LaFrance; Ladder One, a 75-foot American LaFrance aerial ladder; Rescue One, a converted bread truck (Central Station); and Engine Seven, a 1952, 52-foot boat with a 7,500-gpm capacity pump (Fireboat) (Peaks Island Station).

Engine Three Station and Bramhall Station covered the airport on an on-call basis, where an old military surplus MB5 truck was parked unattended. It was parked in an unheated garage, with a partial door (the door opening was ten feet high, but the door itself was only eight feet tall), and the bottom two feet were exposed to the weather. All the apparatus were open cab trucks (with no roofs). All were gasoline engines with manual transmissions. Our largest pump capacities were 1,000-gpm pumps. Our tallest ladder was Ladder Six, at one hundred feet.

We ran with four to six men on each truck. We protected a city with a nighttime population of sixty thousand people and a daytime population of about two hundred thousand. This included a large airport, three and one-half miles of working waterfront with a major shipping terminus for dry cargo and a petroleum product tank farm, a major railroad hub, and a major transportation hub. Our tallest building was ten floors high. We had three large hospitals. We were recognized as the largest American city north of Boston. We worked for a salary of $95 for a sixty-two-hour workweek, or about $1.53 an hour. This was when the federal minimum wage was $1.25 an hour. About one year later, the minimum wage would go to $1.50 an hour, and our pay scale would not change for another year. So we were working for the minimum wage. The retirement policy was that you had to work until age sixty, no matter how many years of service time that you had to work. We had to buy our own dress uniforms from Benoit's Clothing Store in Portland, at a cost of more than $250 (almost a three week's salary). Our work uniforms were dungarees with chambray shirts. Our firefighting clothing consisted of a rubber coat, rubber boots (with no steel toes, steel shanks, or insulation), and helmets made of plastic.

On one particular summer day, a fire equipment salesman came to Central Fire Station to sell an improved fire helmet made of fiberglass to our Fire Chief. Being the kind of firemen that we were, while this salesman was talking to the Fire Chief, we took the new helmet and put it in the station's refrigerator freezer. When the salesman came out of the fire chief's office, we retrieved the helmet and dropped it onto the floor of the station, where it shattered in four or five pieces from being frozen. No sale that day. We had no self-contained breathing apparatus, no gloves (we had to buy our own gloves), and we used leather mittens with wool inserts during the winter months; we had no eye protection, no hoods, no hearing protection, no personal alarms, and the only radios were on the trucks. We had no personnel communications equipment. Fire scene communications tended to be information hollered out of a window down to the truck where the nearest radio was located. Even today my voice tends to be soft because of the damage to my vocal cords from all the yelling.

The Portland Fire Department had a command structure that started with the Fire Chief, Deputy Fire Chief (this occasionally changed to District Chief and then back again), fire captains, fire lieutenants, firefighters. Administration also consisted of Fire Prevention Staff (this varied dramatically sometimes from two to six men, and men who were on extended sick leave were placed in the Fire Prevention Bureau) and Fire Dispatchers.

The Fire Prevention Staff, when I first started, numbered four men. It would later be reduced to one man. The Fire Prevention Bureau's efforts were and are mostly disregarded and shrugged off. But the numbers tell the true story. When I first started, the Portland Fire Department had not lost a person in a fire for more than twelve years. As I worked, and as the Fire Prevention Bureau was reduced in manpower, those numbers changed. They peaked at a point when we were losing three to four people per year to fire. The positive changes didn't begin until some years after we started an aggressive Fire Prevention Program focusing on fire detectors and fire alarm systems. These patterns of fire safety cycles take decades to go through its swings.

There was no Rookie/Drill School when I started on the job. I was on the job for two years before a Drill School was started, and those of us who had been hired during that time had to attend it anyway. It would be another five years before physical training drills would be initiated. It would be around 1980 before physical baseline tests would be implemented and physical training would become mandatory.

During my career, the Portland Fire Department Fire Alarm Sequence was as follows:

A still alarm (transmitted by telephone to the station or by radio directly to the truck) calls out one truck. This was usually for emergency medical service calls or for small fires that could be handled by one truck and four to five men, for example, an accident scene, a car fire, a dumpster fire, or a grass fire. If more trucks were needed or more manpower was needed, then the initial truck could call for more help.

A box alarm, either a street box or a desk box (initiated by the Fire Dispatcher), is transmitted for any fire that the dispatcher felt required a more aggressive response, for example, an alarm from a fire alarm box such as those located on various street corners or from a supervised fire alarm system within a building. Some other examples include a report of smoke in the area of large buildings, a report of a fire inside a building, multiple reports of a fire, an automatic alarm from a building's fire alarm system, and any report of fire from a building or area that has a concentration of people (places of public assembly). Depending upon factors such as the location of the building, the size of the building, the usage of the building, or the life hazard involved in the building, a box alarm response would bring anywhere from two engines and one ladder up to four engines, two ladders, the fire rescue, and the on-duty Deputy Chief. Any report of fire on the waterfront also included a response from Engine Seven, the Fireboat.

Box alarms were organized as a First Alarm, usually from a street box (a single Box Alarm Complement); a Second Alarm (usually twice the complement); a Third Alarm (usually every truck in the city), with station coverage coming into the city by mutual-aid contracts from communities outside the city, which usually included South Portland, Cape Elizabeth, Scarborough, Westbrook, and Falmouth; and a General Alarm, which brought mutual-aid fire trucks and manpower directly to the fire scene. The on-duty Deputy Chief could also special-call additional trucks that he felt were needed. For about ten years, this became a regular practice because of our problems with city-administrated manpower reductions.

Anytime we had multiple fire alarms, they were treated as general-alarm fires, and mutual-aid response from the surrounding communities was called in. We experienced a number of these incidents during my career. We experienced times when we had a couple of two-alarm fires at once, a three-alarm fire and a two-alarm fire at the same time, and one occasion when we had a general-alarm fire in progress and we experienced a series of single-alarm fires at the same time.

By 1975, seven and one-half years after I started, we numbered 180 firefighters, a loss of 140 men, or about 43 percent of our manpower. We were reduced to running with two or three men on each truck. This was a planned maneuver by the city administration. It was part of a policy of retaliation for our gaining a significant improvement in our union contract. We had achieved a forty-six-hour workweek, a retirement policy of twenty years' employment and/or age fifty-five, and a pay raise. Incidentally, during my career, the city administration contracted an outside agency to do four efficiency studies for the Portland Fire Department, at a cost of more than $50,000 each. Each study strongly recommended that the fire department manpower be significantly increased, for safety reasons. Each completed study was ignored and circular-filed.

Deputy Chief H. told us more than once that "You guys are stupid". Because we kept on doing our job even after the city had cut us to less than minimum manning and treated us like a "bastard child." He told us that we should just start letting these buildings burn down (after we resolve any life hazard problems). But we didn't. We kept going in anyway.

Despite our city fire department environment, we were still a neighborhood fire department. Our stations were still focal points in their respective neighborhoods. People in these neighborhoods still came by to visit or brought their children by to see the trucks. We have had people come by with plates of cookies, brownies, or food because they thought that we would enjoy them. People came by to ask us questions or to ask us to do some work on their homes. People in the neighborhoods knew us by name. They invited us to visit their homes. They treated us like family. And yes, we did get calls directly to the stations for fire calls and, sometimes, for cats in trees.

CHAPTER SIX

During my career, I worked for five men with the title of "Fire Chief, Portland Fire Department." Only one was a "real" Fire Chief. The rest were political appointees. Some of them had never even taken formal classes in firefighting or in fire administration. One was a good firefighter, but he had a serious problem with drinking. One of them considered it his priority each day to read the Portland Press Herald Newspaper from cover to cover. One of them practiced a campaign of hate against the rest of the firefighters because of an incident in his early career when he violated a union work slowdown. He was also known to be afraid to enter a burning building. But he did go into a burning building once, in his career, as a Lieutenant, when the Deputy Chief, on the fire scene, ordered him to "join your crew inside that building or be in my office tomorrow morning." Old John "the Big Red Machine" was the best line Fire Chief I have ever worked for. We all decided that he really would have been great in New York or Boston, but he was from Peaks Island and at home with the Portland Fire Department, and that's where he wanted to be. No matter how bad the fire was, he never lost his cool. And if you made a mistake on his fireground, he could chew you out royally, but after the fire was out, he would treat you to a cup of coffee, and it was over just that fast.

CHAPTER SEVEN

When I first retired from the Portland Fire Department, I was seeing a psychotherapist, for a diagnosis of PTSD (Post-Traumatic Stress Syndrome). This major issue is now starting to be recognized by the United States Fire Administration and fire departments around this country. The efforts to begin to address this problem are decades overdue. I was talking to my psychotherapist during one of the sessions and told him that I was thinking about running for a political office in the town that I was living in. I said, "I want to be able to make a positive difference in people's lives." He told me that I wouldn't do any good in politics. When I asked why, he said, "Because you have personal values that you place a very high value on. Your honesty, integrity, ethics, and honor. Those are the first things that you will have to throw away if you get into politics." I thought about that for about sixty seconds and answered, "You're right. I do place a very high value on those personal values." Today, twenty-five years later, I still place a very high value on my personal values of honesty, integrity, and honor. That's the primary reason that this book was written: to set the record straight on some of the things that happened in the years 1967–1989 and to tell the story of those of us firemen who lived through it.

Part of this story talks about the politics of fire administration and the greed, the self-serving agendas, and the narcissism that go hand-in-hand each time politics raises its ugly maggot-covered head out of the slime that it lives in.

This story is true. I lived it.
Why did I become a fireman? I have been told that this story is true.

When I was five years old, my parents and I were visiting one of my mother's uncles, in Walpole, Massachusetts. The home was a very nice Cape Cod–style home on a dead-end street. The home had a fireplace in the living room. My mother was in the kitchen helping to cook. Things in the home quieted down, and my mother decided to go looking for me, to find out why I was being so quiet. When she entered the living room, she saw me standing very close to the front of the fireplace. Earlier, there had been a small fire going in the fireplace, but it had burned down to just a small bed of embers. I had my pants fly open, and I was urinating on the fire and putting it out. At age five, I was already putting the wet on the red.

There was another, more disturbing, incident in my childhood that may have also contributed to my becoming a fireman. When I was ten years old, we were living in an apartment on the West End in Portland, at 70 Winter Street. This was a second-floor apartment. Our only heat was from a kerosene-fired kitchen stove and a coal/wood-fired parlor stove. As the oldest child, I was expected to care for my younger brother, age six, and my sister, age four. I also had to make sure that they were woken up, fed, and dressed in the morning. It was wintertime and cold. The process to light the kitchen stove was to turn on the kerosene valve. This was located at and under the two-and-one-half-gallon kerosene tank attached to the rear of the stove, in an inverted upright position. Wait for about two minutes and lift the cast iron plates on top of the stove. And, using a wooden kitchen match, light the kerosene-saturated wicks, for the burners. There were four burners on this stove. On this particular occasion, my mother turned on the tank valve and then left the apartment and went to work. It usually would take her about thirty minutes to do that. After arriving to work, she called home and told me to light the stove. When I stepped into the kitchen, the kerosene was running out of the stove and across the floor in a stream of fluid. I had to turn off the tank valve, use newspapers to soak up all the kerosene on the floor and inside the stove, and then light the stove. This was an extremely dangerous situation. There were three children in the house, and I, the eldest, was only ten; the youngest was four. If this had been a single occurrence, then I could shrug it off as a mistake. Even if this had occurred two or even three times, it might have been just a mistake still. But this occurred ten to twelve times. I was frightened that my mother was trying to kill us. I would later find out that this was just what was happening. So yes, I was becoming a fireman at age ten.

I guess I was destined to become a fireman. I was not always one to study, but when I became a fireman, I wanted to learn more about the job and how to do it better and to learn more about whatever it was that I was doing or that I wanted to do. I was about one and one-half years on the Portland Fire Department when I encountered the brick wall that was in place within the Fire Administration, an administration that was against anyone taking any classes or going to any schools or learning about the fire service and/or just trying to learn how to do the job better. It was based on a deep fear that someone might know more than they, the Fire Department Administration, knew. I was taking classes in firefighting at a local community college. I had to fight to get the time off to take the classes. I had to take sick days off or use my vacation time to take classes or swap time with someone else, just to improve myself and learn how to do the job better. I had to pay for these classes out of my own pocket. I became one of the first fifty EMTs (Emergency Medical Technicians) in the State of Maine. I became the first in the Portland Fire Department. I taught EMT classes for four years. Later I would become one of the first people to fight to get Critical Incident Stress Debriefing accepted within the fire service in Maine. I was one of the first few to be trained in dealing with Hazardous Materials incidents. And I had Fire Chiefs and Deputy Fire Chiefs who tried very hard to fire me and/or force me to resign just because I was reaching out and forward in the education process.

At about this same period, I encountered a man whom I grew to greatly admire: Don Cady. At the time, Don was the Cumberland County Emergency Preparedness Director. His office was at Bramhall Fire Station. We were standing in the station workshop area one day, while I was cleaning and sharpening tools. It was a beautiful, sunny summer day. As we chatted, I was complaining to him about how the Portland Fire Department was stagnant. Don told me, "There is no such thing as being stagnant. You either progress and move forward or you regress and move backward. Because if you aren't progressing while everyone else around you is progressing, you are really regressing." I thought about this for about one minute, and I told him, "You're right. This fire department is regressing backwards." He just replied, "Yes." We became longtime friends.

I became a thorn in the side of those in the Fire Department Administration who wanted to keep the fire department moving backward. I was the first to grow and keep a mustache. Today, mustaches are considered a signature feature that you are a fireman. I became the first to openly buy a home and move outside the city to live. When I started with the fire department, there was an unwritten rule that you had to live within the response territory of the truck that you were assigned to. For example, if you were assigned to Ladder Six, you were expected to live in the West End of Portland. If you were assigned to Engine One, you were expected to live on Munjoy Hill. With a pay scale that was just above minimum wage (minimum wage was $1.25 an hour, and I was earning about $1.53 an hour. The only way that I could afford to buy a home was to buy one outside the city. Portland, Maine, has always been and still is an area of very high real estate values. In perspective, Portland has always had a much higher housing cost rate than the surrounding area. I say that I openly bought a home outside the city because there were thirty or forty men who had already done that, but they were sneaking back and forth to work and lying about their home addresses (using PO boxes) or a relative's mailing address that was within the city. One man was using the street address of the fire station that he was assigned to. The Fire Chief (Chief D), at one point in time, came to the fire station that I was assigned to and told me that he was going to force me to resign from the fire department. I told him that I was here to stay and that I would still be here after he was gone.

There was another Fire Chief (Chief C). He wanted to fire me because I grew sideburns while I was on vacation. I had been working as an aid at Mercy Hospital's Emergency Room. A television station came in and did a story about the Emergency Rooms and what the ER Staff was experiencing. I was photographed working there, wearing my sideburns. I was still on vacation when he called me into his office. I stood outside his office with a Union Representative for about forty-five minutes. One of the headquarters secretaries went into his office to give him something, and when she exited his office, she forgot and left the office door open. I saw him sitting at his desk reading the daily newspaper. I told the Union Representative that I was leaving, that I had to go to work, and the next time that the Fire Chief wanted to see me, he could do it on fire department time, not on my personal time. One of the Deputy Chiefs, explained to the Fire Chief that I could have my facial hair any length that I wanted to as long as I was on vacation.

At a later date, this same Fire Chief showed up at Bramhall Station one day with the on-duty Deputy Chief. He pointed at a fireman who was working near one of the trucks and asked the Deputy Chief, "Who is that man?"

The Deputy Chief told him the man's name. The Fire Chief then asked, "How long has he been working here?"

The Deputy Chief answered, "He's been on the fire department for a little over four years."

This was a Fire Chief who had so distanced himself from the men on the fire department that he had reached the point that he didn't even know who he had working for him. To give this Fire Chief due credit, he also was able to have two new fire stations constructed.

I was also harassed about the vehicle that I was driving (an old Dodge Power Wagon pickup truck). I was constantly being transferred from one station to another with no warning. When I would arrive to go on duty, at my assigned station, I would be told that I had been transferred to another station, sometimes all the way across the city. Some of the fire officers whom I worked for would receive phone calls and instructions from fire headquarters telling them to harass me and to try to make me quit. One Lieutenant told me to shave my chest hair, because it was sticking up over the collar of my T-shirt, and he had had instructions from Fire Headquarters to watch the length of my facial hair closely. Another lieutenant was instructed to give me a bad evaluation report. He was told that if he did that, he would be placed higher on the promotional list for Captain.

But I stayed. And I stayed for twenty-two years until I had a heart attack in the station and I was forced to retire. I was forced to retire despite my request to stay and my certifications and credentials from the National Fire Academy in Emmitsburg, Maryland, to teach firefighting classes and/or to work as a Fire Prevention Specialist. I later found out that this refusal to keep me on the job was in violation of several Federal Labor Laws. The Union President at that time, Dennis, lied about my termination and told everyone involved that I had refused any offers of other work within the city. I am not a fan of the unions.

CHAPTER EIGHT

Politics in the Fire Service

Each time politics raises its ugly, pus-filled, maggoty head, whatever it touches it destroys, whether it be a municipal administration or a company business or a fire department. It destroys whatever it touches. I have watched countless incidents of someone with moderate skills, who would, with the help of politics, be pushed up the ladder of promotion—"not by what you know, but by who you know." The old saying from the 1980s is very true, about the Peter Principal: "The more that you screw up, the higher that you will rise up." I saw dozens of promotions made that were based not on ability or education or skills but on who you were drinking with and at what bar you were hanging out at night.

Two Fire Chiefs were appointed based on their political contacts at a certain exclusive club in Portland and not on anything else. One man's mother was a power broker at this club. This insidious destruction within organizations is like a cancer; it inevitably causes the loss of everything good about the patient. In the Portland Fire Department, it caused the loss of pride for what was once something very good. The constant belittling of the fire department by the city administration wore down that sense of "we are good." And the *political appointees* were working *with* the city administration to wear down our sense of *self-worth*.

The union became a situation where they were no longer part of the solution, but part of the problem. Many members of the union administration became more interested in *what they could get out of it* instead of *what we can do to make this better for our membership*. There were two Union Presidents, Fred and Leigh, who argued and fought for us, and they quickly were pushed out of office, to be replaced by those who were more friendly with the City Administration. All of these people were more interested in their own greed than in doing something positive and progressive. This greed, as in all cases of greed, were examples of greed for wealth, greed for power, greed for status. The Union President who was in place at the time of my forced retirement was so interested in his own political status that he lied about my case and assisted in my being forced off the job. When I called the New England IAFF Union Representative, he hollered at me over the telephone to never call him again, to communicate with him only through the Portland local representative. He later went on to become very high up with the Boston Fire Department. My adverse encounters with the various unions would continue for decades, culminating with the Union of Maine State Workers, when I became a whistleblower after encountering corruption with a certain State Agency. I was forced into a situation where I had to choose between staying in the corruption or resigning from the department. The Union Representative told me that if I fought it and went to court, then they would go to court and defend the person, who was doing the corruption, against me. So much for honesty, integrity, ethics, and honor. Allowing politics in public safety should be ruled as a criminal felony.

Politics never ever accomplishes anything positive. It always destroys whatever it is allowed to infiltrate. Public safety systems. Health care systems. Public administration systems. All these efforts to help people are always, always, always, destroyed by politics.

During my twenty-two years of career service with the Portland Fire Department, I watched this activity eviscerate the heart out of the department. Those firefighters still did their job, but the heart was gone from that entity that had been the Portland Fire Department. So many good firefighters who were hurt on the job and then forced to leave because of politics, and even some of the circumstances surrounding the LODD of a fireman and the aftermath of that incident, all corrupted and twisted by politics. This all led to the death, of the heart, of that Fire Department.

In my studies today, I have come to believe that all of us will, at the end of this lifetime, have to stand before the Supreme Being, whatever name you wish to call it, and we will have to justify all our decisions and all our actions. That this Supreme Being, whom this writer calls "The Boss," will make you responsible for those actions. Maybe at that time those people who practice politics in places like public safety will finally be brought to task for what they do. I hope so.

In the case of one man who rose to become Fire Chief, this writer is reminded of the comments made by a nun during the buildup to Y2K. This nun wrote, in a newspaper article. "She stated that", "I hope. No I, believe that there is a special room in Hell for those people who abuse other people and then use a Holy Book as a shield to prevent being held responsible for their actions." I hope that she is right.

The Buddha taught a lesson about this issue. He was called to stand before a group of leaders and dignitaries. They questioned him about his teachings of the people, and their questioning became aggressive toward him. As he was standing before them, he noticed a line of ants walking across the floor between himself and the dignitaries. He responded to the dignitaries' questions by pointing at the column of ants and telling the dignitaries that they should become aware of the consequences their decisions and their actions, because they might be reincarnated as an ant. Maybe those who practice politics should pause and remember this lesson. They may be allowed to return as an earthworm or an ant walking across a floor.

Chapter Nine

The nightmare fires
The Wilson School fire, The first week of December 1974
Merry fucking Christmas

In the military, it's said that you can tell who has been up on the line and who hasn't by just looking in their eyes. That person who has seen death (up close and personal) acquires a look called the "thousand-yard stare." When you look into their eyes, they are not looking back at you. They are looking back at the scenes of the horror that they have experienced. These scenes remain in the minds of those persons and never go away. I am one of those people. Today, I still have those memories. Karl Learned, an old friend, said it well.

"Bobby, we have a lifetime full of memories. Some of them we never want to forget. Some of them we wish that we could forget."

And anything can trigger them: a sound, a smell, going past a certain location, hearing someone say a particular word or phrase, hearing or reading a name. Yeah, those memories don't go away. Look up the definition of PTSD.

I recently picked up the Portland Press Herald and read of the death of a certain man. He lived, at the time of his passing, in Millinockett, Maine, about 160 miles north of Portland. That man and I had a special bond. I hadn't sat down and talked to him for twenty-plus years, but we still share a special connection. Only police officers and military soldiers know of that bond that firemen have with each other. Many pretenders call themselves firemen, but they aren't. They say that they know, but they are lying. They are lying to themselves and everyone else. Billy Schweickhardt and I had that bond. Here's the story.

It started as a regular night shift, just like ten thousand other night shifts. I was at Ladder Three Station, at about 5:00 p.m., one hour early, my usual time in the door. I was the Driver, so I met with the man I was relieving. He took his gear off the truck and I put mine on. I started to check the truck out to see if everything was all set. My routine would normally take me about one and a half to two hours. It included the engine, controls, pump panel, cab, equipment, SCBA's, compartments, and the general condition of the truck.

I then went into the Day Room to cook my dinner. We were all talking about the coming Christmas holiday. There were four of us on duty that night.

Billy and I were working on Ladder Three, out of Engine Three Station on Stevens Avenue. Ladder Three was an open-cab, Seagrave, seventy-five-foot Ariel, on a straight chassis. It was the first week of December 1974. It was cold that night, and the air was clear with well below freezing temps, with frozen snow and slush on the streets and sidewalks, the kind of weather that happens in south-coastal Maine from mid-November to about mid-April each year. The officer was Lieutenant Willy G., the senior fireman was Jack R., and I was the driver. Billy Schweickhardt was the rookie; he only had a few months on the department, and it's a really serious learning curve. The Portland Fire Department had a rookie training program at that time, but it was annual and given only once a year. You were hired and you had to go through OJT (on-the-job training) until the time came for the Rookie School. And this Rookie School was for one week only. How much can you learn about firefighting in one week?

We went on duty at 6:00 p.m. The alarm came in at about 7:30 p.m. for the Wilson School on Chestnut Street, across from the side entrance to City Hall. Ladder Three responded on the Second Alarm. We went right to the scene of the fire. I parked on Cumberland Avenue at the corner of Cumberland Avenue and Chestnut Street. My first sight of the fire was looking up Chestnut Street, at the vacant three-story school building. The entire roof area was showing heavy smoke and no visible fire.

The building had been closed as a school for some years and was being used by the Portland School Department as a storage facility. The building was masonry construction (granite stone, brown brick stone, and heavy timber), with a mansard roof and slate roof shingles, and it was about 110 years old at the time of the fire. The building was built shortly after the 1866 Great Portland Fire. The building was rectangular, with a long central corridor, parallel to Chestnut Street, and opening up to rooms off each side, on each floor. The stairwells were at each end. This building was a typical W. L. Stevens–designed school building. The ceilings were all twelve feet high. The interior trim was birch paneling with chair rails. The floors were hardwood at all levels. The stairwells were all eight to ten feet wide. The stairwell landings were located toward the front of the building. Each set of stairs was composed of twenty-three to twenty-four steps. The building was adjacent to Portland High School (the second-oldest public high school in the United States).

At first sight, the building was showing very heavy smoke from the entire roof area. Ladder Six and Ladder One were parked on Chestnut Street in front of the building. Fire Chief D., Deputy Chief M., and Deputy Chief F. were all standing or sitting on Ladder Six. Ladder Three's crew was ordered to enter the building, through the right-hand entrance, and go up the stairwell to the third floor to check for fire extension. Another crew was ordered to enter the building on the left entrance and do the same thing. This resulted in eight firemen (two crews) being inside the building.

Ladder Three's crew reached the third-floor level. We went into the first room facing Chestnut Street. We could see a medium amount of smoke and feel a lot of heat, but no fire. And it was getting hotter. We were opening up the ceiling and walls and checking for fire extension. At this time, Fire Chief D. made the decision to use the water cannons (ladder guns) from Ladder Six and Ladder One to attack the fire from above the roof. These guns (water cannons), put out 250 gals of water per minute each (water weighs just about eight pounds per gallon) at about ninety pounds of pressure (force). This amounts to one ton (two thousand pounds) of water and weight per minute, from each gun, being forced down upon the roof structure, a roof structure that has already been severely weakened by the fire.

Under "Tactics and Strategy within the Fire Service," this is a common practice. We have a saying—"Put the guns to it"—and that is exactly what it means. However, in the fire service, we also have rules of Fireground Safety. One of these basic cornerstone foundation rules in place in the fire service since the late 1800s is that if you use water cannons on a fire the first thing that you do is to make sure that there are no people (victims or firefighters) in the way of these master streams of water. These streams of water can severely injure or kill people. (I know one fireman that was hit by a master stream that was being directed into a window. He was blown across a room and into a wall and sustained several broken ribs.) And if there are people still inside the building, and these streams of water are used on the building, then there is a very serious chance of injuring or killing someone. These streams of water are sometimes used to break apart and blow apart the building itself. Some of these streams of water have been used to break apart (to peel) brick walls a few bricks at a time.

Chief D. instructed Deputy Chief M. and Deputy Chief F. to have the aerial guns from Ladder Six and Ladder One activated and used on the roof of the Wilson School. All three knew that there were firefighters still inside the building. They ordered the guns onto the fire anyway. Not one of them questioned the order or took the time to use our two-way radios to warn those of us inside the building, to evacuate the building. We were given no warning at all until the roof structure of the building started to collapse in on us from the force and weight of the water hitting it. At the time of my retirement on January 29, 1989, there was still no policy in place on the Portland Fire Department for evacuations of burning buildings. No alarm system. No radio calls. No air horns. Nothing.

Ladder Three's crew was still in the first room that we had entered on the third floor to start to search for fire extension. I sensed that something was wrong within the building, and I stepped back out of the room and looked up the corridor toward the other end. I saw very large pieces of the roof and ceiling structure coming down and crashing onto the floor. (This is the same floor that we were standing on.) I turned toward Lieutenant G. and the other men in the room, and I hollered out, "We have to get out of here, this fucking place is coming down around our asses." At this point, Lieutenant G. stepped out into the corridor, looked toward the collapsing area, and said, "Let's get out of here." He and Jack R. headed down the stairs to get out, leaving behind myself and the rookie, Billy Schweickhardt, who had stopped to look up the corridor. He just had not had enough time, on the job, to learn and to recognize just what it was that he was seeing. And what he was seeing was a building in collapse (looking at it from the inside of the building). By this time, the roof and ceiling sections that were hitting the floor were only about ten feet away from us. (Picture an eight-foot piece of framing lumber, a 2" × 4", lying down on the floor stretching away from you.) Each falling section consisted of 12" × 12" roof timbers, large sections of plaster ceiling material, and large pieces of sheet metal (the roof mounted, air-handling/heating units). Each section weighed close to two thousand pounds each. I grabbed Billy and literally threw him down the stairwell. I then turned to see if anyone else was in the area. I spotted the other crew at the other end of the corridor, evacuating the building also. We waved to acknowledge that we were safe and leaving the place. When I turned to go down the stairs, a large section of the roof assembly, including a piece of the 12" × 12" roof timber, and part of a sheet metal air-handling unit, collapsed down on top of me. I have no personal memory of going down those stairs. I only have what I have been told (that I was airborne down the entire stairwell of twenty-three steps to the second-floor landing). I landed on top of Billy Schweickhardt. My next memory is of being led down the outside steps of the building to the sidewalk outside and thinking that I had hurt my foot somehow. As we exited the building, we stepped through a shower of slate roof tiles that were raining down on us, from forty feet in the air. One of the slates came down and cut through the top of my fire boot. I was hurt all right. I didn't know it yet, but I had just lost almost one inch of my body's total height, in a very major compression fracture of my entire spine and skeleton. The pain didn't begin to set in until almost two hours later.

But the real nightmare didn't begin until a few days later, after we were off duty. I couldn't sit in a chair; I couldn't sleep lying down on a bed. It hurt to walk. It hurt to sit. I was in continuous pain. I thought that I had somehow thrown out my back. I went to see a chiropractor. He manipulated my back to try to correct it. Because I was in such pain, I went off duty sick.

The chiropractor continued working on my back twice a week. I returned to duty, but for three months, I couldn't do anything. I couldn't lift or carry anything. I still could not sit or lay down to sleep without serious pain. Over-the-counter pain meds didn't work on the pain. Finally, the chiropractor told me that "this is more than I can handle. You should go see a neurosurgeon."

I was connected up with a Dr. Carl Brinkman Jr., a prominent neurosurgeon at the Maine Medical Center. He examined me and told me that my spine had been very badly compressed and that the discs between vertebra L-3, L-4, and L-5 had been crushed. I had lost about three-fourths of an inch in my height. He did a test on my spine and confirmed his diagnosis. He also told me that if I hadn't been in peak physical condition at the time of the accident, I probably would have died or become a paraplegic before I got to the bottom of those stairs that night. He suggested operating on me immediately, but I was stubborn and I waited through two more days of pain before I called him and said, "Let's get this over with." It would eventually take two surgeries and three months of rehab. Years later, a third surgery would be needed to rebuild my cervical vertebra. I would be able to return to work as a Fire Dispatcher for about one year. I was asked to stay in dispatching because I became very good at it, but I really wanted to return to the trucks. The Dispatchers were being phased out of the fire department and into the new Portland Department of Public Safety; I wanted to stay with the fire department. I spent the following year in the Fire Prevention Bureau, and I was becoming very good at this also, but I still wanted to get back on the trucks. I did eventually return to active duty on the trucks; I stayed for thirteen more years until my heart attack. But I have never been without some level of pain at that injury site, even today, forty years later. The accident also triggered Osteoarthritis in my spine and my joints. There have been more surgeries, including two knee replacements. A total of seventeen and a lifetime of medical help and daily meds to try to offset these problems.

But the long-term nightmare really began with what I didn't know was going on. What I didn't know during the time of my recovery was that Fire Chief D., Deputy Chief M., and Deputy Chief F. were scrambling to cover up the damage from their bad decisions that night. They conspired to try to get me fired. They went to the neighborhood where I lived and questioned my neighbors and friends about my activities. I got repeated calls from friends that said, "Hey Bob, those two fire chiefs were here again asking questions." One friend of mine nicknamed them "Starsky and Hutch," after the television show that was popular at that time. One thing that they did—and I didn't find out about this until more than ten years later—was that they went to Ladder Three Station and talked to the crew I had worked with that night. Two of these men told me about this incident later. Deputy Chief M. and Deputy Chief F. met with the Ladder Three crew that I had worked with. They told Lieutenant G., "If you sign this letter stating that Beane was not hurt that night, we'll take care of you, and you'll be promoted soon." Lieutenant G. did sign the letter, and two years later, he was promoted to Captain. They told Jack R., "If you sign this letter, we'll take care of you." Jack R. told them, "I'm getting ready to retire soon and this guy saved our lives. I'm not going to help you fuck him over." They told the rookie Billy Schweickhardt, "If you sign this letter, we'll take care of you, and you'll have a good career." Billy told them, "That man saved my life, and I'm not going to help you fuck him over."

Jack R. did retire a few years later, and Billy Schweickhardt stayed for more than twenty years. I stayed for another thirteen years, and as a senior firefighter, I worked hundreds of shifts as a fill-in for lieutenants. (Doing the work but not getting paid for it.) Eventually I did achieve a promotion to lieutenant, but I was denied this promotion or any recognition for what I had done that night. It would be another ten years before I would be promoted to lieutenant.

My personal fight with all this was within myself, knowing that I had saved those lives that night, and not only was I not given recognition for it, but the existing Fire Administration tried for many years to fire me or force me to resign to cover up their negligence that night. That has been my personal battle.

In doing my investigations and observations during my career, I noticed that this was a pattern of behavior. Others were forced to resign to cover up bad decisions on firegrounds. Politics is great!

Massachusetts Avenue and Congress Street
Another great Christmas

There is a certain smell around building fires. Sometimes it's as simple as the smell of old finished, painted lumber that has burned. Sometimes it's mixed with that smell of hot, wet horsehair plaster or sheetrock. Sometimes it's the smell of burned furniture, clothing, plastics, and people's belongings. And far too frequently it's mixed with the smell of burned human flesh, that particular acrid scorched meat smell. Similar to what it smells like if someone really badly burns some meat in the oven or on a bbque. Meat that has been burned to charcoal.

It was cold that night, almost zero degrees Fahrenheit. The air was clear. The streets and houses were all decorated for Christmas. Santa Claus was due to arrive in just a few days' time. I was in charge of Engine Four, out of Bramhall

Station. We went on duty at 6:00 p.m. Firefighter D. was driving for me. About 8:00 p.m., we responded to an alarm for Massachusetts Avenue and Congress Street, for a reported fire on the second-floor residence, with people trapped in the building. We were the second due engine. Engine Three was first due. Engine Three was Lieutenant Jimmy F., and Phil Riley was his driver. Engine Three arrived and reported heavy fire showing on the second floor and a report of someone trapped on the second floor. When we arrived on scene, I saw a wood frame, two-and-one-half-story multiple-use building with a convenience store on the first floor and apartments on the second floor. The front entrance and stairs were connected to a hallway that ran to the rear of the building and a second set of stairs to the rear entrance. There was heavy smoke and fire showing from the second floor. The Engine Three crew had advanced an attack line inside the building, at the front entrance, and up the stairs to the second-floor landing. They were stopped, at the landing, by heavy fire in the hallway. Lieutenant F. and two men were on the stairs just below the landing. I took one man with me and went into the building at the front entrance and up the stairs. None of us had on an SCBA. The department rules were that we were not supposed to use them unless we had to for a rescue. I noticed that Lieutenant F. had forgotten to put his boots on, so I told him to go back out to the truck and "get them on, before your goddamned feet freeze." I took the knob (the nozzle). At this time, we still had heavy fire blowing over our heads. This is when the nightmare started. *We ran out of water.* Engine Three's five-hundred-gallon water tank had run dry, and my driver had not laid a water feeder line from the hydrant into Engine Three. Later, I would be told that Deputy Chief R. had to open the driver's door of Engine Four and holler at him to lay the line. But the bottom line is that for three to four minutes, those of us inside the building had no way to fight the fire. We also encountered an additional problem with structural elements of the building itself. The door to the front apartment from the hallway was made of solid hardwood, two and one-half inches of thick oak wood. And it was locked. We couldn't get through it. Finally, Phil T. grabbed a Halligan tool and made the landing long enough to break out a panel in the door so that we could make entry. We also had the problem of opposing hose lines from the rear stairwell. At about this time, we finally received a water supply and advanced onto the landing and into the apartment. It was very hot, well over four hundred degrees. The fire was being pushed back and forth through the length of the hall by the opposing hose lines.

The fire had been confined to the hallway and had not done much damage to the inside of the apartment, but the twenty-three-year-old man lying across the daybed, by the front window, was dead. There was a portable television on a small table about three feet from his head that was completely melted down around its frame. Later, I would be told repeatedly that he was probably dead before we even got the call from Fire Alarm. But this one is my nightmare fire. I suffered flashbacks and nightmares from this fire for more than twenty-five years. I kept asking myself, *Why couldn't I have saved his life?* And I thought for years that I could have saved him if I had pushed myself harder. Even after finding out that he was dead, before we even received the alarm. I was the firefighter who covered the body with a piece of bed clothes and stayed with it until the Medical Examiner arrived, took one look at the body, and said, "Well, the fire killed him." (No shit.)

On a side note: When I stepped off Engine Four that night, at the scene, I only pulled up one of my boots. The other boot later filled with water, and I thought that my foot would freeze solid from the cold. One warm dry foot, the other cold and wet. Well, so much for hollering at Jimmy about his boots. And thank God for learning to keep a set of dry socks at the station.

Later I would learn that one reason we had had such a hard time making the stair landing was because of the fire blowing over our heads, in surges. This was caused by having two attack lines working on the fire from two opposing directions: one attack line from the front stairs of the building and another coming up the rear stairs of the building into the same hallway (the old opposed-lines problem, from Firefighting Tactics 101).

This fire was proved to be arson. And it was a murder. The young man who died had been dating a young woman. Her former boyfriend had stolen a Christmas tree. He then set it on fire and dragged it up and down the second-floor hallway outside the apartment, thereby setting the walls inside the building on fire. He then walked around the corner to the girl's home and told her, "See what I just did." He ended up going to prison for twenty years.

All of us have a nightmare fire scene, an accident scene, or some other emergency scene. This is one of mine. It took me twenty-plus years to finally get over being angry at the month of December and at Christmas. At the time of this fire, we had experienced fatal fires on three Christmases in a row. I still shudder when I remember the fire scenes and shoveling out the fire debris from countless fires. The debris that included people's Christmas trees, Christmas gifts, and sometimes the family's pets, and those many times when we were working around that body that was lying on the bed or the floor. And then to go off duty and go to my own home to celebrate the holiday but to also live with the memories of the destruction that I had just come from.

Chapter Ten

Hot damned days and cold fucking nights

Dates, days, even years are details that I seem to have forgotten. But the scenes are still clear. I can remember that it was a hot day or a cold night, but I can't remember calendar dates, or even what year it was. They all just seem to run together in a swirl like trying to see the details of a tornado cloud while it's spinning. Remembering one tidbit seems to trigger the memories of a dozen others. Part of this is the PTSD. Another is just that there are so many of these memories.

It was summertime, late July or August, and it was hot. It was one of those days when the air temp is ninety-plus degrees and it was 90 percent humidity. The humidity from the saltwater harbor was almost stifling. It was one of those days when just standing up and walking across the room caused you to break out in a sweat. Portland can get like that in the summer. And you wait for sunset when the breeze comes in off the bay and cools things down a little.

It was midafternoon, and I was in charge of Engine Five, out of Central Fire Station. We received an alarm for a building fire on Montreal Street, up on Munjoy Hill. Captain Lloyd was in charge of Engine One, the first due engine. We responded from Central Station and turned right to go up Congress Street Hill to North Street and then left over North Street and then a right to go down Montreal Street. About a one-mile run. Engine One reported at the scene. This was followed by silence on the radio. I was wondering when Captain Cook was going to report it in as a working fire because when we turned onto Montreal Street, I could see two blocks down the street to the fire building, and the fire was blowing halfway across the street. As we pulled up in front of the fire building, I could see that the building was a two-and-one-half-story, single-family residence. The building was wood-framed with a pitched roof. The building had asbestos shingle siding, the kind of siding that explodes like shrapnel when it gets heated up in a fire. The building was about sixty years old and well kept. There was a twenty- to thirty-foot distance between it and the buildings on either side.

I called in to Fire Alarm and reported, "Engine Five to Fire Alarm. We have a working fire." Immediately afterward, Captain Cook called for a Second Alarm. As we pulled up in front of the building and jumped off the truck, I noticed an old man across the street, on the sidewalk. He was rolling around on the sidewalk and laughing his ass off. My thought was that, *He is one sick puppy. This fire is no laughing matter.*

We had heavy fire showing from almost the entire building, but the fire looked different. It was very hot, but there was not much smoke yet. Strange! We made entry with the Engine One crew, and the Ladder One crew set ground ladders to the second-floor windows. We made fast progress against the fire, but it was clear that we were dealing with some kind of an accelerant, and a lot of it. By this time, we were starting to lose guys to the heat. We ended up having five or six men go down with the heat, because of the air temps and the humidity.

And the old man on the sidewalk was still over there laughing.

We knocked the fire down quickly and started to do our overhaul and making up (picking up our equipment and securing the building). That's when we found out why this fire was different. We found twenty-five gals of Naptha, a commercial cleaning fluid, in open top, one-gal cans in a first-floor closet. We also found the remains (the splash patterns) of an additional ten gals of Naptha poured on the floors and stairways throughout the house. This fire was set up to blow up when the fire reached that Naptha that was in the closet.

We were lucky. All old buildings tend to settle as they age. This house was an old building that had settled over the years. The closet with the Naptha in it had a door that had swung closed shut, by itself, because of the way that the building was leaning toward the front. This had prevented the Naptha, in the closet, from igniting and exploding. We were lucky that day. There were twelve of us inside that building when it could have gone up like a blowtorch.

Back outside and making up the trucks, I finally looked across the street at that old man. I now recognized him as a retired fireman, one of the old guys, whom I had worked with years ago, when I was just starting out on the job. I went over to talk to him.

"What were you laughing about? We worked our asses off in that place, and we've got five or six guys down with the heat."

He answered, "I wasn't laughing at you guys. I was laughing at the two guys that started the fire. When they finished pouring the Naptha, and one of them lit the match and then threw it into the doorway. Their clothes were saturated with the Naptha fumes and when the stuff ignited, the fire chased them down the outside stairs and out onto the sidewalk and up the street. It serves them right."

I immediately told the Police Officer on the scene, and he told me that a Portland Police Patrol Unit had picked up the two men about three blocks away from the fire scene, because he had seen them walking along the street, with their clothes partially burned and some of their hair and eyebrows burned off.

It serves them right. There is street justice sometimes. I wonder how long it took before they tried that again.

We were on this scene for a relatively short time, a total of about three hours.

And cold damned nights
The night we burned the top floor off the Salvation Army warehouse on Elm Street

I was working a shift swap for "Smoky." This was a practice whereby one man would agree to work for another man; in return, that man would work for him at a later date. I was driving for the Captain (Stubby), on Engine Four, out of Bramhall Station.

It was winter, January or February. The air temp was seventeen degrees below zero Fahrenheit, and the winds were at about forty miles per hour. I would later research this on a wind chill graph and find that it was giving us a wind chill factor of negative sixty degrees below zero. We came on duty at 6:00 p.m. We received the fire alarm at about 6:30 p.m. for the Salvation Army Warehouse on Elm Street near Lancaster Street. This building was a warehouse of wood-framed construction, three stories tall. The building was sixty feet wide and one hundred feet long, with a flat tar-and-gravel roof and asphalt shingle siding.

Engine Five was the first due engine, and Engine Four was the second. We rolled out of Bramhall Station and turned right to go down Congress Street. By the time we had reached Congress Square, Engine Five had arrived on the scene and called for a working fire and for a Second Alarm. When we turned left onto Elm Street from Congress Street, we saw that the entire top floor of the building was showing heavy smoke and fire. The call went out for a Third Alarm. I took the hydrant at Oxford Street and Elm Street and hand-laid feeder lines to Ladder One and to Engine Five. The ice began to be a problem immediately. Any spray and any water exposed to the air immediately froze. Within thirty minutes, everything was coated with a rapidly thickening coat of ice.

I hadn't seen ice build up that quickly since my days at sea, on the North Atlantic, with the Coast Guard. Eventually we had ice buildup of more than four to six inches thick that covered everything: the streets and sidewalks, the trucks, the equipment, the firefighters, utility poles, power lines, and the other close buildings.

I have never experienced problems with engine pumps like I had that night. The indicator needles in my pressure gauges (glycerin gauges) started to move clockwise, slowly, until they had turned around in a complete circle, two and one-half times that of normal. And the water pressure remained the same in my pumps. It turned out that this is a problem with glycerin gauges in intense cold situations. But boy, was I scared for a little while.

Because I was operating the engine's pumps, I was relatively dry. Cold, but dry. At one point, I gave my spare gloves to Captain Stubby. He made the comment that I could have sold any dry gloves for a good price that night. I noticed at one point that the water leaking from Engine Four's pumps (all the engine companies had problems with the pumps leaking) was freezing as it hit the street. At this fire scene, it caused a column of ice, around six feet wide, to grow from the street level up to and even around the pumps. The ice in the street had built up so that it was even with the sidewalk's curbstones, about eight inches high.

We were relieved on scene the next morning at about 8:30 a.m., fourteen hours on scene. The following day, I was talking to the guys from that oncoming shift. I learned about the difficulties that they had making up that morning. They had to break up the ice from around the trucks just to move them. The ice column under Engine Four had to be broken up with axes before the truck could be moved. Ladder One and Ladder Six had to be driven back to their stations with the aerial ladders down in the beds but still extended and backed into the respective stations in stages, as the ice was melted off the aerials using hot water and hot air from the station's heating systems. The hose lines had to be returned to the stations in frozen fifty-foot lengths on large flatbed trucks (car carrier trucks) and thawed out before they could be hung up to dry.

There was one decision made that night by Fire Chief M. that stands out in my memory. At the height of this fire, he ordered the Portland Police to go to the home of the City Manager and to pick him up and make him to come to the scene of the fire (whether he wanted to or not) so that "He can see for himself what we do for work."

CHAPTER ELEVEN

Bramhall Station

This was my favorite place in the world. Bramhall Station is located on Congress Street, the main street that runs through the Portland peninsula. It is just around the corner from the Maine Medical Center, the largest hospital in Maine. The area is comprised of a mix of two large hospitals, businesses, high-income residences, low-income residences, high-density areas, working waterfront, commercial areas, and downtown entertainment areas. It's the West End. This is also the area of the city that I grew up in. These streets were, at one time, my playground, and the route that I walked back and forth to school passed in front of what would later become Bramhall Fire Station.

When I grew up in this area, there were three fire stations. Engine Four was at the corner of Spring Street and State Street (near the Mercy Hospital). Ladder Three was on Brackett Street near Spring Street (across from what is now Reiche School). Ladder Six and Engine Six were on Park Avenue at St. John Street (near the railroad overpass trestle). Just before I went on the job, these stations had been closed and consolidated into Bramhall Fire Station. "La Casa Grande" (the big house) had been open for just six months. Bramhall Station housed Engine Four, Engine Six, Ladder Six, and the on-duty Deputy Chief. It also included the Cumberland County Civil Emergency Preparedness Headquarters and the fire department's carpenter shop. Ladder Three was installed in its own new station on Stevens Avenue near Brighton Avenue.

These stations were incorporated into one station because of a tragic accident that occurred in late summer of 1961. Two fire trucks, Engine Four from Spring Street (an open-cab American LaFrance) and Ladder Three from Brackett Street (an open-cab Seagrave), were dispatched to the area of May Street and Spring Street for a report of a fire behind an apartment house. (This fire alarm report would turn out to be an unnecessary call; the fire was, in reality, a man burning rubbish in a steel barrel, a common practice at that time.) These trucks were responding from two different directions with lights on and sirens howling. Neither truck could see or hear the other, partially because this inner city intersection was a blind one. Both trucks collided at the intersection of Spring Street and Brackett Street. This accident would be the worst fire truck accident in the city's history. There were eight men on the trucks at the time of the accident. One man would die. Four would be severely injured. Two men would receive lighter injuries. One man, Billy L., a good friend of mine, would be crushed between these two trucks in a space of about five inches. As a result, he would suffer from epilepsy for the rest of his life. Firefighting can be a dangerous business even before you arrive at the fire scene. He would stay with the department as the Department Carpenter and maintenance man until his retirement.

On May 14, 1967, I reported for duty at Bramhall Station. The only prior firefighting training that I had had was in the military service, and it was Marine Firefighting, not city firefighting. On the day that I reported for duty, I was told to do nothing unless I was told to. The Portland Fire Department had just started on a work slowdown to protest stalled contract talks.

But the moment I looked at those big red trucks, I was in love. I felt that I had just come home after being away for a while.

I was painfully shy and very introverted. I was the type of person who could sit in a crowded room for hours and not say anything to anyone. So I sat. If the trucks went out, I would climb onto the tailgate and hang on for dear life. I began to help clean the trucks and the station. I was on the job for about two weeks when one these old guys came up to me and asked, "Hey, kid, are you working here or are you just hanging around?"

I replied that I was working here. He then said, "Well, if you keep your eyes and ears open and your damned mouth shut, you just might learn something around here."

I took that advice to heart, and I practice it even today. That man, Louie Napolitano, became a second father to me. He took me under his wing and taught me a lot. These big, old, crusty World War II Veterans were the best.

I learned to clean up the station (my new home). I learned that a clean, shiny fire truck is something to be proud of. I learned that if you take care of your tools and equipment, then when you need them they'll be there, ready for you. I learned just how much equipment is stored in all those compartments on those trucks and that each truck carries a wide variety of equipment that is special to that truck. I learned about hose fittings and ladder dogs and tormentor poles. I learned about closet hooks and lifelines and a dozen different kinds of ladders. I learned how to repair and maintain all these tools.

I learned how to stay alive in a fire building. How to stay low and breath through your mouth when you are in smoke; we had no SCBAs (self-contained breathing apparatus) at that time. I learned how to follow the walls or follow a hose line to get out of a building. I learned how to determine the right direction to get out of the building, from the hose couplings and from the sounds of the trucks out front. If you become trapped and disoriented inside a burning building, you can die. I learned how to read the fire and to try to understand what it was saying to me. I learned how to listen for the sounds of the fire rumbling upward through the walls of the buildings. I learned how to dance with the fire. I learned how to scramble around on roofs (some of them were burning away underneath us). I learned what a spongy roof feels like and what that means. I learned what it feels like to walk on a roof when the roofing tar is melting under your feet and it's slippery. I learned how to not let my fear of the fire cripple me. I learned how to stare at the fire, face to face, and not let it force me to run. I learned how to set, climb, and work from ladders: ground ladders, from sixteen feet up to fifty feet long, and aerial ladders, some of them one hundred feet high. I learned what it meant to use the ladder dogs on a ladder and how to lock on.

I began to learn how to come out of my shell and talk to other people. I learned, for the first time in my life, how to laugh. We firemen have a strong sense of street humor. It would come out when we would come back to the station from a bad accident, with the blood all over everything, and send someone out for a couple of pizzas. It's a coping skill that firemen use to offset all the grief and hurt that we see. I learned how to watch someone else do a chore and then learn how to do it myself. I learned how to slide the pole, even with a cup of hot coffee in my hand and not spill it. I learned how to cook for myself and for up to sixteen other men, and I became good at it.

I learned how to do courageous things as part of the normal day and to do heroic things when the occasion required it. In short, I learned how to be a fireman.

It's a serious learning curve. Today you need a degree in Fire Science and paramedic training before you can even apply for the job. When I started on the job, all that you needed was a strong back, a weak mind, and a desire to help people.

Deputy Chief H. took over training about one year after I went on the job. One year after that, at the first Drill School, he told us these comment, about what we were doing for work. He told us, "If anyone ever asks you what do you do for work? Give them this answer:

"Ask them, 'Do you watch television?' They will answer, 'Yes.'

"Ask them, 'Do you see the news on television?' They will answer, 'Yes.'

"Ask them, 'Do you see the pictures of burning buildings on the news?' They will answer, 'Yes.'

"Ask them, 'Do you see all of the people running away from the burning buildings?' They will answer, 'Yes.'

"Ask them, 'Do you see all of those damned fools running into the burning buildings carrying tools and stuff?' They will answer, 'Yes.'

"Just tell them, 'I'm one of those damned fools.'"

I would later take these things that I had been taught and in turn teach firefighting classes to other people, young and old, men and women, who were firemen or in the process of becoming one. My favorite class to teach was the one titled "Fireground Survival," a class that I helped create. It was a class in basic fireground safety that covered everything from building construction, fire behavior, vehicle fires, safety gear, self-contained breathing apparatus, size-up and tactics, hazardous materials, live fire training exercises, search and rescue, and staying alive in a burning building. I taught this class for more than twenty-one years to more than 3,500 young firefighters. I loved being able to pass on what I had learned to other firemen who were just starting out on the job.

As firemen, we quickly learn to be creative and to think on our feet. There is an old saying in the fire service: "When the experts can't figure it out, they call the fire department." We also became a testing ground for any innovations in tools for the fire service. Fire equipment companies will send us tools to try out for a while. If you give anything like this to a bunch of firemen, they will quickly figure out if it's going to work or not. And they will quickly figure out how to break it.

Chapter Twelve

Some of the men

These are some examples of the men I worked with when I was a Rookie. Most of these men have made their transition to a better place and are no longer with us except in our memories.

I was told frequently, "Hey, kid, just shut up and follow me."

The Captains:

Jerry Jerome (Cap). He stood about 5'8" tall with gray hair. He was a World War II vet. He had an average build, but the respect that he had earned made him really stand about ten feet tall. The man whose style of leadership I admired so much that I later copied it. He was soft-spoken, polite, and never got rattled, even when while he was watching me as I was learning to drive Ladder Six. He never had to raise his voice. When he opened his mouth to speak, everyone stopped and listened.

Captain Wernick (the Kraut). He stood about six feet tall with a gruff manner. He had a muscular build. He was also a World War II Vet. He was a man of great courage and usually one of the first to enter a burning building. He was the man who introduced me to my second major fire and taught me to not be afraid when facing the fire. I learned this from him one night as we walked up and over the huge pile of smoldering rubble from a general store fire on Munjoy Hill, where we heard and felt the cans of paint exploding under us where we were walking. "Don't worry, kid. That's just the paint cans blowing up." And we kept walking. I followed him.

Murray Roberts (Stubby). One of the best. He was a tall man, just over six feet. He had a wiry build. He never got excited. I have listened to him on the radio as he was pulling up in front of a major fire scene, and he never even raised his voice. He just got the job done, and he had the greatest sense of humor. His story of the difference between helmets and anteaters stays with me even today. He is one of the men who taught me how to not lose my cool at emergency scenes.

I later worked with Rick C., who was as cool as anyone I ever knew. He was of average height. He was muscular (a lot of golf). Rick was in charge of Engine One on Munjoy Hill for years. Rick went in on a bad fire one bitter cold winter night. It was very early morning, around 2:00 a.m. It was clear air, but the temperature was just under zero degrees Fahrenheit. This fire became a fatal fire. It was in a three-story, wood-framed, three-apartment building on Monument Street, one block directly behind Munjoy Hill Fire Station. The building was thirty feet wide and forty-five feet long with wooden shakes for siding and a pitched roof with asphalt shingles. The building was about fifty years old. Upon our arrival, the building had fire showing on the entire rear extending from the ground level to the roof. When Engine One pulled out of the station and turned right to make the corner onto Waterville Street to respond to the alarm, Rick looked over his shoulder, past the station, and saw the sky lit up with the fire. He keyed the radio mic and slowly said, in a very calm, clear voice, "Engine One to Fire Alarm, strike me a Third Alarm on this fire." And then he added, to all the other incoming response trucks, "Pull up your boots, guys, we're going to be here all night."

Joe T. (Joe). He was about 5'10". Medium build—a little on the thin side from a cigarette habit. He was a thinker like me. He was a man who shared my dreams of a better, smarter, safer, and more educated fire department. He tried to get a Hazardous Materials Team on the Portland Fire Department. He started the project, and it took him more than ten years to finally get one. I consider myself so fortunate to have worked for him for a few years. We would sit in the kitchen/day room at Engine Eleven Station and have hours and hours of talk about our dreams for the Portland Fire Department.

Harold B. He was tall and thin. He had a slow way of talking, like he was a little embarrassed to be saying anything. We worked together on old Rescue One, the old bread truck that ran out of Central Fire Station. I drove for Harold, and I was with him on his first CPR save. That call is a lasting memory for both of us.

Lloyd Cook. He was about six feet tall with a quick sense of humor. He always seemed to be on the verge of bursting out laughing. He was one of the survivors of that 1961 fire truck accident. He was another of those quiet, humorous, polite men and was a great teacher. I was there one day when he was once again almost killed on a fire scene, on Fore Street at the Cumberland Cold Storage Plant, by someone with good intentions but with no common sense. He was standing beside a deck gun that had been placed on the street to pour large volumes water at the building. An out-of-town fireman reached up and jerked open the gate valve handles on the truck's pump panel. That deck gun lifted off the street and slammed into Lloyd's chest and shoulders. He would be severely injured and spend months in recovery.

Lloyd Parker. He was more than six feet tall with a muscular build. He was an outdoorsman. He was always hunting or fishing or working in the woods somewhere. He was one of the nicest, gentlest men I have ever met in my life. He was another of those old-timers who never seemed to get excited no matter how bad the emergency scene was. He was a true gentleman.

As I stated earlier, there were 320 men when I started work. To give them all the due respect that they earned and deserve would take a lifetime of writing. These brave, courageous men, these "leather lungs" firemen, they were the best. I can only comment on a few. Within twenty years after their retirements, most of them would die from the physical effects on their bodies from the work that they did. I am so grateful for having known them and to have worked with them.

Chapter Thirteen

It's a sharp learning curve

When I started on the job, we had sixteen men on duty on each shift at Bramhall Station: Ladder Six with five, Engine Four with four to five, Engine Six with four to five, the on-duty Deputy Fire Chief, and the Fire Department service truck and the Fire Department carpenter.

We were working a strange kind of swing shift. It was called Kelly Days. Every other week you had an extra day off so that you ended up working with a mix of men every time that you walked in the door.

Ladder Six's crew was Captain Jerry Jerome; Lieutenant Charlie Thomes; Drivers Jerry Chase, Andy Palazzo, and Carl Godine (Hoss); Ronny Deroschier; Jack Flaherty; Leigh Selleck; and myself. Engine Four's captain was Captain Wernick, the lieutenant was Joe "Shadow" Foley, and the Driver was Les Connelly. Engine Six's Driver was Phil Riley. We also had Bobby Stewart, "Mucka" MacDougal, Dick Foy, Dick Roy, Leo Landry, Chuck Solesky, Ted Axelson, Louie Napolitano, Ray Henderson, John Greene, and so many others.

Driver training. It was summertime, and that's a beautiful time of the year in Portland. It was a nice warm day with a temperature in the 70s, a blue sky and puffy white clouds, and a gentle breeze. The kind of day that you wish would continue on and on. That winter would never return. Captain Jerome decided to take advantage of the weather and begin to have me learn how to drive Ladder Six's tiller. This is one of the best jobs on a fire department and on a ladder truck. You're sitting up high. You don't have to be concerned with throttle pedals or brakes. All you have to do is learn how to steer the thing correctly. If you're in traffic, you have the best view of everything around you, including looking down into people's cars and sometimes seeing some very interesting sights. I have ridden on Congress Street in Portland, leaning back in the tiller seat and hanging both my feet out over the side. *Top of the world, Ma.* When you wave at the kids on the sidewalk, it's like giving them an extra special birthday present.

When Jerry Chase, as Ladder Six's Driver, decided to break me in as a Tiller Driver, he did it in a blunt, unique, effective way. Jerry was an over-the-road tractor-trailer driver in his part-time job. At the time, the Maine Medical Center had an entrance (the old original 1862 entrance) to the building, on the Western Prom, at the intersection with Bramhall Street. This entrance was originally designed for the width of a horse and carriage, circa 1860s. The building had been built just following the outbreak of the American Civil War. It had a horseshoe-shaped driveway turnaround. The height was about twelve feet. It was a beautiful red brick and granite block archway. It was about sixteen feet wide and paved with tar.

We were driving around the Western Prom area in Portland, and I was feeling pretty proud of myself. I hadn't hit anything yet. Jerry Chase picked up his speed, to about thirty miles an hour. He then headed into that horseshoe-shaped turnaround, at that old hospital entrance. He never slacked off his speed, and we went through the entrance and out the other side. I was scared spitless. He drove on without slackening his speed and out onto the Western Prom and went about 1,500 feet further up the street. He then pulled over to the sidewalk and stopped. I got down from the tiller seat and shakily walked up to the tractor. I was going to punch him out. Jerry looked down at me from the driver's seat and calmly said, "Did you hit anything?" I answered him, "No." He then said, "Well, I guess you'll make it then. Go get back up on the tiller." Like I said, It's a serious learning curve. I would learn later that Jerry was the best ladder truck driver on the fire department, and I would later be grateful to have learned how to drive from him. A year later, I would also be taught to drive the tractor, the "Front Half."

A Tractor-Trailer Aerial Ladder is the best truck in the world for city firefighting. When you have two people who can operate that truck well, a Driver and a Tillerman, you will find that they can maneuver that truck into the tightest places that you can ever imagine. We were able to place that aerial ladder into tight alleys and driveways between buildings with turns in them, tight parking lots full of cars, damn near anywhere that we wanted to go with it. We have set that aerial between power lines, over one roof to reach another roof, out over wharves, and up the underside of bridges.

We also cross-trained with engine companies because at any given time, you might be asked to ride on one of the other trucks to fill in. I remember standing in front of the pump panel of Engine Four for the first time and being just overwhelmed by all the gauges and handles. All the name tags for the different gauges were baffling. What did they mean by "primary pressure" or "vacuum pressure"? What was friction loss? And some of the older guys were really defensive about having anyone know more than they did about that pump panel. One old driver would swing an axe handle around at you if you reached out and touched that pump panel to keep "you young guys away from my pump panel." There were others who would call you over to the truck and start teaching you about it. That's when I learned that a water supply, pump panels, water tanks, and hose fittings are all just plumbing systems designed to move water for a different purpose.

All our trucks at that time were open cabs (no roofs), with gasoline engines and manual transmission, and if you were driving a truck with those old manual transmissions, well, if you missed a gear, you had to pull over to the side and start all over again, because the transmissions did not have synchronized gears in them. As you start all over, all those old guys would sit there glaring at you for making a stupid rookie mistake. We rode an Officer up front with the Driver and two to four men on the tailboard. Try to draw a picture in your mind of trying to stay on the tailboard while riding through city streets during the winter weather, with its snow and ice. "Hanging on for dear life" is the phrase that I use. A steel diamond plate backstep covered in snow and ice makes for some interesting rides. We did not use safety straps or safety bars. And no one rode in the jump seats unless you were hurt. The drivers had to get used to scrapping the snow and ice off the driver's seat and off the floorboards and the pedals before they could get back into the truck to drive it. And if you were wet and soaked through from fighting the fire, by the time you got back to the station, your coat, gloves, helmet, and pants would be all frozen into whatever shape you were in for the ride back. It was almost six years before I saw my first truck with a roof and automatic transmission. At that time, we thought that things were getting soft. It was also five years before we saw a self-contained breathing apparatus on one of our trucks. But more about that later.

Chapter Fourteen

Memorable ladder sets

One summer evening, at about 10:00 p.m., we received an alarm for a fire in a penthouse apartment. I was working with Leigh Selleck that night. The fire location was on top of the Eastland Hotel, on Congress Street near Congress Square. We set to the nearest roof edge to where the penthouse apartment was located: on top of the roof of an eight-story office/residential building. We extended the aerial out to its full length, at about a seventy-five-degree angle, and we came up about eight feet short of the edge of the roof of the main building. So Leigh and I decided that instead of bedding the aerial and trying to move the truck closer to the building, we took a ten-foot straight wall ladder, took it to the top of the aerial, lashed it into place with lifeline ropes, and completed the set. We then hauled hose lines and tools up over that jury rig set for about two hours. If we had ever been caught doing it by OSHA, well, who knows, but we got away with it, and it worked.

"Necessity is the mother of invention."

On another fire scene one afternoon down on Hanover Street, we had a fire that was located on the rear of a three-story apartment building. This building was located on Paris Street. The building was a wood-framed, flat-roofed apartment building, with gasoline siding (building siding that was made from asphalt shingles), known to ignite and burn rapidly. The fire had started in the framing of the porches and stairs that were at the rear of the building; these extended upward from the ground level to all three floors and were attached into the rear wall of the building. The only way that we could reach the upper levels of these porches was to move Ladder Six into the parking lot of a building on the next street over and set the aerial across a parking lot, over several parked cars, across the fence separating the properties to the rear of the building where the fire was. Andy Palazzo was the Driver. We had the aerial extended out to about ninety feet. The angle of the set was less than ten degrees, almost horizontal. The book says that you cannot work on an aerial ladder in that position. But we did. One at a time, each of us would walk out to the end of the aerial, sit down on the end rung, with our feet dangling in midair, and work with an axe at the burned wood of the fire building. The tip of the aerial would move up and down in about eight- to ten-foot bounces each time that we took a swing with the axe. So you would end up taking a swing, waiting for the aerial to stop moving, take another swing, and wait for the aerial to stop moving. We did this for about an hour. Sometimes, you just have to push the envelope to get the job done.

We used to practice climbing the aerial ladder by setting the aerial straight up into the air while the truck was parked on the ramp of the station and extending it to its full height (one hundred feet). We would then climb one side of the ladder, cross over, and climb down the other side. We nicknamed this the "Hero Climb." At one time, a certain Deputy Fire Chief used this as punishment for us because someone complained about his heavy drinking while on duty.

I worked with two firemen who were working as steeplejacks in their part-time jobs. Lee and Joe taught me a lot. You don't get over being scared, but you do learn how to do it right.

Ladder Six also carried a full complement of ground ladders including a Bangor ladder. A Bangor ladder is a fifty-five-foot ground ladder that the book says takes five men to set: three raising the ladder itself and two on the tormentor poles (these are outrigger poles to keep it from falling sideways). It took four men just to carry this ladder around on fire scenes. It weighed more than two hundred pounds.

Ladder Six also carried a small booster tank, with 250 gals of water and a 500-gpm pump with a 50-foot booster hose line. We carried pompier ladders. These were poles with a curved slotted steel hook that looked like a large saw blade on one end. They were used to climb the outside of a building, by swinging the pole over your head into the window above you. The slotted hook would catch the windowsill. You then climbed the pole to that window and repeated this activity until you reached the desired floor. I have climbed six stories up and back down on the outside walls of a building using this tool.

We carried some leftover tools from a bygone era. Some of the ladders that we carried were wooden ladders. We carried a life net. In training, I have jumped from a four-story building into this net. On Ladder Six, we carried four leather fire buckets. We also carried a line throwing gun, a rifle that fired a blank 30.06 caliber cartridge that propels a floatable cartridge attached to a long length of small line. This was used in rescue situations. Because of my experience in the military, I already knew how to use this, and in the military, I had used it in real rescue situations to carry a safety line from ship to ship at sea.

During my career, I had the great pleasure to attend classes six times at the National Fire Academy in Emmitsburg, Maryland. These classes were for two weeks each time, and during the middle weekend, you are given the opportunity to go play tourist in the surrounding area. This area included Washington DC and Baltimore, Maryland.

At a class in 1997, during one of those middle weekends, I spent two days with the Baltimore Fire Department's 14 Engine on Hollings Street. At the time, 14 Engine was the busiest engine company in the world. I made two fires with them in one day. But what stays in my memories from that weekend is the sight of two Seagrave Tractor-Trailer Aerial Ladders coming on scene for those fires. I was in heaven. God, I loved that truck. Portland no longer has a tractor-trailer aerial ladder, and that is a loss. That style of truck is truly unique to the fire service.

CHAPTER FIFTEEN

My first working fire and my first save

I had been on the job for about two weeks. It was the end of May 1967. Early summer in Portland. The day was a beautiful day with a clear sky and an air temp of about seventy degrees. In my first two weeks on the job, we have responded to numerous small fires: dumpster fires, car fires, a few mattress fires. This one afternoon, we received a fire alarm for a room fire on Hollis Road, off Brighton Avenue, behind the Brighton Medical Center. It was a long travel for us. The distance is about three and one-half miles. Our response time was about six minutes. When we arrived on scene, we found a stately 2½-story, wood-framed, single-family residence, in the Victorian-era style. We had heavy smoke showing from the second floor, on the right side of the building. This was a single-box alarm. Engine Three was first due; Engine Four, Engine Six, and Ladder Six filled out the box. The Ladder Six Driver was Andy Pallazo, and the Tillerman was Hoss Godine. On arrival, the Deputy Fire Chief, Jim N., called to me and said, "Get inside and do a search."

Meanwhile, Ladder Six was setting the aerial to the right side, second floor, of the building to a bedroom window.

I went into the front door of the building. I was looking at a large foyer area with a wide stairway, on the right side, leading to the second floor. I walked up the stairs while calling out, "Is anyone here?" At the second-floor landing, the area was smoky, and I could hear the other firemen working in the bedroom off to the right. The smoke started getting a little thicker, and it had that classic smell of wet horsehair plaster. I turned to the left and entered a bedroom area. An elderly man was standing there looking scared and confused. I spoke to him and said, "I'm a fireman, sir. Could you come with me, please." I held out my hand, took him by the arm, and walked him down the stairs and out the front door, to the sidewalk. My first save, and it was just that simple.

Years later, we would learn that this elderly man was afflicted with what would later become known as Alzheimer's disease. But at the time, to me, he was just a confused, scared old man.

After doing that, while I was feeling pretty good about myself, that's when I got a little stupid. Hoss was on the aerial ladder, set to the window at the right side of the building, and I heard him holler out, "I can piss more water than I'm getting out of this hose line." The Deputy Fire Chief told me to connect in another line to a Siamese fitting, to get more water to Hoss, and I promptly opened the valve the wrong way and soaked the Deputy Fire Chief from head to toe. Not a nice way to say, "Hi, Chief. I'm the new guy here." For the next few weeks, I was told, repeatedly, to just stay away from any of the hose fittings until I learned what they were for and how to use them. I was then told to take them all out of the compartments and clean and service them and, while I was at it, to hopefully learn what they are used for. Like what is the difference between a Siamese fitting and a "Y" fitting. That first summer was a steep learning curve.

CHAPTER SIXTEEN

My early years at Bramhall

Bramhall had been open as a new station for about six months when I started work. Everything was new and it looked it. One of the things that was mentioned to me by the older men was that whoever had approved the building design had let the contractor install nice white tile floors throughout the living areas of the building. Firemen are always walking around in fire boots that frequently have just come from some fire scene, maybe with melted tar on them. We tracked up those floors constantly. And we constantly scrubbed and cleaned and rewaxed them.

The living areas upstairs were divided up into a day room, a series of two-man sleeping rooms, a library, a kitchen, and office space. Downstairs was the apparatus floor, main floor, watch desk, work areas, and the offices for the Cumberland County Emergency Preparedness staff.

When we were running with a full complement of manpower, there were two men in each room. I roomed with Jerry Chase for two years. I would later change shifts and work just opposite him. It worked out well, because we both snored very badly. Jerry was an over-the-road truck driver, with his own tractor. When I worked opposite him at the station, he would sometimes call me at the station (usually about one or two hours before shift change) and say something like, "Hey, Bob, can you hold up and work for me, just until I get in. I'm headed back to Portland now."

I would respond, "Sure, Jerry. Where are you now?"

He never failed to shake me up by saying, "I'm outside of Springfield, Massachusetts. But I'll be in Portland in two hours."

And he would make Portland in that two-hour time frame, hauling a loaded tractor trailer. (Just don't ask how.)

Lou Napolitano. This is the man who became a second father to me. He lived about six blocks away from where I lived, and I used to go to his home and have breakfast with him and his family and then he would ride with me to the station. I have fond memories of his wife and children in their home. Lou taught me so much about the job. Today, forty-nine years later, I can still hear his voice. "Hey, kid, follow me." We used to joke about blue uniform sweaters. The one that I bought for myself was exactly like his. And he would holler at me, "Hey, kid, have you got my sweater on?"

I also joined four other men on my shift, and we cobbled together a set of free weights and started working out together. Joe, Dick, Lee, Donny, and myself. It was a good mix of weightlifting styles. Two of the men were into bodybuilding, one man was into powerlifting, and one man was interested in overall maintenance. I began building with no set goal. Eventually I reached a point where I was bench-pressing 280 pounds and bicep-curling 45 pounds. My body weight at that time was 175 pounds. Everyone helped each other out. I was bench-pressing a 260-pound bar one day. Dick was spotting for me, standing behind me as a safety man in case a problem occurred. What I didn't know was that my persistent sore throat that was about a week old was really tonsillitis. I had the bar up over my head when my right shoulder collapsed out completely. If Dick hadn't been there for me, I would have dropped the weight down across my neck and died. Thanks, man. I had my tonsils removed three weeks later. It was three days before Thanksgiving. That year I ate turkey soup.

We all worked some kind of part-time jobs. We had to because the pay was so bad. Two of the men I worked out with were steeplejacks, men that worked at high heights, such as the tops of factory chimneys. One of these men used to do one-handed pull-ups from the staging railing, one hundred feet above the ground. One of these men asked me to help him on a job site one day. He said the job paid good—$50 per lightbulb. We would be changing the lightbulbs in the Raymond Communication Tower: eight lightbulbs spread out over 1,700 feet of height. And it was all climbing a ladder, no hoist. At that time, the Raymond Tower was the tallest man-made structure in the world. I had to refuse because I was already committed to a house-painting job. But I have wondered for years about that challenge and whether I could have done it.

At one time, those of us on the fire department also worked at all the jobs in the building trades as electricians, plumbers, carpenters, sheet rockers, roofers, concrete workers, painters, equipment drivers, truck drivers, warehouse work, hospital aid work, teachers, and everything in between. We even had an airplane pilot (he flew, at night, for an airline that carried cargo throughout New England). We had men with Merchant Marine licenses; these men frequently worked as professional fishermen. We had men who had degrees in education and law. We could have stepped into almost any occupation out there. Some of the men did group together and work in the building trades as a company. There were at least two construction companies in the Portland area that were made up of just off-duty Portland firemen.

Like a lot of the others, I ended up working a lot of part-time work, frequently seventy- to eighty-hour workweeks. There were multiple times when I would work for five or six or even seven months straight without taking a day off. This kind of work schedule did cost me. Eventually I would crash. And when I did, I usually ended up sick or injured. But I would rest up and go back out and do it again. At that time, I was working seventy to eighty hours a week, and my wife at that time was working sixteen hours a week, and when I got home, she would tell me all about *her* shows on the television. Today, I still get angry when someone uses that phrase. This was also a part of the finishing touches on my first marriage. I remember frequently leaving home for work on a Monday morning and not getting back home until Friday evening. I worked as a house painter, carpenter, heavy-equipment operator, truck driver, anything that I could do to pick up some extra income. At one period of time, I had a business with a partner. We repaired large boilers, the kind that you climb inside of and walk around inside of. I would work at the station, leave and go to a job site, work until I had to leave to return to the station, work my shift, leave again and return to the job site, and do this over and over again for two, three, or four days in a row. It's not a good life for a marriage. Eventually my first marriage failed, for a lot of reasons, and this was part of it.

CHAPTER SEVENTEEN

Cooking at the station

Lou taught me how to cook for a sixteen-man crew. Our diet in the station was high on carbs, and we burned it off almost faster than we ate it. Firefighting research has shown that a fireman, in the first ten minutes of a working fire, demands more from his body than someone working forty hours in a factory. We ate hard and burned it off just as fast.

One of the recipes that Lou taught me was for an Italian meal called pasta fasul. I still make that today, and I have many friends that request that I make it for the social events that my wife and I attend.

We had guidelines for cooking meals. Some of us were good cooks, and some of us weren't. The bad cooks were told after one try to please don't cook here again. The good cooks kind of rotated around. It depended on what everyone felt like eating that day. Usually, right after shift change in the morning, someone would ask, out loud, "Hey, what do you guys want to eat?" The discussion would be guided by the weather; by how much it was going to cost (we paid for all our own food); by what everyone wanted: meat, fish, soup, Italian, whatever. We had to figure out how much the meal was going to cost and then divide that by how many guys were eating. It was a simple formula. We also had to bring in the meal, at the cheapest cost possible, usually under $2.50 each. Because of these guidelines, we became really creative at planning meals. In 1967 dollars, $2.50 was a lot for lunch. I have one memory of having some Deer meat hamburg that I had brought from home. I had made it into a mincemeat pie. The only mistake that I made was to put it on the table and turn my back for fifteen minutes to answer a phone call. When I returned it was gone. I didn't get a single slice. (Boy, you guys are like a bunch of walking-around seagulls.) I did take the record for a low-priced meal once. I had some ham shoulder leftover at home. So I made a green split pea soup, and the price on the meal came out to be about $0.25 per bowl. One guy ate six bowls full. I also learned how to make a good chili. I used a very large pot, like a three-gallon canning pot. I used to make it and almost fill it full. And by the end of the shift there weren't any leftovers and the guys had cleaned up the pot.

We also had what we called the "House Fund." Everyone chipped in $2 each week, and this covered coffee, sugar, creamer, condiments, the daily newspaper, and other small items. It usually worked out very well. But it's funny about some of the guys. We had one guy who refused to donate to the house fund, but he would go across the street to the convenience store at the corner there to get his coffee because the store owner gave it to us free, and so he wouldn't have to pay for it. Boy!

We had another guy who refused to donate, but after the meal was over, he would come into the kitchen as we were cleaning up and make up a plate of leftovers for himself. We stopped his game by putting any leftovers down the sink and into the garbage disposal unit and grinding them up in front of him.

During the early 1970s, we experienced a beef shortage in the Northeast. This became my introduction to horsemeat. It was cheap at the time and tasted good. It is kind of dry, like moose meat.

Usually the cook didn't have to wash the dishes. But everyone else helped to prepare and clean up after. That's when I learned how to have a real family.

I used to chuckle whenever we had a dry spell in fire calls (not many runs). I used to see the guys start to act like a bunch of old hens with each other. They would start to nitpick at each other. "He used my coffee cup." "He won't clean up his room right." "Who took my stuff?" "Why can't he help out some more with the housework?" Boy! Sometimes it would get bad. As a Lieutenant, I used to tell my crew that I am not a babysitter. Work this out between yourselves. But then, when that bell rang, everyone would come together like a family of brothers. All the separate personalities would go away, and everyone became firemen together.

CHAPTER EIGHTEEN

Those rookie years

One of those fond-memory things, from those early days, that have gone by the wayside, that I have seen and been told about, is the gathering together of men either at the front landscape retaining wall, beside Bramhall's apparatus ramp, or by the front apparatus doors, with the doors up. We used to sit out there for hours and wait for calls. Sometimes we ended up sitting on that wall until 1:00 a.m. or 2:00 a.m. Just sitting and talking and watching the city life flowing past. It gave us a connection with the people from the neighborhood. That doesn't happen much anymore. That's a great loss.

One day, I was standing there with "Shadow" Foley. He was the lieutenant in charge of Engine Four. He was a special friend of mine. We were standing at the doors talking, and a car pulled up into the middle of the ramp and stopped. The driver shut off the engine. Then she and the passenger got out, locked the car, and started to walk away. Shadow spoke to her and said, "Hey lady, you can't park that car here. This is the driveway for this fire station."

She responded, "It's okay. I'm only going to be a little while. We're having lunch at the Roma restaurant, just down the street."

I tend to be a wiseass sometimes, and this was one of those times. I spoke up and said to the driver, "Hey, lady. Do you see that fire truck right there behind me?"

She said, "Yes."

I then said to her, "Lady, I drive that truck, and if we have an alarm and your car is in my way, I'm going to use this truck to push your car across the street out of my way, before I go on to the alarm."

Boy, was she angry. But she came back and moved her car off the ramp.

One of the other stories about Bramhall's ramp is not as humorous. The fire station's dumpster was located in one corner of the ramp. For a period of time, we used to see a street person picking through the dumpster looking for bottles and cans to turn in for money. He was Hispanic, and we nicknamed him Ramon. After a while, those of us at the station would save up the bottles and cans in the station and give them to him to help him out. Every winter, he would find some place to hole up, and in the spring, we would wait to see him again. One winter, he dropped out of sight, and we thought that he had again found a safe place to hole up in. About the end of March, we received a call to check out something suspicious, in a snow bank, on State Street about four blocks from the station. It was Ramon; he had ended up collapsed in that snowbank, sometime that winter, and froze to death there. The snow had covered him over. No one knew it until the snow started to melt that following spring.

I have seen dozens and dozens of deaths, but the deaths that bothered me the most were those where the person was alone when they died, and no one knew or cared. Or if the death was that of a child. They were the ones who never had a chance to live a life. Today I can close my eyes and the memories of them still are there, in living color.

Another ramp story happened when I was not there, but I know the men who were there. It was summertime, and the building directly across the street from Bramhall had a little neighborhood store; it also had an apartment upstairs. The store owner was a good guy. The apartment was rented to an asshole who had committed himself to living his entire life on welfare. Now, about 75 percent of the people on welfare are on it for just a few short months. Usually until they can get back on their feet again. But some people make it their lifelong ambition to stay on it. These are the same people who tend to create two, three, or four generations in that family that live on welfare. I have no sympathy or patience with these people. This one family we nicknamed the Clampets, from a television series at the time. They abused the system. One day, Lieutenant S. came down the stairs inside the station and saw Steve and two other men building a contraption, just inside the apparatus doors. It included a support system and a piece of single wall woodstove smoke pipe, about eight feet long. They had capped off one end and drilled a small hole in that end. Steve was pushing handfuls of nails, bolts, and pieces of chain into the open end of the pipe. He also had a railroad flare sitting on the floor ready to light. Lieutenant S. asked him, "What are you guys doing?"

Steve never batted an eye when he answered, "We've built a cannon and we're going to blast that son of a bitch Clampet out of that fucking apartment. We're tired of having to watch his shit and not being able to do anything about it."

Lieutenant S. never said a word. He just turned around, and carrying his coffee cup, he walked back upstairs. If that had been a real cannon, I think that the neighbors in that area would probably have cheered Steve on.

One day, the on-duty Deputy Chief had just pulled up onto the ramp and was just getting out of his car when Ladder Six had an alarm. The Chief stepped to one side and waited for us to pull out. I was sitting in the jump seat behind the driver, Hoss. There was a slight problem though: the guy who was the Tillerman for the day, Ronny, had been outside the rear of the station, in the fire station parking area, and didn't hear the alarm. So here we are on the truck, headed across the ramp, and the tractor portion is just starting to make a right turn onto Congress Street, when I look back and there's no one in the tiller seat. I start pounding on the driver's shoulder and pointing at the empty tiller seat. Hoss stopped the truck, and I started to get down off the jump seat and to go back and take over the tiller. Then came Ronny, running out of the station and trying to get his boots on at the same time. The Deputy Chief just stood there watching, shaking his head as if saying to himself, "I don't even want to know what this is all about," and turned around and walked on into the station.

On another occasion, one man was outside the rear of the station sunbathing. A call came in, and he didn't hear it. The truck made the run and came back, and he was still laying outside soaking up the sun. Years later, he would miss a two-alarm fire because he was in his bed at the station sleeping off a drunk. We took all the particular information on the fire, for the reports, and gave it to him in the morning.

One evening, I was on duty at the watch desk, which is located on the apparatus floor. It was summer and about 10:00 p.m. It was a nice quiet evening. I watched a car pull up onto the ramp and stop. The man-door entrance at the left front of the station opened up, and a man casually came into the station. He seemed in no hurry. He walked past the trucks, looking at them and coming toward me. I thought that maybe he was a friend of one of the other men who were on duty at the time. They were all upstairs watching TV. As the man approached me, I asked him, "Can I help you, sir?"

He said, "Yes. May I speak to the man that's in charge of the station?"

I reached over and picked up the telephone and called upstairs to the Dayroom. I asked for Captain Wernick, the Station House Captain. While I was doing this, the man just stood there watching me and said nothing. When the Captain answered the phone, I said, "Cap. There's a guy here to see you."

I still thought that this man was there to visit someone. When Captain Wernick came walking down the stairs and introduced himself to the man, the man said, "I have a problem."

The Captain responded, "Yes, sir, what can we help you with?"

The man then said, "Well. My car is on fire."

Things got a little exciting about then. I sounded the alarm, and everyone in the station responded. We all ran out to the car, and we found a smoldering fire in the front seat cushion. It seems that the man had been smoking a cigarette while driving down the street. It fell down into the seat cushions and started to burn. We removed the seat from the car and put the fire out. We checked out the rest of the car for any fire extension and found none. We searched the storage area in the rear of the station and found an old milk crate for this man to use as a car seat; we then sent him on his way home. Hey, it's just another quiet evening at Bramhall.

Hanging together on the ramp was such a connection for us all. It's a loss that this type of activity is gone now.

Chapter Nineteen

Some of the rescue calls

I remember the bums living under the aqueducts under the old Million Dollar Bridge, which connected Portland and South Portland. We went on rescue calls there for quite a few of them. Many of them were dead when we arrived. Many of them had been chewed on by the rats, and some of these people were still alive even with missing toes and fingers from the rats. Some had died from drinking canned heat. The alcohol strained through bread, from small cans of heating compounds. The rats in this area were wharf rats from the Portland waterfront, and down there on the docks, they grow to be larger than small dogs. It is not unusual to see a ten- to twelve-pound rat running around on or under those docks. Do not piss them off; sometimes they don't run and hide, they attack. I was in dress uniform one day, standing beside Ladder Six, while the rest of the crew was doing a fire inspection at a building on the West Commercial Street docks. One of these rats ran out from under the building and headed straight at me. It ran up to me and ran partway up my pant leg, before it turned and headed off in another direction. It took me five minutes before I could breathe normally again.

When I was in the United States Coast Guard, we had a saying about going on rescue calls. We had to go out to sea, on the call, but we didn't have to come back in.

Working as a fireman was the same. Every time that the bell rang or the phone rang, we knew that we were going out, but we didn't know where to, for how long, or for what. It took me four or five years, after I retired, before I stopped jumping up and running to answer the telephone by the second ring. It becomes such an ingrained habit.

I remember waking up, in the middle of the night, while I was at my home, from having nightmares that the fire alarm had rung and I couldn't find my turnout gear, so that I could get to the truck; I was stumbling around my bedroom and looking for my boots. Some of these things stay with you for a long time afterward. Even today, after twenty-seven-plus years of retirement, I still stop and look if I hear sirens and air horns. I still want to step up and help if the situation calls for it.

When the alarm rings, it's part of the adrenaline rush. You don't know all or what it is that you are responding to. A report of smoke in the area can end up as a multiple-alarm fire or someone burning leaves, especially in the fall. Or a report of a fire in a building can end up as a candle in a window; we had dozens of these, and many of these were in college dorm buildings. Accident scenes can include hazardous materials or fatalities. Dumpsters can hold anything including explosive materials like spray paint cans or ammunition and sometimes human bodies. In the fire service, we have found, sometimes tragically, that vacant buildings can be the homes to street people. This can create especially dangerous situations. For a period of time, each fall we would visit the vacant buildings in our respective response areas and roust out the street people living in them, hoping that they would then find a safe place for the cold weather months. We were just tired of finding them dead, from a fire that they had started, inside the rooms that they were in, while they were just trying to stay warm.

We went through a period when we encountered a lot of late-night car fires in certain sections of the city that were vacant. These cars all had out-of-state license plates on them. Investigations showed that there was a problem in some of the areas outside of Maine, that unwanted informants, people from these areas, would be taken to Portland, in the trunks of cars. Once here, the cars would be set on fire, usually in the very early morning hours and in vacant areas. The person in the trunk of the car would be left there.

My worst rescue calls were the ones involving kids. I always thought that if the dead person was over twenty or so, then they had had some chance to live for a while. But if they were younger than that, then they had never really had that chance, and this saddened me. I also have a hard time with the memories of the people who died alone and no one cared. No matter what the cause of death, they died and no one cared.

When I was a Lieutenant on Engine One, Munjoy Hill, we responded one hot summer night to a report of a bad smell in an apartment house on Cumberland Avenue on Munjoy Hill. It had been hot and muggy for about two weeks. On arrival, I saw a two-family apartment house in good repair. The owner met me on the sidewalk. He lived on the second floor and rented out the first-floor apartment. He told me that he smelled a bad odor in the first-floor hall. He also told me that he hadn't seen the first-floor tenant for four days. I smelled that strong, distinctive odor when I was standing outside the building on the sidewalk. I knew what I was going to find inside. But I had to check everything out first. I told my crew to stay outside. No sense in putting them through this too. The owner and I went inside, and as soon as I stepped through the door into the hallway, I knew what was causing the smell. I am a firm believer in having and showing respect for the dead, no matter who they are. I asked the owner if I could use his telephone. I did not want to use my radio. I then called the Fire Dispatcher, "Scary Gary," and told him that Engine One was at the scene and that we had found an unattended death. I told him to *not* put it out over the fire department radio because I didn't want "scanner land" to know about it. I wanted the Police Sergeant to come to the scene and see the body at the same time that I did so that we could verify the death. As soon as I had hung up the phone, the Fire Dispatcher called the on-duty Deputy Chief on the radio and told him, "Car Three, Engine One has a dead body up there on Cumberland Avenue." I was pissed. I had just finished telling him to not put it out over the radio. When the Police Sergeant arrived, we entered the apartment and found a male who had been dead for about four days. He had apparently died from natural causes. It looked like either a heart attack or a massive stroke. He was lying on the bed partly covered by bedclothes. I was so sad for him because he had died alone, and no one knew about it or cared about it for four days.

On another incident like this, one late summer day, I was in charge of Engine Four, out of Bramhall Station. It had been hot and muggy for three or four days. We received a call to assist the police at an address on Spring Street near Brackett Street. The building was a brick, two-and-a-half-story apartment house with a pitched roof. It had three apartments in it. The police officer said that he wanted us to make entry into the apartment. I think that what he really wanted was for someone else, instead of himself, to go to the top-floor apartment and open the door. As he and I entered the building, I could smell the problem. I went back out to the truck and got a little kerosene cleaning fluid from the truck compartments and put it on two pieces of cleaning rags from the truck. I gave one to the cop and used one myself. Just hold it under your nose. We found that this was a way to block the smell of dead bodies that had been around for a few days, especially in the summer months. The cop and I walked up the stairs to the top floor. I did my legal B&E (breaking and entering) on the door. We entered the apartment and found the body of a young man who had committed suicide by drugs. It looked like he had been dead for at least three or four days. So sad. Again, no one knew or asked.

Some of the calls hit close to home. It was summer, and I was driving Engine Four for Stubby. I had just come on duty for the day shift. It was about 7:30

a.m. It was a sunny day with an air temp at about seventy degrees already. We received an alarm for a car accident on Elm Street and Lancaster Street, near the Bayside area of Portland. The accident was reported to have happened in front of the Portland Unemployment Office. We responded, and our response time was about three minutes. The distance was about one and one-half miles. On arrival, we found that a car had hit a building. The building had originally been an old printing company shop, and the walls were brick and three layers thick. This made the wall a twelve-inch-thick masonry construction. The car was an old Plymouth Fury, one of the full-sized American cars. The car had hit the building straight on, and it had hit the wall so hard that it had compacted like an accordion into the wall of the building. After impact, the car's length had reduced from eighteen feet to about eight feet long, front bumper to back bumper. All we could see of the driver was a section of his skull and hair about eight inches long and three inches wide. As we waited for a wrecker to remove the car, we questioned the bystanders. It seems that this man had been talking to them while waiting for the Unemployment Office to open. Everyone was there to collect their collect their unemployment checks. This man had suddenly told his friends, "Hey, watch this." And he climbed into his car and drove away. As he drove around the block, he accelerated his speed. When he turned back down Elm Street from Cumberland Avenue, toward his friends, his speed was about thirty miles an hour He quickly accelerated to about fifty-five miles an hour and drove straight into the wall. It was his way of suicide. The wrecker driver/owner, Charlie, was well-known to us, and he was told to be careful because of the body that was still trapped in the car. He would later tell us that he took almost five hours to cut the car apart to remove the body. It was after that that I learned the identity of the man in the car. He was one of my cousins.

An interesting note is that a few years later, I read a study was done involving fatal car accidents. It was reported that a significant percentage of them are thought to be suicides. The cynic in me speaks up and says that if you want to die, go ahead, but why take someone else with you? That is selfish.

CHAPTER TWENTY

Some interesting grass fires

We considered any fire involving less than one room to be a small fire. Usually, when the responding truck arrived, the officer would call in to Fire Alarm and report what they had and if they wanted help.

But over the years, we had a couple of grass fires that because of the circumstances escalated to multiple-alarm fires. Portland is a major railroad hub. There are three railroad lines coming into Portland. One grass fire in particular was caused by a passing railroad train. One of the railcars in the train had a "railcar truck wheel" bearing that had overheated and was melting as it went down the track. This is not an uncommon occurrence. It was spitting out pieces of melted liquid steel all over the sides of the railroad bed. This caused a grass fire that stretched out for more than two miles. Things get a little exciting when that happens. This fire was interesting because we ended up with the equivalent of a three-alarm fire response for a grass fire.

At another alarm, the fire was a grass fire started by vandalism. This particular day was sunny, but we had thirty- to forty-mile-per-hour winds. The fire rapidly spread throughout the entire length of Capisic Pond Park. The park is about one quarter of a mile long by about one-eighth of a mile wide. The area is mostly saltwater marsh with tall grassy foliage. This is an area that is used for walking and recreation. The park area is located within and surrounded by an area of a heavy concentration of single-family homes. Because of the winds, this fire quickly spread and became another three-alarm fire for a grass fire.

A third instance of a multialarm grass fire was a fire in the area of Pierce Street, in the Stroudwater area of Portland adjoining Westbrook Street. This area is another salt water marsh that meanders through and into an area of heavy concentration of residential dwellings. The area is about one third of a mile wide by one half of a mile long. This was another day of heavy winds. The fire was started by vandalism. And it quickly spread to almost the entire area. We ended up with a two-alarm complement of fire equipment and, interestingly enough, some airport crash rescue trucks, but they proved to be worthless because they quickly bogged down in the saltwater marsh mud and had to be towed out with a bulldozer. We were on this scene for two days and nights.

On another occasion in that same area of the city, it was another hot, windy day. This was another grass fire that was started by vandalism. At one point, I was standing on steeply sloped area, off Capisic Street, in between two houses looking out over the marsh area, and I watched Jimmy, a good friend of mine, leave his bunker coat on the grassy bank in front of me and walk out into the burning field. This dried grass was about four feet tall and burning. He got about five hundred to six hundred feet out into this field when suddenly the wind shifted and began to blow the fire at him. Just that suddenly the fire was licking at his ass. I never saw him run so fast in his life. And the fire chased him right back to his bunker coat. I later chewed on Jimmy a little, and I asked him, "What the fuck were you thinking?" He just shrugged and walked off.

Some of the grass fires were so comical. We received a call for a grass fire late one evening. The call was for the rocky beach area at the base of the eastern promenade facing out toward the entrance to Portland Harbor. This area is a very steep embankment that descends about one hundred feet down from a city monument parking area, to a railroad bed and then about fifty feet across to the shoreline. When we arrived and started to look around for the fire, we saw a campfire on the rocky shoreline. I walked down the embankment and had the truck go around the long way to the railroad bed access road and meet me at the campfire. When I got to the campfire, I found a young man there. I told him who I was and asked him what he was doing there. He said that he had just arrived after hitchhiking and walking from California to Portland, Maine. He said that he was going to camp out for a few days. I worked hard at not laughing out loud at him. It seems that he had never, in his life, experienced an area where there was a saltwater tidal effect. He had placed his campsite about three feet above the low-tide level. In Portland, our saltwater tides average nine feet in height. This young man's campsite was going to be underwater in about another three hours. We informed him about the problem and told him that he should really pack up his things and leave. Right now!

You never know how things are going to turn out beforehand. No two fires or emergency incidents are the same. This is a tough lesson. They are all slightly different. And the fire never acts the same way each time.

Sun Tzu, a Chinese philosopher, wrote a book titled *The Art of War* more than one thousand years ago. In the book, he wrote that "no plan of battle survives first contact." His book is required reading at military academies all around the world. This statement also applies in the fire service. We firemen become so good at thinking on our feet in emergencies because we quickly learn that we have to.

Delano Mills Fire

Another fire that started as a grass fire and quickly grew into something much larger. One of the large fires that I was at, early in my career, occurred on St. James Street, in the Libby Town section of Portland. The right side of St. James Street is all commercial buildings. The left side of St. James Street is a large open field, a city-owned swimming pool, and an elementary school.

This area is mixed commercial buildings that are adjacent to a railroad line. The other side of this single-track railroad line is concentrated multiple-family residential buildings. This railroad bed, the old Boston and Maine Rail system, is about fifty feet wide. The buildings are of different ages. Some are fairly recent and some are old. There is a large open-field area that used to be the city dump and is nonbuildable. It is now used for sports practice. Some years later, the city did build an elementary school there, but it had to be abandoned later because of the methane gas seeping up through soil and into the building. This proved to be an almost disastrous situation.

The Delano Mills building was an old factory building. It was one hundred feet wide by four hundred feet long. The building was heavy timber construction, with a flat tar and gravel roof. The building also had a full basement area. These old mill buildings have common factors from a firefighting perspective. They are old heavy timber construction; many of them pre-date World War I; they are usually vacant or being used for storage; their interiors are usually saturated with oil-soaked wooden floors; and they frequently have twenty- to forty-foot-high ceilings inside. The interior walls are usually unprotected bare wood. Any windows are usually covered by heavy wire mesh screens or metal grills. The mechanical systems are usually out of date. Any plumbing and electrical systems have usually been stripped out. Any fire alarm systems are not functioning or have probably been scrapped out. Any fire suppression systems are usually either nonexistent or not functioning. The exterior siding of this particular building was asphalt shingles, better known, in the fire service, as gasoline siding. New England is riddled with these buildings. Almost every town in New England that is located on or near a river has at least one of these buildings, usually masonry and heavy timber construction. One of the largest fires in New England, occurred at Chelsea, Massachusetts, on a quiet Sunday afternoon, on October 14, 1973. The Great Chelsea Fire involved a series of old mill buildings that extended for eighteen city blocks, and it burned over a three-day period. The fire response for this fire was from sixty-seven fire departments. At the time of the last fire at the Delano Mill building, the building was being used to store hundreds of new tires, in the basement, from a local tire dealer. We had had a series of small fire problems in the building, but nothing serious.

It was an late spring day, just before the schools had stopped for the summer. We received the fire alarm for a grass fire along the railroad tracks behind the Delano Mills building. Engine Six responded first; they were about one and one-quarter miles away and doing building inspections (block Inspections), with a response time of about three minutes. And by the time they were halfway to the scene, they could see a very large amount of black smoke in the area of the building. They called for a working fire and a Second Alarm at the same time. At the same moment, a Street Box alarm was also struck for that fire scene. Eventually the Fire Dispatchers would receive more than twenty fire calls for this fire. By the time Engine Six arrived at the scene, the Officer-in-charge, Lieutenant Kenny, called for a Third Alarm. A grass fire had ignited the asphalt siding on the building beside the railroad tracks. Within five minutes' time, this fire had gone from a grass fire to a third-alarm building fire for us. There were two men that were sent to the roof to get ready to receive a hose line. The fire exploded throughout the building almost trapping these men on the roof. The fire spread so rapidly that within fifteen minutes from ignition, the entire building was involved. The fire was being fueled by the old oil-soaked timbers in the structure and then by the hundreds of new tires stored in the basement. The fire was burning so hot that the Ladder Six truck, parked more than one hundred feet away from the building, started to burn. Two of the lights melted, the leather seats began to burn, and some of the truck body paint began to blister and burn. Lieutenant Kenny saw what was happening and jumped into the driver's seat and drove the burning truck out away from the heat of the fire. It was good luck that the aerial ladder had not been set and that he was able to move the truck with no one in the tiller seat. This fire ended up consuming the entire building, right into the foundation. We had no chemical suppressant available to use on those tires in the basement; we just pumped water into the fire until the basement filled up with water. This place burned and smoldered for three days.

But thanks, Kenny, you saved that truck. This fire was my first experience of having to wear my helmet on backward to shield my face from the heat. It was also the first time that I was at a surround-and-drown fire. We eventually used four guns on the fire, and it was still a couple of days before we had it out. This fire was one of four third-alarm fires that I experienced in my first year as a fireman in Portland.

Chapter Twenty-One

My first major fire
The Elks Club on Free Street

I had been on the fire department for about four months when I went to my first major fire. The Third-Alarm fire at the Elks Club on Free Street, in Portland.

This was a large wood-frame building. It was eighty feet wide by two hundred feet long. It was a two-story building with a flat roof, with a tar-and-gravel surface. The building was in good repair and was used as the Elks Club headquarters and an event center. It was late afternoon and I was at Bramhall Station, in the night watch room, shining my uniform dress shoes. One of the men had installed an emergency radio scanner in the room. I was listening to the Portland Police Department frequency. I heard the Police Dispatcher give an assignment to a patrol car to "check the area behind the Elks Club on Free Street for a fire in the trash barrels." I walked out into the dayroom and asked the crew, "What truck has the Elks Club for a response area?" The guys said that it was Engine Four. I said, "Engine Four is going to the Elks Club for a fire in the trash barrels." I had no sooner finished speaking that when the bells went off and the Fire Department Dispatcher called for all of us to go to the Elks Club on a First Alarm. We got geared up and on the trucks. As we started out the door, I heard the Dispatcher call us and say that the Police Department had relayed to him that we had a working fire. Engine Four was leading the line of trucks with Engine Six and then Ladder Six at the rear. We turned right onto Congress Street, and as we entered Longfellow Square, about three-tenths of a mile from the station, I heard, over the radio, the Captain, on Ladder Six, call the Dispatcher on the radio, "Strike me a Second Alarm for this fire." I thought to myself, *Oh, oh, we're in for it now.* When we reached Congress Square, about another three-tenths of a mile, the Captain on Ladder Six called the Dispatcher on the radio, "Strike me a Third Alarm for this fire." By that time, we could all see the smoke rising over the skyline. As we turned down Free Street from Congress Square, we could see that the entire building was heavily involved with fire and smoke. That first report to total involvement was in less than five minutes. Ladder Six pulled up into the parking lot, off the Free Street side building and immediately set the aerial to the roof. Andy was driving. Lee, Hoss, myself, and Jack climbed to the roof and started to look for any way to start ventilating this fire. Suddenly, Hoss turned around and looked down at his feet. We all did the same. That's when we noticed that the roof tar was melting like ice water and even beginning to bubble under our boots. Hoss said, "We better get out of here. This place is getting ready to let go."

So we all went straight back to the aerial and started down. Jack went first, then Lee; Hoss told me to go next because I was the rookie, and he brought up the rear to make sure that I would be okay. As we were descending the ladder, we heard a loud rumbling noise from the roof. It was that close for all of us. The entire roof had just collapsed into the fire. We all almost took a one-way trip into hell. I learned a lot that day. Not one of those men that I was with got excited or worked up at all. We just took it calm, cool, and collected. Boy, I was working with some great men. The decision was then made to fight this fire from the outside, and we did. Hose lines were set up, water guns were put into place, and we just did a "surround and drown." At one point, I watched as a captain, Bob, tried to use a large (2½") hose line on the fire; he was standing on a shed roof that was attached to the fire building. He was forced backward by the water pressure until he was knocked off the roof to the ground. He was injured and would be out of work for a few weeks. We would be on this fire scene for two more days. Lou Napolitano came up to me as I was working on a water cannon, flowing 250 gals a minute onto the fire, and said, "So kid, do you still want to be a fireman?" I quickly answered, "Yes."

This was a comment that I came to expect from some of the old guys for about two years, every time we were at a bad fire scene someplace. One of these guys would wander by and ask me that question, "So kid, do you still want to be a fireman?" After about two years of asking me that question, I think that they finally got the message, that "Yes, I did." These old "leather lung" guys were a tough bunch, but after you had proven yourself to them, they accepted you as one of themselves. They were the best.

On a side note: the city's water main system, at that time, was badly in need of an overhaul, as we were pumping with multiple engine company pumps from the same fire mains and demanding hundreds of gallons of water flow, each minute, from these hydrant mains. Well, some of the mains on the side streets were still made out of wood—yes, wooden fire mains that were still in use in the late 1960s. Because we overloaded the system, we collapsed residential water tanks in a few of the buildings in the area. By pulling such a draft on the water system, it sucks the tanks into themselves so that they collapse like an empty soda can. Over the next few years, the Portland Water District would make an all-out effort to update and upgrade this system to the point that Portland's water system today is the envy of most of the cities in the eastern half of the United States.

CHAPTER TWENTY-TWO

Private support services for the fire department

I should make some comments about support services for firefighting in Portland. At Bramhall Station, we also housed the Salvation Army Mobile Kitchen. We kept it clean and ready to go to any emergency scene where it was needed. When it was needed, there was a dedicated group of volunteers from the Salvation Army who would turn out, take it to where it was needed, set it up, and serve hot fluids and munchies to firemen at the emergency scenes. These folks did this for us firemen free of charge. For this, I still have a warm place in my heart for the Salvation Army. These people showed up at hundreds of fire scenes in Portland and stayed with us for the duration of the emergency. Rain or shine, cold or hot, they were there.

As much good as the Red Cross has done for people—and they have done a lot, whenever they showed up on a fire scene, they also served hot fluids and munchies, but they charged us for everything that we used. I can't forget that part of it either. And just to qualify myself, I have periodically done work for the Red Cross as a teacher of emergency skills. But I won't forget being at some fire scene, at 3:00 or 4:00 a.m., cold, soaked to the skin, exhausted, with icicles hanging from my helmet, and having to scrounge around in my pockets for some money to pay for a hot cup of coffee or some soup from the Red Cross mobile kitchen. They have wonderful people there, but they need to review some of their policies.

In Portland, we also had a group of fire buffs, the "Box 61 Club." This group's name came from the fire alarm box that was struck for the Great Portland Fire. Fire Alarm Box 61 has never had a recall struck for it. Technically it is still an active fire alarm. This group of dedicated people were great. They were the people that operated the Salvation Army Mobile Kitchen at emergency scenes. They showed up after some bad fires and helped us reload trucks, clean hose, and hang hose to dry—the heavy grunt work. They also saved an old vacant fire station, Old Engine Four, on Spring Street near State Street by Mercy Hospital, in the West End area of Portland. They operated it as the Portland Fire Museum. They were influential in supporting us whenever the city tried to cut us some more. Today, the Old Engine Four Building on Spring Street is home to the Portland Fire Vets Organization. And it is still operated as a Fire Museum for the Portland Fire Department. Today you can find regularly scheduled monthly meetings of this group, the Portland Fire Vets. They have open houses, and they bring in kids to show them the antique fire apparatus. Today the group is made up mostly of retired Portland firemen.

The old general store on Munjoy Hill

My second major fire occurred just a few months after the Elks Club fire when I had been on the job for about eight months. It was an old general store on top of Munjoy Hill. It was located at the corner of Congress Street and Waterville Street. This building was a landmark for the area. The "general store" was a leftover concept for the nineteenth century. In this store, you could buy anything: some groceries; some clothing, such as coats, boots, gloves, and hats; or some hardware items, such as paint, nails, lumber, tools; guns and ammunition; knives; archery equipment; just about anything you might need. It was a true old-fashioned general store. This building was wood-framed, 3½ stories tall, with a pitched roof with asphalt shingles and wood clapboard siding. The store portion of the building was within the first and second floors. The top floors were residential and storage. The basement area was heating, with an old coal-fired steam furnace, and storage. The building was about sixty feet wide by eighty feet deep. It was located at the sidewalk, on Congress Street. This fire was in the evening; it quickly became a General-Alarm fire, calling for mutual-aid response, from the South Portland Fire Department and the Falmouth Fire Department. This became a surround-and-drown fire because of the explosives (guns, ammunition, paint cans, aerosol cans) that were stored in the building. After the building had collapsed in on itself, we just sat back and poured water on it. In the later stages of the fire, Captain Wernick called to me and said, "Hey, kid. Come with me." We walked up onto the huge pile of debris that was still smoldering and burning underneath our feet. As we walked across it, we heard and felt explosions. I started to leave, and the Captain said, "Don't worry, kid. That's just paint cans exploding under where we are," and we kept walking. He was as cool as a cucumber—a good role model for me. We were at the scene of this fire for an additional two days.

CHAPTER TWENTY-THREE

Emergency rescue calls on Ladder Six

Prior to the implementation of MEDCU (the city ambulance service), medical emergency calls were handled by the fire department and the police department. This was a time of little or no training for EMS (emergency medical services). This was the time of the "bag 'em and drag 'em" mind-set. Ladder Six had an Emerson Resuscitator. This was oxygen tanks, regulators, and masks in a large travel trunk–style box. It weighed over forty pounds. We would respond to the emergency call, grab this "suitcase resuscitator" and go into whatever situation we had to.

One winter night, in a heavy snowstorm, we received a call to respond to a man having a heart attack at a local restaurant. It was snowing at the rate of two inches an hour, and we had ten inches on the ground already. The restaurant was located at the intersection of Congress Street and St. John Street, about one-half mile from Bramhall Station. Andy was driving Ladder Six and Hoss was tillering. Andy was able to get Ladder Six partway to the scene. He got bogged down in a snowdrift at the intersection of Gilman Street and Congress Street about two blocks from the restaurant. Hoss, John, and Teddy grabbed that Emerson resuscitator case and started wading through almost waist-deep snowdrifts to the restaurant. They saved the man's life, but Hoss would later say that the first people to really need some of that oxygen were themselves.

On another cold winter morning, we noticed that we would always get really busy on the mornings after a snowstorm. This would be for the elderly people who were outside, in the intense cold, shoveling the snow from their sidewalks and driveways, particularly old men who wanted to prove that they could still help. Snow blowers hadn't been invented yet. Later I will comment on missing fingers from snow blowers. This particular morning was sunny but cold. We had received about six inches of snow the previous night. The call came in about 9:00 a.m., for a man down on the sidewalk with a possible heart attack. He was said to be on the sidewalk at the certain street address near the University of

Southern Maine campus. I was tillering and Hoss was driving. Before we even left the station, Hoss was very upset. And when we arrived at the scene, we found out why. The victim was Hoss's father. And he was beyond our help. Hoss had told him to wait until he got home from being on duty to do the shoveling, but he had gone outdoors and started it anyway. Those kinds of calls can be rough. But it's so much worse when it's someone close to you.

On another incident, we had a call at 7:00 a.m., on a sunny summer morning, for a man having a heart attack. When we arrived, at the home, a single-family residence on Capisic Street near Bancroft Street, we found a man sitting in a chair, in front of the television. When I examined the man, I discovered that he had passed away sometime during the previous evening. (Rigor mortis and pooling of the blood were already occurring.) The lieutenant was told to go by the rules no matter what. So he told me to administer oxygen to the body. We administered oxygen to a corpse for more than an hour before we were relieved at the scene. What a waste of our resources and what a trauma for the wife.

Not all rescue calls are traumatic. Sometimes the rescue calls were funny, in a street humor kind of way. When no one dies or no one is badly hurt, it can sometimes be funny.

The elderly people used to keep an eye out for each other. They would call each other or stop in and see each other every day. And if someone dropped out of sight, they would call the Fire Department to come down and check on that person. We received hundreds of these calls each year, and we didn't mind going to them.

We received a call one summer evening to go to an address on Grant Street in the West End area of Portland. The building was one of those three-story brick apartment houses. We had dozens of buildings just like it in the West End. This evening, we were called to check on one of the tenants, an elderly woman who lived alone. Her friend lived in the next apartment to her, and she was the person who had called us. As we entered the building, the woman who had called us said, "My friend in that apartment hasn't answered my calls for the last two days. And she doesn't answer the door either." We stepped over to the door, and Lieutenant Charlie knocked on the door and hollered out, "Mrs. Smith, this is the fire department. Are you all right?" There was no answer. The lieutenant tried this again. Still no response. The lieutenant told Hoss, "Hoss, take the door." This meant to kick the door in. We had no key for the lock. Hoss stepped in front of the door and placed a good kick into the door just above the door handle. The door burst open, breaking the lock set. What happened next sounds funnier today, but at the time we were afraid that we had hurt someone. As the door burst open, we could see someone flying backward across the room and bouncing backward over the sofa. The door had burst open, swung closed, and then opened up again. When it opened the second time, we all crowded into the room and ran over to the figure that was sprawled across the top of the couch. It was the elderly woman. And she was knocked out cold. We revived her. Hoss thought that he had killed her. After a few minutes, when she was able to talk to us, she told us that she was very hard of hearing, and her hearing aid had broken. She couldn't hear who was at the door, but she thought that someone was there. So she went to the door and was peeking through the door lock keyhole at the same time that Hoss kicked open the door. The doorknob had hit her in the forehead, thrown her backward, knocked her out, and left a big lump on her forehead. She was okay. Her friends were okay. And we were okay. But Hoss was shaken up. For a few seconds, he thought that he had badly injured her.

CHAPTER TWENTY-FOUR

Dogs, cats, and other pets

As a rookie fireman, I was told early on by the old guys that we no longer responded to calls for cats in trees. But we still received calls from little old ladies who would call us at the station and very nicely ask us to please come to her home and get her cat down from the tree. I was coached to respond with this standard answer, "Mrs. Jones, have you ever seen the skeleton of a cat in a tree? No! Good, because when your cat gets hungry enough, it will come down from the tree." Nevertheless, we sometimes still responded to calls for animals that were just a little worse off.

We received a call one day for an injured dog. This was summertime and a beautiful day. The area of the call is still a place of beautiful old Victorian-era homes, many of which were built by and for sea captains in the days of the windjammer sailing ships. This particular incident occurred on Pine Street in the Western Prom area of Portland. When we arrived, we found a bloody, tragic situation. The homeowner's dog had been chasing the owner's cat around the inside of the second floor of the home. The second-floor windows had been open. The cat jumped out of the window and landed on a narrow ledge, about twelve inches wide, that ran around the outside of the second floor of the home. The dog jumped out of the window also. The dog, being larger and heavier than the cat, weighing about seventy-five pounds, overshot the ledge and sailed out of the second-floor window and landed on a decorative cast-iron spike fence that surrounded the front yard of the home. The dog was long dead when we arrived. He was impaled on six or eight of the iron spikes. We removed the dog's body from the fence, washed the fence down with water, and left the dog's body with the owner.

One summer day, I was in charge of Engine One from Munjoy Hill Station ("the Hill"). We received an alarm for fire in an apartment on Vesper Street. The house was a two-and-one-half-story, wood-framed, two-family apartment house. The fire was in the front two rooms of the second-floor apartment. We got in and did a fast knockdown. The owner of the apartment was a young woman; she was standing on the sidewalk in front of Engine One. As we were overhauling the fire and checking for any fire extension, I went to the rear of the apartment, in the kitchen area, and found a dead cat and a dead dog. We also found a twenty-gallon aquarium, with about fifteen gals of water still left in it. The fish in the aquarium were still alive. I picked up the aquarium and took it downstairs to the street. George and I walked across the street and gave it to the owner. I told her, "I'm sorry about the cat and dog, but we saved the fish."

No chapter on pets can be complete without this story. Every time that I read about someone somewhere having an unusual pet in an apartment, I am reminded of this incident.

I was working on Engine Four out of Bramhall one summer day when we received an alarm for the Lafayette Hotel on Congress Street between Longfellow Square and Congress Square, in the West End of Portland. This building is a very old apartment building that had been a former hotel, with about thirty one-room and two-room apartments. The building is four stories tall, masonry construction, with brick exterior walls and a flat tar-and-gravel roof. The alarm was for a fire in a basement apartment facing out onto Congress Street with the entrance door at six feet below sidewalk level. The response was Ladder Six, Engine Four, Engine Six, the fire rescue, and the on-duty Deputy Chief. As we were pulling up in front of the building, we saw light smoke coming out of a doorway leading into this basement apartment. The owner of the apartment, a young man, was standing on the sidewalk. As we started down the stairs to the apartment door, it was the usual cram of firemen trying to get into the fire area. It's always "Who's going to be first? Get out of my way." In this instance, we had the usual situation of six or seven firemen trying to get through the door of the apartment at the same time. The owner of the apartment took this opportunity to casually mention to the Deputy Chief that he was worried that his pet snake might have gotten out of its cage and would be free inside the apartment in all the smoke. It cracked me up to see all these brave firemen scramble over each other to get back up to the sidewalk and then to stand there saying to each other, "You go first." "No, you go first." "No, please, you can go first." Just for the record, I am not afraid of snakes. I happen to think that they are very interesting creatures.

On the subject of dogs in burning buildings. I was told this story by the guys that I worked with, when I first started on the job. It was winter and about three months before I came on the job. They were working on Ladder Six. It was in the evening. They received an alarm for a room fire in a nursing home on Emery Street near Cushman Street, in the Western Prom area of Portland. This building was a two-and-one-half-story, wood-framed, pitched-roof building with individual rooms for about ten residents. There was about two feet of accumulated snow on the ground, and it was cold. When they arrived, they saw smoke and some small amount of fire showing from a room on the second floor. They made entry and began to evacuate the residents and to fight the fire. The fire itself was small. It was just one room. But as they evacuated the residents, one elderly lady began crying out about her "baby." She kept crying out that her baby was in her room. The guys thought that perhaps she meant a grandchild. They set a ground ladder to the window, and Leigh climbed the ladder and pried open the window. This was when they found out what her "baby" was. As Lee reached into the window, he was met by a seventy-five-pound German Shepherd that was scared from the fire and smoke. The dog lunged at Lee, and as he did, Lee grabbed the dog by the scruff of the neck and threw it over his shoulder and out the second-floor window. Thanks to the two feet of snow on the ground, the dog was unharmed when he landed on the ground, and the last that they saw of the dog was as it was running up Emery Street.

I had a similar incident with another dog about ten years later. I was on Engine Five out of Central Station. The area today is called Bayside and is located in the center of the peninsula of Portland, facing Back Bay. It has always been a rough, low-income area. It is comparable to any ghetto in any city anywhere. We responded to an alarm on Anderson Street near Oxford Street. On arrival we found a three-story, wood-framed, flat-roofed apartment building having six apartments in it. The fire was in the apartment on the second floor in the rear of the building. I went up the stairs to make entry and found the door locked. I forced entry, and as I opened the door, I was met by a very frightened sixty-pound dog. The dog bit into my coat sleeve, tearing the coat but not quite making it to the skin. I did what Lee had done years before. I threw the dog over my shoulder, and it went airborne down the stairs to the sidewalk. This time there was no snow cover on the ground. The dog must have been okay, because the last anyone saw of it, was as the dog was running down the street away from the fire building.

The last call that I will mention about pets has to do with those in vehicles. I was driving Ladder Three out of Stevens Avenue Station. It was a summer afternoon, and we received an alarm to respond on the Second Alarm to a fire on Sherman Street near Deering Avenue Hill, just down Deering Avenue from Congress Street. This location is in the West End of Portland, in an area now called Park Side. This area overlooks Deering Oaks, a park in the middle of Portland. My response route was to go in Deering Avenue past King Middle School, partway up Deering Avenue hill, and then left onto Sherman Street. As we got closer to the scene, we could see large amounts of smoke and fire from the building. In my firefighting classes, I always teach my students to always watch the skyline. You can see the good ones from miles away. As I started to make my turn onto Sherman Street, a car was in the middle of the intersection. The woman driver was panic-stricken because of the activity around this fire scene, and she froze at the wheel. She had been looking over her shoulder at the fire trucks behind her, and when she looked back to the front, here comes another fire truck trying to get around her car. I couldn't make the turn because I just didn't have enough room to get past her car without hitting it. I started waving at her to move out of the way, but she just froze. Mark was riding in the jump seat behind me. He saw what was happening. He climbed down from the truck and ran up to the car. He opened the driver's door and saw that the woman was just panic-stricken. He grabbed her and pulled her from the car, and as he jumped into the driver's seat to move the car himself, he faced an immediate problem. There was a large dog in the backseat. Mark is good. He put the car in gear, pulled it out of the way, got out of the car, and told the woman, "Please get in your car and calm down the dog." This fire scene I will mention later, because it became a lesson in structural collapse.

CHAPTER TWENTY-FIVE

Some of the other men I worked with while I was a rookie

Lt. Charlie Thomes, Les Connelly, Chuck Solesky, Ted Axelson, Dick Foy, Stan Lynch, Dick Roy, Bobby Stewart, and Leigh Sellick.

Most of these men are no longer with us; they have made their transition to that much better place.

Leo L. was a wiry man, about 5'9" and about 160 pounds. He was one of those tough guys who had come home from World War II and gone to work on the fire department. He was of French Canadian background, from a tough Maine mill town family. He was also a good friend. I learned a lot from him. Leo was one of those men whom I remember saying to me, "Hey kid, follow me," as we ran into a burning building before breathing apparatus. Leo had a favorite saying that I have adopted as my own. Leo would say, "I calls 'em, like I sees 'em, and if some people don't like that, too bad, I still calls 'em like I sees 'em." Today I still take that same attitude.

Charlie T. was the lieutenant on Ladder Six when I started work. He was about 5'8" and about 160 pounds. He had a face that looked like it had been carved out of stone. Charlie was a little excitable. As he would start to get excited, he would start hollering and swearing. He knew what he was doing in a fire. He was a bull with any hand tools that we had. I was on his crew for about two years. I remember, whenever anyone asked him, "Hey, Charlie, how are you doing?" he would always respond, "God damn it! I'm tired and Shirley's tired too."

Shirley was Charlie's wife, and they had a wood furniture store in Westbrook. They both worked very hard at. Their business made and sold pine wood furniture. I have many memories of Charlie, including the evening shift change when he had a heart attack; he almost died right then and there. We did CPR him. He did survive, but he retired and died a few years later.

Remembering Charlie, I remember this incident. During the first month or so of the winter season, we would have a lot of small fires in automobile engine compartments. These fires would always start the same way and involve the same car engine components: the carburetor and the air filter, which is attached to and located just above the carburetor. The carburetor would flood with excess fuel, the vapors would fill the air filter, and the engine would try to ignite. Finally it would backfire, and the flash would ignite the excess vapors in the air filter, and it would start to burn. We had these fires by the dozens in cold weather. They occurred almost always at the start of the winter season; after that, the people would remember how to do it right. Sometimes, the fires would spread to the entire engine compartment and through the firewall into the passenger compartment, and the vehicle would be a total loss. It depended on how much old grease and oil had accumulated within the engine compartment. In some of the firefighting classes that I taught later, we did a fire set in a vehicle engine compartment and timed it to see how long it would take to spread to the passenger compartment. The usual time was about three minutes.

This incident was in the first strip mall in Portland. This strip mall was Arlen's Shopping Center. It was built on the site of the old Union Railroad Station at St. John Street and Congress Street, Union Station. The city administration, in one of its more stupid moves, decided in 1961 to have that beautiful old classic, Victorian-era train station building demolished and turned into a strip mall. The irony is that the strip mall's anchor store only lasted for about five years before it closed, and it has changed ownership about six or eight times over the years. As a child, I played in that old train station. There are some pictures of that building that still circulate today. It was comparable in beauty to Union Station in Boston, Grand Central Station I New York, or Union Station in Washington DC.

Back to that car fire call! We responded with Ladder Six. This incident occurred in the week before Christmas. It was in the evening, about 9:00 p.m. It was cold, below freezing, but the streets were clear with no snow or ice yet. This strip mall is about one-half mile from the Bramhall Station. Our response time was about three minutes. We entered the parking lot and noticed that it was full of parked cars. We also noticed that we could not see any visible fire or smoke. This parking lot held about 150 cars. We started to slowly cruise through the parking lot looking for the person who had called us. We had on our emergency lights but no siren. We made three passes through that parking lot before a woman stepped out from between two cars and flagged us down. The lieutenant said, "Are you the person that called us?"

She said, "Yes."

The lieutenant stood up in the cab of this open-cab fire truck, with five other firemen there, and hollered at her, "Jesus Christ, lady. How many fucking times were you going to let us cruise through this parking lot before you said something?"

Oh, Charlie! Some people just get excited and don't think. The fire in the engine compartment of her car was confined to the air filter. We removed it and sent her on her way.

Les Connelly was the driver on Engine Four. At that time, it was the busiest truck in Portland. Les was one of the old guys when I first went to work. He was a tall, good-looking man with white hair. He was also one of the gutsiest firemen I had ever met. Les had been driving Engine Four for almost his entire career. When Bramhall Station was built and Engine Four Station was moved to Bramhall and Engine Four Station was shut down, the Deputy Chief in charge of personnel decided to transfer Les to a different truck at a different station. Les was called at home and told to report to the other station the next morning. Les just didn't show up for work. After two days, the Deputy Chief called him at home and said, "Where are you? You are supposed to be at the other station. Les told him, "I drive Engine Four. That's what I do, period." The Deputy Chief called him back a few hours later and told him that he had been transferred back to Engine Four. The next morning, Les was back on duty on Engine Four. Les became a good friend because he was one of those drivers who was willing to teach you about the engine truck operations. He taught me the basics of engine pump operations.

He also had some great stories about the days when he started with the fire department at the old Brackett Street Station. Les told me the story about one of the men who almost got himself shot by the United States Secret Service. It was at the old Park Avenue Station. This building was located at the intersection of Park Avenue and St. John Street, a T-intersection facing east onto St. John Street. This was at the time when John F. Kennedy was campaigning for president. He came to Portland on a tour in the fall of 1959. Park Avenue Station was the home of Ladder Six. It faced Park Avenue at the intersection of Park Avenue and St. John Street. This fireman was an avid hunter. He was also a gunsmith who picked up a little extra money by repairing guns for people. This particular day he had just finished repairing a rifle for someone, and he was checking it out while he was looking out the second-floor windows of the station. These windows faced up St. John Street toward the Western Prom area. He noticed a parade of cars coming up the street toward him. He didn't know who or what they were. As they went past the front of the station, well, here he is standing in the window of the station, with a rifle in his hands, looking down onto the car carrying John F. Kennedy. The Secret Service people got really excited. And then we are all familiar with Dallas, Texas, a few years later.

CHAPTER TWENTY-SIX

Practical jokes

When firemen get a little bored, or when things are a little slow, and there's not much going on, watch out. This is when the practical jokes come out, and some of them are classic. One very special friend of mine "Mucka," holds a PhD in practical jokes. He has been retired for more than twenty years, and his reputation is still talked about. I will mention just a few of his "doctoral thesis" jokes.

Around 1970–71, we had two terrorists living in Maine. They were responsible for blowing up some government buildings within the midstate area of Maine. On the Portland Fire Department at this same time, one of the daily duties was standing telephone watch from 6:00 a.m. until midnight. The watch stander's desk was located on the apparatus floor near the trucks. It was at the outside man-door leading in from the street. This desk was at the foot of the set of stairs leading down from the living areas. We were all concerned about the bombings because we just thought that it was only a matter of time until these bad guys got to Portland. Usually the watch desk area was busy. During the daytime, there were people coming in and out of the station and lots of activity. But at night time, especially after about 9:00 p.m., it gets really quiet. Everyone except the watch stander would be upstairs in the living area. On this particular summer evening, Wally O. was on watch at the desk. It was about 11:30 p.m., and he was having a hard time staying awake. (We all did.) Mucka peeked down the stairwell and saw Wally, kind of dozing off. He turned around to a few of us and said, "Hey, watch this."

He went to his room and came back with an M-80 firecracker. He lit the fuse and dropped it down the hole in the floor for the brass sliding pole on the far end of the apparatus floor. When that firecracker went off, Wally came up about two feet into the air, from his chair. We thought that he was going to have a heart attack. He told us later, after he had calmed down a little, that he thought that the terrorists had blown up the back wall of the station. Those two terrorists would later be caught, tried, and convicted, and they are still in prison.

In another incident, the lesson is that sometimes it's best not to brag too much around the fire station. One young fireman was involved in the rescue of a dog that had wandered out onto an ice flow in Back Bay in Portland. This area is a large saltwater bay that is surrounded on three sides by the city. Water access is under a large bridge. There is a park that follows the shoreline named Baxter Boulevard. This bay is round and about one mile across. Because it's shallow, it tends to partially freeze over in the winter. And in the early spring, around the end of March, the ice melts and breaks up into large pieces. We have frequently had to rescue children and dogs that wandered out onto ice during this time of melting. The ice slabs (flows) would start to drift out away from the shore with the passengers on them. Then we would be called to help. This usually would be nothing more complicated than having us put the small rescue boat into the water and retrieving the person or pet that was on the ice flow. All part of a winter day's work.

On this particular call, we found a very frightened dog out on the ice. We performed the rescue with our small rescue boat. The dog was brought to shore and released to the owner, a small, frightened ten-year-old boy. When we returned to the station, the young fireman involved in handing the dog to its owner started bragging about his great rescue. We listened to this for about two days. Then the plot was hatched. The wife of one of the other firemen worked at the Maine State Capital Office Building in Augusta. She was asked to bring home a blank sheet of official State of Maine stationary with the letterhead on it and an envelope to match it. Two or three guys got together and typed up a beautiful-sounding letter, telling this young fireman that his efforts during the recent rescue of the dog on the ice flow had been noticed by the state legislature, and they wanted to show their appreciation of his work. The letter asked that he present himself at the state legislature's chambers, at a certain time, on a certain date, to be formally presented before the legislature. The letter was then sent to his home. He did travel to Augusta, and he went to the state office building to receive his "award." He didn't brag much after that. Our efforts are team efforts and not just that of any one person.

Be careful how you word things to some firemen. Central Fire Station is a granite block building with a flat roof. It is a very active station and it also houses fire headquarters. More about this beautiful old building later.

One summer day, on a weekend, during a quiet spell when we were in a slow time for responses, well, the firemen got bored. The old saying is "And when the cat's away, the mice will play." A certain Deputy Chief who liked to drink a lot ordered one of the firemen to hook up a series of spare fire hoses and pour water onto the flat roof of the building. His intent was to check for water leaks in the roof. He then went away someplace to have a few beers. This fireman did just exactly what he was told to do. This roof has a three-foot parapet wall around the roof. The building is two and one-half stories tall, and it's sixty feet by one hundred twenty feet. The hose lines ran very well. All day long. Late in the afternoon, this Deputy Chief came back to the station and wanted to know what had happened to the roof test. When he was told that the water was still running, well, we thought that he was going to have a heart attack. We're lucky that the roof didn't collapse in on us. The water level had risen up to almost that parapet level. The weight was estimated at over 150 tons. Just be careful what you ask for; you might get it.

On another occasion, the Deputy Chief told one of the men to make sure that the flower beds in front of the station were watered every single day without fail. Well, one day, it was raining, and the Deputy Chief called the station on the telephone and reminded the men to water the flower gardens. One of the men went outside the station, dressed in his turnout clothes and helmet, and started watering the flowers (in the rain). The Portland Press Herald newspaper was located in the building right next door. One of the newspaper photographers took the picture, and it was printed in the newspaper the next day. Oops, Chief. But that's what you told me to do.

One more story about Mucka. Just before he retired, Mucka was a lieutenant at Bramhall Station. One night, one of the new young guys was "ragging" on him. This went on all evening long. The older guys kept telling the young guy to "leave him alone or he'll get you." The new guy shrugged them off and said something to Mucka, "Hey, old man, do you go to bed at sunset or do you dare to stay up a little later?"

That was the wrong thing to say. Mucka didn't say anything; he just smiled and responded by saying, "I'll stay up later than you."

At about 2:00 a.m. the young guy finally dropped off to sleep. When he woke up at six, he got some breakfast and got himself cleaned up. At 7:00 a.m., he went out to move his car from the parking area behind the station, getting ready for shift change. That's when he found out that Mucka had stayed up a lot longer than he had. This young guy's car was a Volkswagen Beetle. He found that it had been jacked up, the wheels had been taken off, the car had been set back down onto the tire rims, and all the lug nuts were missing. On one of the tires was a note. It instructed him to go to a certain place in the station, and he would find the first lug nut. At this spot, he also found another note telling him where the next lug nut was located. This scavenger hunt continued for all the twenty lug nuts. Each one was located in a different place in the station, including the top of the hose tower. It took this young fireman until early afternoon before he got the tires back on his car and he was able to leave. He didn't harass Mucka again.

Mucka was one of the best, and he kept us laughing for years.

Chapter Twenty-Seven

Some interesting calls

Some of the calls were just so funny, in a street justice kind of way. I was in charge of Engine Four one evening. It was midfall with cold weather, but it hadn't snowed yet. So it was probably in late October or November. We received an emergency call for an attempted suicide. The location was on Revere Street, in the Woodfords Corner area of Portland. With suicides, the police were always dispatched at the same time. We arrived at the same time as the police. What we found was so funny. A young man had gotten drunk and had a fight with his girlfriend. She had thrown him out of their apartment. He had then driven his car over to his father's house, on Revere Street; they had had a fight. His father had thrown him out. He decided to suicide out. He took a hose from the trunk of his car and hooked it up from the car exhaust to the rear window of the car. He climbed into the car and started it up and sat there waiting to die. Well, things just weren't going his way that night. He had left the lights on in his car, and a neighbor who lived across the street had seen the car sitting in the driveway with its lights on at 2:00 a.m. The neighbor had called the police. As the police were responding, this young man's car ran out of gas. When we arrived, the police were pulling the driver out of the car. The young man was arrested for attempted suicide, and he had the king of all headaches (a carbon monoxide hangover). These headaches last for about three days. It just wasn't his time to die.

In another incident, I was driving Engine Eleven for Captain Joe. It was a beautiful summer day. Blue skies and about seventy-five degrees. It had been a slow day, and we were just taking it easy. A nice quiet day shift in a single-piece house. The emergency call came in for a vehicle accident with people trapped in the vehicle, on Martin's Point Bridge, about three miles away from the station. We rolled out and headed in that direction. Our response time was about five minutes. When we arrived on scene, we found an old Plymouth Valiant car on the bridge. This bridge is two and one-half lanes wide with protected walkways on both sides for joggers and fishermen. It is part of US Route One and runs between Portland and Falmouth. The walkways are protected from the traffic by Jersey Barrier–style barricades. There is a four-foot-high fence separating the walkways from the water. The space between the barriers and the fence is about eight feet wide. This bridge is almost one-half mile long over the inlet to a salt-water bay, and it is used all summer long by people fishing, walking, or jogging. The young man who was driving the car had just picked up a working girl from the area of the city where the hookers walked the streets. He was on his way to a motel, and he was a little anxious. He was driving way too fast for the approach to the bridge, and the car tipped up and rolled up onto the passenger side and started sliding down the short grade onto the bridge. It slid in between the fence and the barriers. The car continued to slide on the passenger side for almost two hundred feet out onto the bridge, still between the guard rail and the fence. As I stopped Engine Eleven beside the car, Captain Joe jumped down from the truck, ran over to the car, and climbed up onto the driver's side of the car; he reached down and pulled upward on the driver's door. He looked down into the car and saw the driver and the young woman all crammed together in a heap against the passenger-side front door. Joe spoke to the driver and said, "Are you all right?"

The young man just smiled and answered, "Man. What a fucking ride."

The working girl hollered out that she couldn't swim. Captain Joe told her, "You're not going to get wet today."

No one was injured. We pulled them from the car and called for a wrecker. We waited until the wrecker arrived, and the wrecker driver hooked onto the car, pulled it up and, over the concrete barrier, set it down onto the street, upright on its tires. A short time later, the young man climbed into the car and drove off. That was one tough car. The working girl? She went back to work.

During my early career, I was transferred from truck to truck on a regular basis. For about two years, I was driving for Lieutenant Ed, on Engine Eleven, out of Ocean Avenue Station, in the East Deering area of Portland. Lieutenant Ed and I quickly became friends. He taught me a lot, and I adopted parts of his leadership style later on. It was cold weather, but it hadn't snowed yet, so it must have been November or early December. Engine Eleven was an open-cab Maxim, with a 750-gpm pump, with a gasoline engine with a manual transmission. It was a great truck. We ran with four men: the officer, the driver and two men on the tailboard. The First Alarm sounded at about 10:00 p.m. It was followed almost immediately by the Second Alarm and then the Third Alarm. The location of the fire was on Commercial Street at the intersection with Clark Street in the West Commercial Street area of the city. This intersection no longer exists, but the sharp corner on Commercial Street still does. This location is a sharp corner that bends around a two-story brick building on one side, and at the time of this fire, there was a large warehouse on the other side. At Engine Eleven Station, we stepped out onto the ramp and looked in that direction. We could see the glow in the sky, and that was more than five miles away across the entire city. We started in toward Commercial Street in response to the Third Alarm. As we crossed Tukey's Bridge, on Washington Avenue headed toward Franklin Arterial, the Fire Dispatcher put out a General Alarm on the fire. The route that I used was across Marginal Way, up over Franklin Arterial to Commercial Street and then over Commercial Street to the fire scene. This was about a six-mile run for us. As we drove, we heard on the radio that a tractor-trailer tank truck had overturned and ruptured the tank. It was a twelve-thousand-gallon tank of gasoline. The product ignited. We faced a section of street between two buildings that was awash with a pool about eight inches deep of burning gasoline and spread out over more than two hundred feet of street. One of the buildings was a brick office building for an oil company. The other building was a one-and-one-half-story wood-framed warehouse that measured seventy feet wide by three hundred feet long. In the middle of this intersection was the closest hydrant and a storm drain manhole that emptied directly into Portland Harbor, about four hundred feet away. Commercial Street is a major street that runs for almost four miles. It's wide and it follows the Portland Waterfront. It includes both vehicle traffic and railroad traffic. It feeds all the working waterfront area in Portland. This fire had quickly extended to include the warehouse building and then through the storm drain system, and out into the harbor, there was a burning gasoline slick flowing through the harbor toward the commercial dock systems. Things got complicated real fast when the responding mutual-aid fire apparatus was stopped at the drawbridge of the primary bridge between Portland and South Portland. The drawbridge was up for a passing ship. All traffic was stopped including the responding fire apparatus.

On Engine Eleven, I was rolling along Commercial Street toward the fire scene at about fifty miles an hour. I was still about one mile away when the Deputy Chief called us on the radio and said, "Engine Eleven, lay a feeder line into Engine Four." Engine Four was on the other side of this fire from where we were. And the hydrant that the Deputy Chief wanted us to use was one hundred feet past them. And there is no quick straight route to get around this fire scene. Any route would involve numerous side streets. I asked the lieutenant, "Which way do you want me to take to get to Engine Four?" He never broke a sweat. He said, "The shortest distance between two points is a straight line." And that's what I did. I drove this old open-cab fire truck with four men on it right through the intersection that was wall-to-wall fire with a very large pool of burning gasoline and a tipped-over tractor-trailer truck in it. I didn't find out until later that the manhole cover for the storm drain had blown off and made an open three-foot-wide hole in the street. Just out of plain good luck, I straddled it. One of the men on the tailboard told me later that his sideburns had scorched off. But we made it, and we made history. Someone was filming the fire, and the film shows Engine Eleven coming through the burning pool of gasoline. Like I said before, "You get up close and personal with the Demon."

We found out later, from an interview with the trailer truck driver, that he was going way too fast for that corner and that he had his girlfriend with him. After the truck rolled over, they both got out, and he told his girlfriend to leave because he didn't want his wife to find out about her. Right after she left, two guys in a car stopped at the accident scene and when they found out that no one was hurt, one of them flipped a cigarette butt into the pool of gasoline, and that action started the fire. They then drove off. They were never caught.

CHAPTER TWENTY-EIGHT

Fires on the waterfront

In Leo Stapleton's book, *Thirty-Five Years on the Line*, he mentions one of the most important lessons to be learned in marine firefighting. For every gallon of water that you pump onto that vessel (boat/ship/barge), it has to be pumped off it; if you don't, the boat sinks.

We had a very limited amount of AFFF, and what we did have was donated to us from the military surplus. It was all in five-gallon cans that were more than fifteen years old. They were leftovers from the Korean War when we received them. We also were given cases of MREs from World War II. Some of the cans were already leaking from rust holes. We had no Class A foam or Class B foam. All we had was water, and on the waterfront, it was all saltwater. Still, we had our moments. Portland had a very busy working waterfront. At its peak, we had around twenty large fishing boats and fifty or more lobster boats operating out of Portland Harbor. We had a steady stream of tankers and freighters operating in and out of the harbor. Today, that number has sadly been reduced to almost none. We also had cargo ships coming in all the time. Ever since the late 1930s, Portland has been a major seaport for oil. The Portland Pipe Line Corporation is a direct oil pipeline from Portland to Montreal, Canada. At any given time, there are anywhere from one to five oil tanker ships in Portland offloading product. Most of this product goes to the Pipe Line, but millions of gallons per week are put onto tractor-trailer trucks and driven throughout New England. One traffic survey that I saw in 1980 showed one million gallons per week leaving Portland and traveling west just on Route 25 toward Northern New Hampshire and Vermont.

Portland's wharves were pretty run down and neglected and suffered from a major lack of repair and maintenance. These docks were all more than 150 years old. They were all wooden, heavy timber construction that had been soaked in oil and creosote for decades trying to keep them usable. Most of the buildings were just wood-framed warehouse buildings. Any fires that we had in these buildings, if they were found early, could be kept under control. But some of them turned into major fires, and that usually meant three to four days on scene. Many of these buildings were heavy timber construction with sheet metal siding and roofs. None of them had any fire alarm or fire suppression systems.

Some of the lessons that I learned in fighting boat fires has to do with barges. In Portland, we have a steady stream of fuel barges coming in to load product and transport it to other locations on the coast or up the rivers. These barges range in size from one hundred feet long to over three hundred feet long, and most are around sixty feet wide. The interiors are usually thirty feet in height. The cargo tanks in these barges are only accessible from a single manhole located in one end. Workmen would climb down into the tank and walk around inside it to do whatever they were assigned to do. There were also ventilation piping holes, but these are usually only four- to six-inch pipes. The safety policy is supposed to be that the tank is opened up and power ventilated for a given period of time before any entry is made. Sometimes the safety policy is used and sometimes it isn't.

It was a fall night, and we received a call for the Fire Rescue to go to one of the docks, at one of the fuel tank farms that dot Portland Harbor. There are four large tank farms in Portland Harbor. When we arrived, we found that two workmen had entered a barge tank to inspect it for water leaks from rust holes. This barge was two hundred fifty feet long and sixty feet wide by thirty feet high. The workmen were in a hurry, and they didn't wait to ventilate the barge before making entry.

Ambient air has a 21 percent oxygen content. If a human being is in an atmosphere that has less than 21 percent oxygen content in it, what happens is this: At 20 percent oxygen content, the person starts getting a little short of breath. Nineteen percent oxygen content, the person gets groggy. At 18 percent, the person starts to become disoriented. At 17 percent oxygen content, the person may become unconscious. At 16 percent oxygen content, the person dies.

The atmosphere inside that barge that night was less than 16 percent oxygen. The two workmen entered the tank and made it about one hundred feet into the length of the tank before they passed out and died. The third workman started into the tank. He advanced about thirty feet, but when he started to become dizzy and short of breath, he came right back out and called for help. We arrived and put on our SCBAs, entered the tank, and the scene quickly became that of a body retrieval and not a person rescue.

I took this lesson and used it in my classes because this mistake by these workmen is still made every once in a while by firemen and rescue workers doing confined space rescues, and they sometimes die from it.

On Commercial Street in Portland, near the intersection of Commercial Street and High Street, there used to be a company that sold animal feed and supplies. This company, New England Feed Company, had closed the Commercial Street location, and the property included a large wooden silo that was used to store a molasses mix that was used in animal feed. The company moved out of that location, and the property was vacant for about eight years. A developer bought the property and demolished the buildings. As the demolition work crew started to demolish the old silo, a problem was created. The crew was using cutting torches to remove iron piping, and they started an accidental fire inside the silo. The day was a hot summer day, and it was early afternoon. We received the fire alarm and headed toward the scene. On arrival, we found a small amount of smoke coming from the top of the silo. But we had a problem with accessibility to the fire. There was no easy opening into this silo. And we had no idea of what the fire might be doing on the inside of the silo. The Deputy Chief told me to try to open a large manhole opening that was built into the base of the silo. This was a steel plate, and it was held in place by thirty one-inch-thick bolts. This opening was three feet by three feet. I grabbed wrenches from the toolbox on the truck and started to remove the manhole cover. It took almost thirty minutes to loosen all these old rusted bolts. We still had no idea of what might be in the silo. As I removed the last bolt, the cover blew off, and I was drenched up to my chin in old rotted molasses, about two hundred gallons of it. It left me drenched with a product that had a distinct, certain, and very unpleasant aroma.

We used a hose line to put out the fire and to wash me down, but the damage was done. The Deputy Chief just shook his head and told me to order a new set of fire gear and a new work uniform. No one wanted to ride with me on the trip back to the station. I could understand why. I was made to ride on the tailgate of the engine truck, back to the station. When I got home that evening, my wife made me get completely undressed outside my home before she would let me into the house, and my clothing was thrown away in the trash.

We have experienced some very interesting wharf fires in Portland. The Grand Trunk Wharf comes to mind first. I was on my way to my home after day shift, shift change, one summer afternoon. I was at the Portland/Westbrook city line when I happened to look out over the city skyline. About seven miles away, I saw this huge column of black smoke rising over the skyline. I just turned to my wife and said, "I'm headed back to the station. I'll see you in a couple of days." I called the Fire Dispatcher and identified myself to him. He just said, "Bobby, I'm real busy. I've got a general alarm going." That was enough for me.

The Grand Trunk Wharf was the site of the railhead complex for the Canadian National Railway in Portland. At its prime, ships would come into Portland Harbor and unload at the wharf. The cargo would be placed on railcars and moved to Canada. This facility was shut down right after World

War II. It went into disrepair, and by the time of this fire, around 1969, the old wooden structure was in really bad shape. These old wharfs had been treated for decades with oil and creosote to prevent decay of the timbers. Grand Trunk Wharf included an overhead, enclosed, heavy, tramway structure that had been used to move truckloads of cargo from the dock to the warehouse. The fire started on the dock structure itself; we never found out why. The weather that day included a moderate wind coming on shore. Within ten minutes' time, the entire dock was involved, and the fire was spreading to the overhead tramway. This quickly became a surround-and-drown fire. But even then, we had serious concerns about extension to buildings as far as one-quarter mile away. We had three men that were almost trapped on that tramway by the fire; they just made it away from the rapidly advancing fire. The Portland Fireboat had a pump capacity of 7,500 gals a minute, and they were losing ground to this fire. All told, we were on scene for three days and nights. There were no deaths from this fire.

Portland has three miles of these old wharves and an additional two miles of residential saltwater waterfront.

A final note about the waterfront: Portland Police helped us a lot with this area of the city. They were always on patrol, and they would call in anything that looked unusual. The patrol unit called for us very early one fall morning. While doing his rounds, he found a pickup truck with license plates from a southwestern state. At first, he didn't think that it was out of place, but a short time later, he went back to check on it. The truck was parked in the middle of a vacant lot on the waterfront, near some old wharves. As the patrolman walked around it, he looked at a homemade camper that had been built into the back of the truck. The patrolman knocked on the door of the camper and received no reply. He tried to open the door, and it was locked on the inside. His intuition went into overdrive. He called for the fire department to come down there to break open the door. When we arrived and did the legal B&E, we were stunned. Inside the camper were a man and a woman and three children. They had used a charcoal grill stove to heat the camper, and they had gone to sleep with it burning. They were all dead from the carbon monoxide fumes. Not a good way to start the day at 6:00 a.m.

Other work on the harbor

Portland's Fireboat also served as the primary EMS rescue boat for the waterfront and for the islands that were located in the city limits. As such, there were times when it was really busy. "The Boat" was built in 1956 and was fifty-one feet long. It was built to that spec because any vessel at fifty-two feet or larger had to have a USCG Merchant Marine–licensed pilot operating it. And the city didn't want to have to pay to have someone trained for that license. "The Boat" had a pump capacity of 7,500 gals per minute, and there were times when this was really needed. It had a crew of three, and sometimes, this was augmented by firemen and/or EMTs. The boat had a very slow overall speed. Its top speed was only about ten knots. This was sometimes a problem on rescue calls to the islands. It would sometimes take twenty-five minutes to an hour just to get to the island scene, and then more time to evaluate the situation, then load the people and then twenty-five minutes to an hour to get back. During the time that I was stationed at Central Station, either on Rescue One or on Engine Five (I was the only certified EMT on the fire department at that time), I made numerous runs with "the Boat." Some of them were memorable: lobster boat accidents, car accidents, drunks, pregnant women. We had them all. The population of the islands in Portland Harbor at that time was around twenty thousand people. Some of these families have been living there for eight or ten generations, since back before the time of the American Revolutionary War. And like a lot of small, old communities, sometimes the attitudes would get in the way of anyone asking anyone outside for help.

It was early fall in Portland, and the weather can be changeable at the drop of a hat. There is an old saying about Maine weather: "If you don't like the weather in Maine, wait a minute and it will change." This was a sunny day in the early evening on a weekend. The Casco Bay Lines, the ferry service that covers Portland Harbor, had one of its ferries leased out for a company party and Sunset Cruise. This usually meant that the ferry would load up just before sunset and cruise the harbor and the islands until about 11:00 p.m., return to the dock, and discharge its passengers. The ferry boat usually ran with a crew of four. This particular evening went well until the sea fog set in. At the time, Casco Bay Lines was having a problem with scheduling. If the fog set in, they wouldn't operate; if the wind picked up and created waves in the harbor, they wouldn't operate. The city and the public were putting a lot of pressure on the Casco Bay Lines Company to install radar on the ferries. But the CBL Company was stonewalling and refusing to comply. This ferry that night did not have radar on board. So when the fog set in, they had a problem. In addition to that, the ferry boat captain and his crew had stopped what they were doing (operating the ferry boat) and had gone down to the party with the passengers and had a few drinks with them. And they had left the ferry boat underway (moving along), while they were at the party. Well, it didn't take long for the ferry boat to go aground on a large rock pinnacle named Pumpkin Knob. The call went out on the radio for help. The Coast Guard patrol boat that night also did not have a functioning radar; it was broken and being repaired.

Johnny P. was the pilot on the Fireboat, and he was the best. Because I was the only EMT at Central Station, I was taken down to the boat, and we got underway. The fog had set in thick enough that visibility was down to less than fifty feet. Johnny used a compass and a stopwatch and the Fireboat's radar to navigate through the harbor. A USCG patrol boat pulled in behind us and followed us to the rescue scene. The trip outbound took us almost an hour, because of the slow speed that we had to travel. I had no idea where we were, but I trusted Johnny. When we came out of the fog onto the rescue scene, Johnny had put us alongside the grounded ferry boat as neat as a pin. I went aboard the ferry boat and started to work. I had more than twelve injured people. Most were only bumps and bruises, but one had a broken leg, and another had a broken wrist. There were some minor head injuries. I ended up treating all the injuries. We ended up transporting two back to the mainland and to a hospital. Like I said, Johnny was the best marine pilot that I had ever known.

I never did find out what happened to the ferry boat crew, but this incident was the final impetus to cause Casco Bay lines to install radar on their boats. And about twelve years later, the fire department had another boat built for just rescue work and transporting people. It was named for a Portland Fire Department firefighter who had been killed in the line of duty, Joey Cavalaro.

CHAPTER TWENTY-NINE

Scattered memories about some of the men I had worked with
Those that have made that transition to a better place

Jerry Chase. One hardworking man. He was an over-the-road truck driver who had his own tractor for years; it was an old Mack twin-axle with an air starter. Jerry was the best truck driver that I have ever met. His son-in-law became a Portland fireman and is still a good friend. Jerry would work his shift at the station, leave and drive truck all day or night, return to the station, and work another shift.

Ted Axelson. Ted was one of the guys who had come to work straight from World War II. He was another one who was good at what he did. I learned a lot from him. I remember him working as a manager at a movie theater as a part-time job.

Dick Foy. Dick worked part time as a salesman for Hoover Vacuum Cleaners, and he had the personality for it. He was always talking a mile a minute and trying to sell you on some idea. He was a good fireman though. I have one memory of him talking to his wife on the telephone. The telephone in the dayroom at Bramhall was located underneath the alarm bell. If Dick wanted to go and do something else, he would take his ballpoint pen from his shirt pocket and tap on the alarm bell so that it sounded into the telephone. He would then tell his wife, "I've got to go, that's an alarm." And he would hang up the phone.

Bobby Stewart. One of my best friends. Bobby and I rode back and forth to work together for a while. He had a great sense of humor. One incident remains in my memories. At Bramhall Station one evening, we were all watching television. The particular show was an old comedy sitcom named *Gomer Pyle*. It was about a platoon in the Marine Corps. Bobby had been in the corps, so had Leigh. The television was in the Dayroom of the station. We were all sitting around the tables and watching it. Bobby walked through the room, and without missing a beat, he just calmly said, "You guys don't know it, but that show is a documentary." We all cracked up laughing. Please remember that we were all military vets. Leigh, however, was furious. He had been a Fleet Marine.

He stood up and said, "If you hadn't been a Marine, I'd put you through that wall right now." That comment just made us laugh even more. Boy, firehouse humor. We used to tease Bobby about his plastic pocket protector, full of five or six ballpoint pens. After Bobby retired from the fire department, he went to work driving a school bus. We couldn't believe that he could have the patience to put up with the antics of the kids on a school bus. But he just told us that when the kids acted out, he would turn off the radio in the bus, and when they behaved, he would turn it back on again. Easy and simple. I really miss him.

Bill Perry. Bill and I were hired together and were in Rookie School together. We didn't work together much after that. We ended up on opposite shifts and at opposite ends of the city. I remember one of the evolutions in rookie school was to rappel off the roof of a six-story building, pick up a person on the fourth floor, and descend to the ground. It was my turn, and, well, Billy was always kind of a heavy build, about 260 pounds. And at the time I weighed about 170 pounds. I went off the roof and stopped at the fourth floor to pick him up; we started to descend, and the safety man on the ground started playing a game with the lifeline. He pulled it tight so that we stopped in midair. He then let it go completely slack, and we dropped like a rock toward the ground. I remember Billy's eyes. They looked like saucers. The safety man learned what it was like to have the training deputy pissed at him. Bill ended up being one of the founding crew members at the Portland Jet Port Fire Station, when it became a full-time fire station. Bill was a great cook, and he had this great sense of humor, but he never did like working on heights.

Stan Lynch. Stan was one of the guys who came to work right from World War II. He was kind of quiet, but he was a good fireman. Just one of those people who were really good at what they did. And he taught me a lot. He was one of those firemen I remember hearing saying, "Follow me, kid," as we were running into the burning buildings and dragging hose lines up flights of stairs. No big drama. Just get in and do the job. I went to Stan's funeral a few weeks ago. So many of them who are no longer with us.

CHAPTER THIRTY

Runs with Ladder Six

I tillered or drove Ladder Six for three and one-half years. During that time, it got really interesting sometimes. Winter was the worst because of the cold and snow. Being inside a building, getting wet and hot, then coming outside into the subfreezing cold, making up the trucks, then the ride back to the station while sitting eight feet up into the freezing cold air make for some memories.

We had no real protective clothing. We had a plastic helmet, a rubber coat, boots with no steel toes or shanks, and work gloves that we had to buy for ourselves. And in the winter we had to buy a pair of Navy surplus foul-weather pants and leather mittens with wool inserts. We had no SCBAs, no hoods, no face shields. A flashlight was just that—something that you carried in your pocket—along with some small tools and dry gloves.

I remember standing under a hot water showerhead, on the apparatus floor, at Bramhall Station with my full gear on and letting the hot water thaw out and melt the ice on my gloves, coat, and helmet until I can get the buckles loosened up enough to take them off. I remember riding the tiller seat and praying that Ladder Six would make it up some of the hills as the truck wheels churned their way up through six to eight inches of falling snow. This was even with the tire chains on.

Any alarm run to the airport—this was before there was a crash station at the Portland Airport—called for a full first-alarm response. Bramhall was the second due response apparatus. We made many runs to the airport. It was a seven-mile response distance, and the response time was between ten to fifteen minutes depending on traffic and weather. For a long period of time, we had a Fire Department Mechanic who should have been working somewhere else, doing something else. He personally ruined many good fire trucks. Ladder Six was one of these. I remember tillering Ladder Six one cold night on an alarm run to the airport. The truck had been starting hard and running rough. On Congress Street, between Stevens Avenue and Frost Street is a railroad crossing. We had made it to that point when the truck engine stopped. We were straddling the railroad tracks. The ladder tractor was on one side, and I was in the tiller on the other side. I could hear Hoss trying to get the truck started again. (Come on, baby, please start.) I look up the tracks, and here comes a freight train moving toward us and blowing its horn. Hoss was still trying to get the truck to start again. As the train started to get closer, I climbed off the seat and started to get ready to jump off the truck. Suddenly the truck started. I sat back down, and we finished our response to the airport. Whew.

On another night, I had been sleeping when the airport alarm came in. I had been sleeping on my right side. My right arm was all numb. It got interesting that night as I tried to tiller with just one arm that was working correctly and that I could feel with. These are some of the things that are not written about in the job descriptions for firemen. I can see it now. The preferred candidate must be able to jump off trucks stalled at railroad crossings.

It would be another ten years before the city decided to build and man a station at the airport, only after the FAA ordered them to do it.

Some of the memorable runs with Ladder Six included an alarm one morning to the corner of Summer Street and Clark Street. The building was an old three-story apartment house. This area of the city is where I was raised as a child. This particular afternoon, we received an alarm for a funny smell at this address. When we arrived, a person on the sidewalk told us that there were three children in the first-floor apartment and that the door was locked. As we walked into the building's entry hallway, we could smell a very strong odor of natural gas. Portland has a very large natural gas system for heating buildings. The captain told us to "take the door." I used a Halligan tool, and as the broken door opened up, we encountered a very heavy natural-gas smell. Three of us went in and started to search the apartment. We found and brought out three unconscious children who had been overcome by the gas. The youngest was about six, and the oldest was about twelve. The parents were at work. All three children recovered.

The beat cops really helped us out a lot. They were constantly moving during their patrols, and they saw things that we couldn't. A lot of drunks and bums living on the streets owe their lives the beat cops who saw them when they were in deep trouble and called us to help them. A lot of small fires were called in to us before they became big fires. And every so often the body floating in the harbor or curled up under the viaduct of the Million Dollar Bridge, sometimes being munched on by rats.

Summertime

So much to do in the summer months and not much time to do it in. Outdoor training, driver training, station work, block inspecting (fire inspections of homes and businesses), maintenance of the stations (paint and repairs), the chance to really clean the apparatus floor area (sweep, wash and repaint the floor, and clean out the floor drain system). And the fires.

Springtime also brought its share of warm weather fires. Every afternoon at 2:10 p.m., we would all gravitate down to the main floor and hang around the trucks. Because within minutes after 2:10 p.m., the first calls would come in for grass fires. It was when the kids would get out of school. And on their way home, it was common for a "Hey, let's start a fire in the dry grass."

We would also see an increase in calls for campfires and leaf fires. People would still clean up their yards and rake the leaves out to the street and burn them. We had one fire call when a worker, installing cable TV into a home, didn't watch what he was doing, and as he drilled an access hole through the sill plate of the building, he drilled right into the primary power wire as it entered the distribution box inside the cellar. It knocked him on his ass and started a fire in the wall of the house. Or the guy who started a leaf fire went inside his home to get himself a beer and burned his garage down, with his car inside the garage. Or the charcoal-fired BBQ grills. We had lots of building fires that started with someone's BBQ grill on the back porch.

CHAPTER THIRTY-ONE

Speaking of drunks

One guy finished his day shift job at 8:00 p.m. He left work and went to a neighborhood bar, drank until 1:00 a.m., and ordered a pizza and some take-home beers. He went home, put the pizza in the oven to warm it up, and went into the living room to have some more beer and watch TV. There was one slight problem: when he put the pizza in the oven, he left it in the box. About thirty minutes later, he noticed that there was a lot of smoke coming from the oven. In his inebriated state, he took the burning box out of the oven, threw it on the back porch, and went back to his beer and TV. He then passed out from the beer. One of the neighbors called us when the whole back porch of this three-story apartment house was burning. Oops.

EMS calls involving drunks and people doing really stupid things. Any emergency worker will tell you that they watch the almanac, and when there's a full moon, everyone gears up for the unusual and just plain odd calls. We responded to more calls for drunks falling off the wharves and getting scared when they found themselves standing in cold chest-deep saltwater, with the tide coming in, and being literally face-to-face with the wharf rats. (In Portland Harbor, they grow to be as large as some small dogs, about ten to twelve pounds.) Or people getting drunk and cutting off toes or fingers with lawn mowers, snowblowers, or saws.

I was on a rescue call on New Year's morning at about 7:30 a.m. The call was for a man injured. When we arrived, we found a man dressed in his pajamas, outside his home in subfreezing cold. He was also suddenly missing two fingers from his right hand. It seems that he was still very drunk from the night before and he wanted to snow blow his driveway. The snow that morning was a little wet. It clogged up his snowblower, and he did the classic maneuver. He stuck his hand into the snowblower chute while it was still running. He was crying and screaming that it hurt so much. We dressed the wounds and transported him to the hospital. He continued to complain about the pain and that we were taking too long to get him to the hospital. Finally, I just said to him, "Shut the fuck up. You brought this on to yourself."

The missing toes is another common incident. Usually a drunk would be out mowing his lawn in bare feet or wearing slippers. Occasionally, they would either pull the lawn mower back over the top of their feet or kick the mower from the side with one of their feet. It's guaranteed to cost them some toes.

Hundreds of car accidents were caused by drunk drivers. One in particular that stays in my memories: It was winter, and at about 2:00 a.m., we received the call for a rollover, with a person trapped in the vehicle, near the railroad overpass on Park Avenue and St. John Street. When we arrived, we found the car up on its passenger side, against the sidewalk, in front of a business building. As we were opening the doors of the car, the Police arrived. We found that the driver was very drunk and unhurt. The police took him into custody and left. We looked at the car and decided that we could not leave it up on its side. If it ever fell down, someone could get hurt. So we all got on one side of the car and pushed. It rolled back onto its wheels. We left and returned to the station. Later that day, one of the Police Officers told us that when they took the driver back to the car in the morning, he just climbed in, started it up, and drove home.

Chapter Thirty-Two

People not cut out to be firemen

Over the years we encountered a few people who were just not cut out to be firemen. The hiring process for the fire department is long and complex. First is the application for employment. Then the background checks. Next is a written exam; this is only held annually. After that is a physical exam with strict requirements. Then comes a physical test. The applicant has to be in excellent physical condition. After all this effort, the applicant has to wait for an opening before being actually hired into the job. This process can take anywhere from three months up to one, two, or even three years.

I was working at the old Engine Nine Station on Arbor Street, in the Morrill's Corner area of Portland. This was a single-piece house. It was an old building that was over one hundred years old. The building was a red two-and-one-half-story brick building. Station's living quarters were on the second floor. The first floor was the apparatus area, a workshop, and the watch desk. This station would later be closed, and Engine Nine would be moved to a new building about one mile away. It was considered a quiet station. Some runs, but not like in town. One summer day, a new guy showed up for work. He seemed like a nice guy.

We usually had shift change at 8:00 a.m. We had some coffee and chat time and then about eight-thirty, we would start housework, cleaning up the station and the truck and doing anything else that needed to be done. Repairing tools and equipment, making sure that everything was all set on the truck. This usually takes about three to four hours to do. At about noontime, we take a break for lunch. Someone might make a run to the store to pick up lunch stuff, but at this station, most people brought their own lunches from home.

On this particular day, the new guy worked with us until noontime. When we broke for lunch, he told the captain that he was going down to the corner neighborhood bar, the Brass Rail, and get something to eat and have a couple of beers. The captain told him that he was a fireman now and that drinking on the job was not allowed. This guy got really pissed off. What did you mean that he couldn't have a liquid lunch? He told the captain, "I quit," and walked out the door. We never saw him again. He went through all that work to get hired, and he left because he couldn't drink on the job.

At the same station on another day, a new guy showed up and only lasted part of the day. This guy came on duty, and at eight-thirty, when we started our housework to clean up the station, he told the lieutenant, "I came here to fight fires, not to do housework and clean bathrooms." The lieutenant told him that housework and station work is part of the job. This guy told the lieutenant, "I quit," and walked out the door. We never saw him again either.

There were a few others who came to work, stayed for a while, and then left. One such man was Freddie. I had known him from high school. He was a good fireman, but he had a serious problem with alcohol. He ended up getting into a series of scrapes with law enforcement officers, and eventually he resigned. He later died as a result of his alcoholism.

Another man, Bobby, was the son of a fireman I worked with. Bobby had a problem with drugs. He eventually spent a few days in jail, where he started a fire in his cell. He resigned and moved out of the area. He eventually ended up in California.

One man worked with us for about eight years and was stationed at the airport fire/crash station. He was a nice guy and a great cook. On his side job, he worked as a cook in an upscale restaurant. He served up some really good meals in the station, but he had another little problem. He was caught by the DEA dealing drugs out of the Portland Jetport Crash Station. He spent three years in the Danbury Federal Prison in Connecticut. It became sad, interesting, and funny, because when he was released, he came back to Portland and asked the Fire Chief for his job back. His request was denied, and he was almost literally thrown out of the chief's office.

One memorable case was of a man whose father had been a fireman. He came to work with us, and it just wasn't working out. He had some emotional problems. He had a long series of problems with the other men, including some fights. It finally reached a point when he wrote a letter threatening the President and signed another man's name to it. He did this to get back at the other man. The investigation by the Secret Service identified him, and they visited the Fire Chief's office. During the interview, the Fire Chief was told to do whatever he wanted to do with the man. The Secret Service would put the man on a list of people who have threatened the President. And his name would stay on that list until he died. This man was told to resign.

Another man was on the job for about eight years. He just couldn't stay out of a bottle. He was calling in sick all the time. He was seen drinking at a bowling alley next door to the fire station, all one day, and when he called in sick, the men in the station were watching him from the window of the station. He was told to leave on his own or he would be fired.

One man worked with us for exactly ten years and six months. Just exactly long enough to collect his vested interest in the pension system. Bill always seemed to be in some kind of trouble. He took his pension money and bought a taxicab. He ran it in Portland for about four years. He was involved in some prostitution work. He lost everything and moved somewhere upstate Maine.

And then there were those people who were just wannabes.
In my lifetime, I have met a few people who thought they would be firemen, but they weren't.
"Two-alarm Terry." Terry was a Sergeant with the Portland Police Department. Terry built a reputation for trying to do police work and trying to be a Fire Department Deputy Chief at the same time. After my back injury and the surgery that followed, I was dispatching for a period of time. For about one year. One summer day, I received a call for heavy smoke showing in an area on Walnut Street, in the Munjoy Hill area. I struck a box alarm for the call. The response called out Engine One as first due truck. Engine Five, Ladder One, Engine Eleven, and Rescue One. As the trucks were moving out of the station, I received a radio call from Sergeant Terry. He was on Cumberland Avenue near High Street, and he told me that he was responding to the fire call. His location was approximately two and one-half miles from the site of the smoke. Terry demanded a Second Alarm on the fire call. I refused. I told him that the fire units had not arrived on scene yet, and when they did, they could determine if an additional alarm was needed. He again demanded a Second Alarm on this fire call. I again refused. By this time, he was on Cumberland Avenue near Cedar Street right at the rear of city hall. He became very excited on the radio. I again told him that any requests for additional fire response would be made by the Fire Department units. At this time, Engine One reported at the scene. About two minutes later, the officer on Engine Zone called me on the radio. He told me to put out a recall on the box alarm. It seems that the property owner at that house had an incinerator furnace in his basement. He had recently had the roof of the house reshingled. He had all the leftover shingles, and he thought that he could save some heating money by burning them in his

incinerator instead of taking them to the transfer station. All the heavy black smoke in the area was coming from his chimney. Engine One put out the fire and told him that the shingles had to be disposed of properly. When Terry got back to Portland Police headquarters, also the site of all emergency dispatching in Portland, he came up to the dispatch area and became belligerent toward me. All of a sudden, the Deputy Police Chief stepped into the dispatch area. He ordered Terry to go with him to another office in the building. He had some strong words with Terry about the duties of a police sergeant. It was explained to him that his duties did not include interfering with fire calls.

CHAPTER THIRTY-THREE

Men who left because of injuries

Some men were injured or traumatized on the job and left because of that. These men were good firemen, and the most difficult and understated hard parts of the job caused them to leave. Two of these men left with very bad third-degree burns on their hands from attempting rescues; more about these men later.

The first of these men to leave whom I knew was Chuck. He was on the job when I was hired. As things happened, just a few weeks after I was hired onto the job, Chuck slid down the pole at Bramhall Station and hit the bottom pad badly, injuring his ankle. He didn't think much about it, but the injury didn't want to clear up. He went to see a doctor, and after some tests, the diagnosis was bone cancer. This was in 1967, when a lot of the cancer treatments had not been developed yet. The doctor told him that the only way to prevent the spread of the disease to the rest of his body would be to remove his leg at the hip joint. Chuck had the surgery done, and his days as a street fireman were over. I have encountered Chuck at various times over the years, and his injury didn't slow him down at all. I saw him one night about six or seven years after his surgery. He was into drag-racing snowmobiles. He also rode motorcycles. He raced snowmobiles on grass racetracks and across water. He worked hard and put his daughters through college. For a period of time, he was back working for the city as an Emergency Dispatcher (during the mid-1970s). He was one good guy, and I learned a lot from him about courage and how to live with injuries.

In another incident at Pearl Street and Congress Street, the building was a three-story apartment house. It had six apartments. It was wood-framed with a flat tar-and-gravel roof. One very cold night in January, the oil-fired steam boiler literally blew up and took out the entire center of the building. Right up through the roof. As it blew upward, it spread fire throughout all three floors of the building. Three children died that night. One of the men, a rookie, climbed a ladder into a second-floor window to conduct search operations. As he crawled into the window, he went across a bedroom. He thought that he was crawling across bedding material. He went on into the apartment. Later, as he came back toward the window, someone else brought in some area lights and lit up the room. This rookie saw that when he thought he was crawling across the bedding, in reality he had been crawling across the dead bodies of the three children. That trauma caused him to resign about three months later.

The fire department administration and the city administration, at that time, believed in a denial policy of Critical Incident Stress Debriefing. "We don't need that shit. That stuff doesn't happen here." I will remark later about PTSD and the mind-set of the Fire Department administration and the city government on this issue.

One man who had burned hands, Johnny, was an old special friend of mine. Johnny went into an apartment house fire on Munjoy Hill one night. The report was people were trapped on the second floor. He went into the building before any fire attack could be started. He encountered heavy smoke and very high heat, but he kept going. His attempt was unsuccessful, and he received third-degree burns on his hands; his gloves had almost burned off from his hands. He left the job and never was able to return.

Warwick Heights. This fire was in the winter. The building was a single-family residence. A split foyer, with bedrooms in the basement. On the night of the fire, the owner had friends, two adults and two children, staying over for the night. They were sleeping in the basement bedrooms. The fire started in the basement. It was well involved when we arrived. The on-duty Deputy Chief, who had been drinking and had a well-known alcohol problem, told two men to get into the basement and get those kids. They started down the stairs to the basement bedrooms, and the intense heat started to melt their plastic helmets and the hoses on their SCBAs. The banister railing was burning their hands through their gloves. They made it to the basement floor, but it was too hot to go any further. They had to back out. One of the men had second- and third-degree burns on his hands through his gloves, and his helmet had melted down onto his coat collar. The Deputy Chief, who had been drinking, was standing on a snowbank in front of the house. In front of a crowd of bystanders, he was screaming at these men and calling them "fucking cowards." The newest of these men ended up going out on sick leave until his hands healed up and then resigning from the department. That was the loss of a good fireman. His helmet and SCBA were picked up at the station by that same Deputy Chief. The items just disappeared and were never seen again.

Chapter Thirty-Four

So many memories

One year, the Fourth of July celebration was coming up, and I am remembering the City of Portland Celebration. This is usually held on the Eastern Promenade. The crowd usually numbers around twenty thousand. This one year, I was stationed on Engine One, on Munjoy Hill. Those of us on duty watched the show from the roof of the station (about two-tenths of a mile away). The show ended about 10:00 p.m. At around 1:00 a.m., we received an emergency call from a taxicab driver. He was in front of the cathedral, about seven blocks down Congress Street from "the Hill." He reported hearing someone yelling for help from the steeple of the cathedral (about one hundred feet in height). We arrived and found a man on the ledge that ran around the church bell tower platform at the top of the steeple. We set the aerial for Ladder One and rescued him from his perch. We found out that he was very intoxicated. He and his friend had gotten drunk, broken into the church, climbed to the top of the steeple (to watch the fireworks show), and passed out drunk. His friend left him up there. He woke up and couldn't get down again without help. Well, we did our thing and got him down, where the police were waiting and they arrested him. We never heard from his buddy.

Another loser

We received a call for a fire in a three-family apartment house in the Woodfords Corner area of Portland. This was a daytime fire, about 2:00 p.m. When we arrived, we had smoke showing from the basement area and from the first floor. The fire was found in the basement. It seems that the evening before, the tenant on the first floor had had a party. Someone had spilled a drink on an overstuffed chair. In the morning, the tenant's wife was housekeeping, and she found the wet cushion. She had taken the cushion down to the basement to dry it. She had placed it on top of the building's oil furnace. Shortly afterward, the cushion began to smolder and then it ignited, filling the basement and the entire building with smoke. There was not much fire but a lot of smoke. The humor in this fire incident comes from, as Paul Harvey, the radio commentator, used to say, "the rest of the story." Mark and I were ordered into the building to search the upper floors for any victims. We worked our way upstairs through the building; as we arrived in the attic space, we heard a cat crying. As we searched for the cat, we opened the door to a room within the attic space and found an indoor, third-floor agricultural project. Complete with grow lights, drying racks, and forty to fifty plants (read this as "marijuana"). Because there was no longer any danger we called to the Deputy Chief and told him to send up the cop who was standing near him on the sidewalk. The cop came up, and we showed him the scene of the agricultural project. What we didn't know was that at that time, the owner of this agricultural project had been sitting in a bar at the other end of the city, about three miles away, drinking. The bartender had a police scanner on, and this patron heard the fire call go out for his home. When he heard that the firemen were going into the building to search it, he knew what they were going to find. He ran from the bar to his car and left to go home. Not only was he in a very big hurry, but he was also very drunk. In his intoxicated drive home, he ran several red lights, sideswiped two cars, and, just a few blocks from his apartment, ran into a minivan with a woman and small children in it. He bolted from his car at the accident scene and ran the last few blocks to his apartment. He arrived just in time to meet the cop who was walking down the stairs from the building. When he told the cop who he was, the cop just said, "Well, sir, you're under arrest. Come with me, please. We would like to talk to you."

Speaking of drugs and other things

We had a nighttime fire on the corner of Deering Avenue and Cumberland Avenue, in the Parkside area of Portland. Just a few blocks from Bramhall Station. It was a small fire on the second floor. Just two rooms involved, but it was hot. As we made initial entry, the tenant for the apartment came up the stairs with us. We had him taken back down to the sidewalk. He then came right back into the building and started up the stairs again. Once again, we had him taken down to the sidewalk. Once more he came into the building and up the stairs in our footsteps. We took him down to the sidewalk and asked the Police Officer to keep him there. When we had the fire knocked down and we had some area lights set up, we found out why this tenant was so anxious to get into his apartment. We found approximately $5,000 in cash on top of his dresser and three one-gallon jars full of illegal drugs. This guy was a drug dealer, and he was worried about his stash. The cop escorted him to a cruiser and then to jail.

After a while, we just didn't even bat an eye. We just told the cops about whatever we found. If it wasn't fatal, it didn't even rate a note in our reports.

Some of the things that we found at fire scenes were worth mentioning in the reports: explosives, guns, hazardous materials.

We went to a small fire one night in the North Deering section of the city, off Maine Avenue off outer Washington Avenue. It was a single-family home, a center-stairwell Cape Cod–style house. The fire was in the upstairs bedroom (upstairs and to the right). I was driving Engine Eight. As the men were making the initial entry, I overheard the building owner tell the Deputy Chief, "Boy. It's a good thing that that fire is in the bedroom on the right side. I'm a gunsmith and the room on the left side of the stairway is my gun shop and it's full of gunpowder and ammunition." Yeah, it's hard enough fighting the fire without having to deal with stuff that can shoot back.

Another incident occurred when I was working in the Fire Prevention Bureau, and I was called to a home on Presumscot Street in the East Deering section of Portland. The owner had just inherited the home from his father. He was cleaning out the attached garage. He found a one-gallon jar with some strange-looking items in it, and he called the Fire Department. I ended up going to the home. As I was talking to the owner, his partner came out of the garage holding a one-gallon clear glass jar in one hand. The jar had a screw-on lid. I took one look and carefully took the jar from him and very, very, very carefully set it down on the ground. What I saw inside the jar were six sticks of dynamite that were sitting in about two inches of a clear oily fluid that had leached out of the dynamite. I called the Dispatcher and had him call the Bomb Disposal Squad at Brunswick Naval Air Base. Whew. Take a deep breath, don't get excited, and *do not* knock that jar over.

At another scene, during the time I was doing building inspections, I went into the old American Can Company building on Read Street, in the Morrill's Corner area of Portland. One of the other firemen had asked me to take a look at this situation that he had found. But he wasn't sure what to do about it. This building is approximately two hundred feet by four hundred feet and three stories tall. The building was built of brick and granite, with a flat tar-and-gravel roof. It had been built during the 1920s to manufacture tin food cans. It had been vacant for ten years or so, and at the time of this incident, it had become a mixed-use occupancy. What I found was frightening.

On the second floor, in about the center of the building, was an area of about two hundred square feet. This was separated from the rest of the occupancies by a wooden framework covered by a chicken wire mesh, open to the air and secured by a cheap padlock. The tenant for this area was operating a business that cleaned and recycled solvents. He had a series of open fifty-five-gal steel drums (old oil drums with no tops on) full of cleaning solvents. I asked him what was in the drums, and he told me that it was MEK. MEK is methyl ethyl ketone. The vapors are explosive, and the liquid is flammable. I was looking at about 150 gals of this product, in open fifty-five-gal drums. These drums were open to the air of the entire second floor of this building. If this had ignited, it had the capability to destroy the entire building in one blast. And this tenant really didn't know what he was looking at or what the product could do. And he became quite upset when I told him to cover the drums and move his business to another fire-safe and approved location. Sometimes they just don't know, and God does look out for fools.

CHAPTER THIRTY-FIVE

Women in the fire service

I learned a valuable lesson about women in the fire service in 1982. I was teaching my first class in fire safety. The title of the class was "Fireground Survival." I had accepted the assignment from a friend of mine, David. He handed me a pickup truck full of equipment (damaged helmets, burned fire gear, handouts, VCR tapes, slides, hose couplings) and a class outline and told me that the class was in Ellsworth, Maine, about ninety miles away from Portland. He also told me that I would be teaching the class alone. "But don't worry, Bob, you'll do all right." Yeah. Don't worry! Right!

I arrived at the school and met the school's facilitator, Billy. He was a good guy. I set up my classroom, and on Saturday morning, I started to teach my class. I had thirty students, and about fourteen of them were women. They were from a Volunteer Fire Department in Orland, Maine. I would find out later that during the weekdays these women *were* the Fire Department. During these weekdays, the men in the town from the fire department would be away working on fishing boats. I taught my class all that day. On Saturday evening, all the instructors would get together and eat dinner. It was at this dinner that the facilitator came up to me and said, "Bob, those women in your class are all intimidated by you, because of who you are." This bothered me a great deal. I wanted to be a teacher of fire safety. My goal was to pass on information to my students to try to help them and not to intimidate them.

On Sunday morning, in the classroom, I started off by telling my students this: "I don't care who or what you are. You need to answer this question. Do you want to be a fireman? Do you really want to be a fireman? Because it's one of the hardest jobs that there is. But, if you really want to be a fireman, then *go for it*. Because there is no job anywhere that can match it. If you ladies want to be firemen, welcome to the fire service. I'll try to give you some help to get you started in this business." And that has been my attitude about this issue of women in the fire service from the start.

At the time of this class, there was a great controversy in the fire service about women in the ranks. I have listened to both sides of the issue, and my feelings are the same; I have met women in the fire service who can hold their heads up with the best, and I have met women who, like some of the men that I have met, shouldn't be allowed in a fire station, let alone on a truck or at a fire scene. But the women who are in the fire service and doing the job and who want to be there are just as good as the men.

Throughout world history, there have been many cultures that welcomed women as equals with men. These cultures recognized that many women had the natural skills and the desires to become great warriors, leaders, healers, and war chiefs. Native Americans long recognized women as valuable members of their society to the extent that women were the ones that inherited property. If a man married a woman, he moved into her family and not the other way around. And if he treated her badly, she could divorce him by simply by throwing his possessions out of the door of the lodge. If a woman had the skills to learn tactics and strategy, then she could be voted in as the War Chief, and the other warriors would follow her orders in battle. The same if she wanted to become the healer of the tribe (the Medicine Woman).

The Celtic culture was similar. There are numerous recorded instances of women being great leaders. And in the Druidic community, there were schools that were just for women who were trained as healers, teachers, priests, and scholars. And those who completed the training (it took more than twenty years of classes and learning) were accepted as valuable members of the Celtic culture.

The same practices were used by those counterparts of the Druids in South America, the Toltec.

In the area of what is now India, at that time, the same things were happening.

Some will argue that women don't have the physical strength to do the job. I would counter that by reminding them that someone with a smaller stature can do search and rescue a lot better than someone who bench-presses 280 pounds but who can't crawl through a two-foot-diameter pipe. Or get through the sixteen-inch opening between the wall studs in a conventional house construction with their firefighting gear on.

If a woman has the natural skills and the desire to become a firefighter, then she should be welcomed as a member of the Brotherhood.

I was teaching another firefighting class in live fire training. The evolution was as follows: The fire had been ignited in a first-floor room. I waited until the room was fully involved. I had nailed the exterior door shut with four sixteen-penny nails to simulate a locked door. The student had to be geared up, with SCBA, and have a charged 1¾" attack hose line ready. They then had to take the door. One of the students was a young woman who weighed about 110 pounds. She came up to me and said, "Can I take the lead?" I asked her, "Do you think that you can do this?" She didn't hesitate. "Yes, I can." I told her, "You have the lead." Her fire gear, SCBA, and hose line weighed almost as much as she did. I knew this woman and her husband. He was a full-time fireman with a city Fire Department across the harbor from Portland. I also knew that her family had a long history with the fire service.

When I said, "Go," she stepped up to the door and kicked it just below the door lock. The door smashed open, hit the wall, and swung closed again. As it bounced open, the second time, she was on her knees, pulling the hose line, and had crawled inside the door headed for the fire room. She knocked the fire down. After the evolution was completed, I took her to one side. I told her, "You are a fireman. No matter what you might end up doing with your life. You are a fireman. And you are ten times the fireman that your husband is." Later, she would divorce him, return to school, get her college Degree in Nursing, and become an Emergency Room Nurse in one the best hospitals in New England in Salem, Massachusetts.

She is an example of what some women can bring to the fire service: that natural talent and desire to be *a fireman.*

There are issues and problems with two different genders living in close quarters. But nothing that cannot be worked out if we want to try. We are firemen. (When the experts can't figure it out, they call us.)

And yes, about 90 percent of the people in any group try hard and do the job. And there are about 10 percent in any group that should be thrown out the door. That holds true for men and women of any age group. I have personally known of three women who should have been thrown out the door of the first fire station that they walked into. They were trouble from the start, and it just got worse. A lot of good firemen suffered because of what they did. But that's not all women who want to be on the job. Most of them work hard at it and pay their dues. And because they are willing to work hard at it, they deserve that chance to do it and the respect that comes from doing the work.

Chapter Thirty-Six

Speaking of the elephant in the living room of the fire service

There are some things that come with being a fireman that no one wants to talk about, either up front when you are hired or even later after it happens. In the fire service and in any job involving Public Safety—Fireman, Police, EMS people—those of us who are in it, we see things and experience things on a daily/nightly basis that most average people don't see except on television. And seeing something while you are sitting in the comfort of your living room, with a drink in your hand, while you are warm and dry, just doesn't count as real experience. That's not even close to reality. Those of us who work the streets, we experience the worst that people can do to each other, and we experience it again and again and again. We see what life hands out to nice people who were just in the wrong place at the wrong time. And we see what happens to people who just do really stupid things to themselves or others. And we see what some people do to other people on purpose. We are the ones who get called in to try to save lives and then to clean up the bloody, gory mess, and we rarely, rarely ever receive even a "thank you" for our efforts.

These experiences do things to us: PTSD (Post-Traumatic Stress Disorder), high substance abuse rates, high suicide rates, high divorce rates, and high disease rates (heart disease, pulmonary disease, cancer in all its many forms).

I was one of the first people to be involved with the effort to start Post Critical Incident Stress Debriefings in Maine. I had experienced the trauma myself, and I knew what the after effects could do. I worked at my first fatal at age eighteen. And it just kept going from there. I was diagnosed with PTSD at age forty-four, after fighting alcoholism for twenty-six years.

I was lucky to be connected with a Counselor who had extensive experience in treating military vets with PTSD. It took him less than five minutes to diagnose me with PTSD, and that diagnosis saved my life. I had been borderline suicidal for the previous six years, and I was just starting the process to complete a divorce from my first wife. Today, it has been twenty-eight years since that diagnosis, and now my life has been on a path of healing for some time. In the book *DSM IV*, Post-Traumatic Stress Disorder is described as "a normal reaction to an abnormal situation." Firefighting, Police Work, and Emergency Medical Service work are inherently asking people to work in abnormal situations. Burned and dismembered human bodies are not normal situations. I have been told by military vets I know and have as friends that they wouldn't think anything of going into combat again, but they wouldn't go anywhere near a fire scene, let alone go into that burning building. Firefighting is just a different version of combat. You are going into battle against a foe who has the capacity to harm or to kill you. Firefighters use weapons that have different names but the same purpose: to kill that foe who is trying to kill you and/or to harm others.

PTSD is not just a small problem in the fire service; it's an pandemic. It's a problem that has to be recognized and dealt with. No longer hidden and ignored. It is the basis for other problems. Alcoholism is common, as is drug abuse. The divorce rate is upward of twenty times the national average. Suicide rates are ten times higher than normal. I saw this frequently in my career. I encountered perhaps eight out of every ten firemen who had a problem with alcohol and another one or two who abused drugs.

In 1968, at the National Fire Chiefs Conference, a comment was made about the high suicide rates among firefighters. At that time, the rate was four times the national average. Divorce rates were twenty to thirty times the national average. These rates have not changed that much. It is rare for a fireman to stay in their first marriage. I didn't. Portland has had its share of suicides involving firemen and police officers over the years. I knew some of them.

The trauma that we experience is such that we can't talk to anyone else about it. This means that we experience these things and then go home and can't talk about it. My worst times were fighting fires in the weeks just before Christmas. Seeing death and destruction around a burned Christmas tree, with people's hopes and dreams destroyed, and then going home, and my wife couldn't understand why I was not happy and joyful over the holiday. And I couldn't talk about it. Those people who are around us but are not in the business have no personnel reference point to turn to about what the fires look like or feel like. So they cannot understand what it's all about. That destroys relationships. It destroys that firefighter from the inside out.

There is another common factor between firemen and combat soldiers. This has been described as the "thousand-yard stare." We have that in common. And anything can trigger it: a random sound, a random sight, a smell, a comment by someone. If you watch a group of firemen sitting around talking, and someone makes a comment about a fire, watch and see when half of the group just stares off into space for a minute. They are reexperiencing a bad emergency scene. And they are reexperiencing it in all of its details: sounds, sights, smells, feelings, all of it. This is the thousand-yard stare. Combat Vets go through the same damn thing. And these memories don't go away with time. They are always there, just under the surface. Always. I have been retired for twenty-seven years, and the memories are still there for me. I can still see those emergency scenes and some of the other things: the rigor mortis of a burn victim, that "angel wings" of fire swirling through the air, at the ceiling level, in a hot hallway, telling me that the place is getting ready to blow.

Cancer and other diseases

I was recently informed that 85 percent of retired firemen from Portland, Maine, have some form of cancer. Eighty-five percent! I am a cancer survivor. I have also attended or read the obituaries for dozens of retired Portland firemen in the last fifteen years or so. They made their transition from a short list of diseases: cancer, heart disease, Parkinson's disease, pulmonary disease.

We breathe in more gases, smokes, and particulate matter than most people even know about or care about. There are things that would scare the daylights out of normal people and things that science doesn't even know about yet, because these smokes and gases that we breathe in are from materials that have been heated up and burned, and in that process, it changes into other things. Who would have anticipated that pulverized concrete could kill you if you breathe it in and that the deaths could come both fast or slow? And that it would not be just from respiratory failure? There have been more than five thousand deaths by disease in the aftermath of 9/11 just from exposure to the concrete dust from the Twin Towers.

These are some of the issues that should be made into a mandatory class in all rookie schools and even at the National Fire Academy at Emmitsburg, Maryland. Maybe, *maybe*, if we open these issues up to discussion, we can come up with some ways to deal with them instead of pretending that they don't exist until it's too late and it's just another wake to attend and maybe a history lesson.

In Portland, Maine, we were not allowed to talk about these things. Instead, what happened was that each individual man had to come up with his own way of dealing with it. Some of us drifted into alcohol abuse. Some of us just isolated from relationships or anything that required a commitment. Two of the men I knew ended up getting married for more than ten times each. Some of us, the lucky ones, myself included, found ourselves in counseling for extended periods of time, and doing this saved my life. And some of us suicide out, including drinking alcohol enough to die from it. Or men who die in tragic motor vehicle accidents that are really intentional and just a way of ending the hurt and pain.

Within the fire service as a whole, we have to come up with better ways of addressing this problem. We have to protect and take care of our own. No one else will. City or town administrations don't even want this issue raised. It scares them. All they can think of is, How much will this cost the city or the town? Fuck the firefighter or police officer or that paramedic. How much is this going to cost us in money?

Within the fire service, we have to remember the brotherhood. We will take care of our own. And this raises some problems of its own. Those of us in these fields are by nature very strong-willed, intelligent, resourceful, think-on-our-feet types of personalities. This can also be our downfall. When we are in a position of needing help (not if, but when), we tend to take on the attitude that "I don't need any help. I can take care of this myself," when, in fact, what we really need is some guidance and help in resolving whatever problem is infecting us, be it substance abuse, major disease, or emotional problems. And we need that special brand of courage that will let us reach out and ask for that help. A very good friend of mine once described that courage to me. Ron said it this way: "Bob, I was asked what do you think courage is?" I told the man, "Courage was the city corner in Revere, Massachusetts, that I grew up on." He answered, "No! Courage is walking up to and stepping into that door and sticking out your hand and saying that I can't do this alone and I need help. That is what courage is." Maybe that's the kind of courage that the leaders in the fire service need. Maybe they should have the kind of courage that it takes to reach out and teach this lesson to others. Hopefully, some of you who read this will have the courage to act on this problem.

CHAPTER THIRTY-SEVEN

Dispatchers
Jimmy Hughes

The best Emergency Dispatcher I have ever encountered in my forty-some-odd years in public safety was Jimmy Hughes. As part of my rookie training, I had to spend a few hours in the Fire Department's Emergency Dispatch Center. At that time, in the old county jail building at Middle Street and Franklin Street, near the Old Port area, in Portland. The Dispatcher was Jimmy Hughes. Jimmy was an ex-Marine with service in Korea. He wore a hat that said "The Frozen Chosun." Later, when I did duty as a Dispatcher, I would be told that a good dispatcher can make or break an emergency scene. If the dispatcher can keep his cool and not get rattled, his calmness will be transmitted out to everyone at the emergency scene, and things go really smoothly. Or if the Dispatcher allows themselves to panic, then that is what is transmitted to the emergency scene as well, and things can get really bad, really fast. Jimmy never lost his cool, not once. He handled multiple multialarm fires in Portland when the telephone was ringing off the wall with people calling in, and he never lost his cool. I have encountered some dispatchers who would try to micromanage a fire scene from the Dispatch Center—not Jimmy. He knew what information he could provide for the responding trucks, and that's what he gave them. He knew that if he was receiving multiple telephone calls for an alarm, then that meant that it was probably a serious fire. And he would tell the responding trucks, "I'm getting multiple calls on this one."

When I was a rookie and first stationed at Bramhall, and I was on floor duty at the Watch Desk, the telephone would ring, and I would answer it. Jimmy would say something like "Hey, Beanie. Here's what I want you to do. Now don't get scared. Just do what I tell you to do. I want you to tell all those old guys sitting around upstairs watching television to come downstairs and get on their big red trucks. Then I want you to tell them to take their trucks and go to __________________ Streets and take care of the fire that's been reported on the second floor. Now tell them not to hurry. I don't want them to hurt themselves. They're getting old." That was Jimmy.

A few years later, when I was stationed at Engine One on Munjoy Hill, in the old original wooden building that dated from 1870, I was awakened one night about 2:00 a.m. by the telephone, and it was Jimmy. The telephone was located so that the person talking on the phone could see out the second-floor window facing the intersection of Waterville Street and Congress Street. Jimmy did his speech about waking up the old guys and getting them to take the truck out to a dumpster fire in the parking lot of the convenience store, right next door from the fire station. I could see the fire from where I was standing, at the telephone. I responded (half-asleep) to Jimmy, "Yeah, Jimmy, I see the fucking thing." When we returned to the station, I had to call the dispatcher to get all our response times for the fire report. Jimmy was laughing at me on the phone. I asked him, "What are you laughing about?" He told me that the Dispatcher Center had just that day upgraded some of their equipment, and part of it was a recording system for all the telephone calls, in or out. He played back, for me, my comment to him about my seeing the fire and the swear words that I used. Was I ever embarrassed.

Years later, when I was dispatching while recovering from my injuries from the Wilson School fire, I remembered the lessons that I had learned from Jimmy, and I earned a reputation as a damn good Dispatcher.

Unfortunately, not all our dispatchers were like Jimmy. We had a few who would try to micromanage emergency scenes from the dispatch center, and it usually resulted in confusing the scenes. One Dispatcher who was usually very good had a smoking habit (marijuana). And he tried to grow his preferred smoking product in the break room of the dispatch center. When the plant got to be about six feet tall, the police department major came down to the center and very firmly told the dispatcher that people were complaining about that plant; they could see it from the Franklin Arterial which passed by the side of the building, and they could see what kind of plant that it was. This new building also housed the Portland Police headquarters. The major told the dispatcher, "Get that damn plant out of here now."

Another Dispatcher was so bad that he was scary. He regularly sent trucks to the wrong locations. On one occasion, he put out a fire alarm for a fire on Munjoy Hill. I was working on Engine One, on Munjoy Hill. When we asked for a location for the fire, he said that he could see the smoke from the dispatch center and that it was on Munjoy Hill; he could see it from where he was. But he couldn't tell us where on Munjoy Hill it was located. Munjoy Hill is a dense residential area that measures about one mile long by three quarters of a mile wide. Engine One and Ladder One left the station, and we drove all around Munjoy Hill, about a three-mile loop, and couldn't find anything. What we did find was an oil tanker out in the Portland Harbor at the location where most of the large ships anchored. It was cleaning its boilers, and there was a large column of black smoke rising into the sky from its smokestack. This was what the dispatcher saw, and he reported it as a large fire on Munjoy Hill.

One of these dispatchers was the one who had ordered Portland's Engine Seven to put on its tire chains to get ready for a snowstorm. Portland's Engine Seven is the Fireboat.

But Jimmy, you were the best.

When I was working as a Dispatcher, the Portland Fire Department's Dispatchers were transitioning to a Public Safety Dispatch Center. This meant that the fire dispatchers had to work part of their shift with the Fire Department and emergency medical services and part of their shift with the police department. I got the chance to meet and get to know a lot of really good Police Officers. Some of these men are still friends today, thirty-five years later. We still draw attention whenever we encounter each other and sit down and trade stories. People just kind of look at us and shake their heads in disbelief at what they are hearing. This street humor that comes through is sometimes just sick, but often it is just how we dealt with it all. Like some of these stories:

I was working a summertime day shift when a patrol officer stopped a vehicle on Brighton Avenue in Portland (one of Portland's major commuter routes). He had stopped the vehicle for traveling at the speed of fifteen miles an hour (posted speed is thirty-five miles per hour at that area) and holding up a long line of other vehicles. The vehicle had Michigan license plates. The officer asked the driver, "Where are you coming from, sir?" The driver answered, "Detroit, Michigan." The officer asked him, "How long have you been on the road, sir?" The driver replied, "About ten days." Detroit, Michigan, to Portland, Maine, at fifteen miles an hour.

Or another incident in the wintertime on a late night shift, when a patrol officer stopped a suspected drunk driver on Commercial Street in Portland, on the waterfront. The officer noticed an automatic weapon and an open briefcase full of money on the seat beside the driver. He arrested the driver and later found out that the man was a drug dealer who was passing through Portland, on his way to Canada, and had stopped at a bar, in Portland (for just a couple of beers). The weapon and the money were seized, and the man was released to return to his home out of state. We wondered what he had to say to his employers when he got home. And we were taking bets on what his life expectancy was.

We put in ten-hour day shifts and fourteen-hour night shifts. But it was never boring. There is something going on at all times, somewhere in the city.

CHAPTER THIRTY-EIGHT

Engine Eight

I was stationed on Engine Eight, at Allen's Corner, in the North Deering section of Portland, for two years. I drove for Stubby and for a short time for Lieutenant Wayne. We had a good time. We were in a primarily suburban residential area with some commercial buildings and some strip malls. We had a good crew. While I was at Engine Eight, I had some really interesting experiences. The truck itself at that time was a brand-new American LaFrance Quint (read "American Can Squint"—if you squint hard enough, after a while, it starts to look like a real fire truck). This truck was so misdesigned. It weighed in at 38,800 pounds on a single-axle chassis, and we were never able to keep a suspension system intact or brakes under it. In addition, about two months after delivery, the paint began to peel off the truck in big strips. It seems that the stainless steel body panels had never been special prepped or primed for the paint.

One morning in the summer, I was driving for Captain R. when we responded to an alarm at one of the commercial buildings. There is a major intersection about three hundred feet from the fire station. It was rush-hour traffic at the time, and as I approached the intersection, I had to swing left to pass by both lanes of traffic. The traffic was stopped at the red light. As I started to pass on the left side of a one-ton box truck, he decided to turn left and into me. I locked up the brakes. One of the bad features on this American LaFrance truck was that if you stepped on the brakes hard and they locked up, the engine stalled. I did this, the engine stalled, and the truck lost all control and started sliding through the intersection. I kept the truck straight, but I was sliding right toward this poor guy in a small SUV on the other side of the intersection. All he could see was this large fire truck sliding toward him out of control. I stopped Engine Eight about ten feet from this SUV. I took a deep breath, shifted into park, and restarted the fire truck; I backed up a little and then proceeded to the alarm call. Later I talked to the guys in the jump seats, and they said that the one-ton box truck had missed the side of Engine Eight by less than two inches. Captain R. didn't bat an eye. He just quietly said, "Good job. I'm glad that you don't have to do this all the time."

Steve G. is a great guy. He has a great sense of humor. He was the driver on Engine Eight, on the off shift from me. At shift change one evening, as he was going off duty, he made the comment that those of us on my shift were a bunch of Kamikazes. He was referring to those Japanese fighter plane pilots from World War II. Well, I couldn't let that one pass by. During the evening, I found an old pillowcase that we were cutting up for rags. I cut it into four strips and marked them like the Japanese fighter pilot head scarf that they wore in World War II. At shift change the next morning, we all wore them on our heads. Steve came in the door, looked at us and just shook his head, mumbled something, and walked off.

On another occasion, Steve took a short length of rope and tied nine knots in it at regular intervals. When the Deputy Chief drove up to the station that morning, Steve took the rope and walked out to meet the Chief. He held the rope up by one end in front of the Chief. The Chief asked him, "What's that for?" Steve said, "I just want to find out how strong the wind is today. You know. One knot, two knots, three knots." The Chief just turned around, got back in his car, and drove away.

It was at Engine eight when I started to realize that I was getting cynical about some of the people that I was encountering at emergency scenes. The station was located at one corner of a strip mall parking lot. Sometimes, in the evenings, a couple of the local kids who were losers would race their dirt bikes up and down the parking lot in between the cars. I mumbled about this for a while, but there wasn't much that we could do. Until one evening.

The building next door to the fire station was a bowling alley. On some evenings it was really busy, especially with tournaments. On this particular evening, these two punks were racing through the parking lot at about 10:00 p.m. (long after sunset). A woman was backing her car out of a parking space at the bowling alley when one of these punks broadsided her car. I happened to be looking out the window of the station at that moment. I yelled to the fireman on station watch, "Call for the ambulance for next door, for a motorcycle/car accident." I ran next door to the accident scene. The kid on the bike was on the ground with a broken leg, screaming. The woman was in her car crying. I checked the kid out for further injuries. The woman was unhurt. The kid kept screaming, "Will someone kill me to make my leg stop hurting."

He just kept screaming this. After about five minutes of that, I told him, "This accident is your own fucking fault, and if you don't shut up, I'll give you your goddamned wish."

I turned around to the woman and told her that I was a witness to the accident and that it was not her fault, and I would make a statement for the police report. But later, it bothered me that I was starting to get cynical about things.

Engine Eight was a good station. After we got the "Squint" American LaFrance Quint, we had some interesting calls. One night, we responded to Falmouth for a mutual-aid call. The fire was in an old Knights of Pythias hall, off Route 26, going toward Gray, about eight miles from the station. When we arrived at the scene, Falmouth Fire Department was already set up, but they didn't have a ladder truck. Our aerial was seventy-five feet. The building was long and narrow, about forty feet by one hundred feet and three and a half stories tall with a small window at the peak. It was wood-framed with a pitched roof and asphalt shingles. The building was more than one hundred years old. We had heavy fire showing from the entire building. The Deputy Chief was Jimmy R. He knew his business. I set the aerial to the peak window about forty feet up and set up to pump a master stream into the window for a "blitz attack." I talked to the two pumper operators from Falmouth about feeding me a water supply. I told them what I needed for water pressures and the volume that I needed. We went at it and knocked the fire down. We then made ready to enter the building. George W. and I climbed the aerial, and George got ready to climb into the window. The interior was not lighted, so we could not see beyond a couple of feet into the space. I was not sure about doing this, but George said something that sticks in my mind to this day. He said, "Hey, Bobby. No guts, no glory."

He stepped into the window. I put both hands on his coat collar, and I wouldn't let go until he said, "I'm okay." He stayed next to the window opening, and I handed him my helmet light. When he turned on the light and looked around, it was an adrenaline rush. Everything inside the building had burned away, all the way from the roof to the cellar. George was standing on a burned wooden ledge that was mostly burned away to about four feet out from the wall, and that's all that was left of the flooring for the entire building. The hole was about eighty feet long by thirty feet wide. It was a forty-foot drop to the cellar. I'm glad I held on to his coat collar. Yeah, George. "No guts, no glory." But let's be a little careful.

Yeah. We did some really great work.

Deputy Chief Jimmy showed his knowledge of tactics again one night at a three-story office supply store on Free Street near Cross Street. The building was completely filled with dark, heavy smoke. Jimmy had six trucks at the scene: four pumpers and two ladders. He made everyone wait until the ladder truck crews had vented the roof before he allowed anyone to make entry. He was a progressive thinker for our department, and he was one of a minority. There were only a very few of us who read the books and studied to try to make the changes. This fire turned out to be some office furniture that was smoldering and had been smoldering for hours. The fire was knocked down with a minimum of fire damage and some smoke damage in the building. This was a three-story brick downtown building.

I worked with Jimmy for two years to reinstate a heavy rescue for the Portland Fire Department. Jimmy fought for it, and I worked to set it up and drove it. When we started, it was only used for large fires and then, after a while, it was used for all working fires. Today it's a mainstay and runs on all fire calls.

CHAPTER THIRTY-NINE

Fatalities

Trends in fire safety tend to take years, sometimes decades, to evolve. When I started on the job, Portland had not lost anyone in a fire for twelve years. When I retired, we were losing three or four people a year to the "Demon." Why? Because when I went on the job, we had an active Fire Prevention Bureau. And we had been lucky.

During the first few years of my career, the Fire Prevention Bureau was reduced in size down from four men to one man and was restricted in its work, and it received no support from city administration. It also suffered from some people working at it for personal gain only. And any extra manpower came from those firemen who were out on sick leave and were placed in the Fire Prevention Bureau for light duty with no additional training or classes for that work.

As a consequence, we started to lose ground in Fire Prevention for the city. And we started to lose people to fires. We also acquired some slum landlords. All fire departments know about these clowns. They come into an area, buy up some property, and use it irresponsibly. They collect rents and put nothing, or a bare minimum, of effort back into the buildings. They stall on fire safety upgrades or just flatly refuse to implement them. We've had our share of these clowns. Our fire rates started to go up, and injuries and deaths started to increase.

At this time, we were still not allowed to use SCBAs. The Fire Administration had stated that it cost too much to refill them at the local dive shop, so we didn't use them. Still we got in, took a beating, and did our job. Later the bureau would get a couple of men who worked hard at it and learned their job. Another guy named Jimmy took leadership in the bureau and became a fighter for an active, progressive Fire Prevention Bureau. He attended classes to learn how to do it right. He started taking cases to court and winning. And over a period of time, his work paid off. But, again, these trends take years to evolve. In the meantime, we were losing buildings and people to the "Demon." We also had an area of the city that was being slowly cleared for a low-income project, the first of these projects in Portland. This area today is known as Kennedy Park. The slow clearing of this area was not done by demolition; it was done with fire. At one period of time, this area looked like a duplicate of South Bronx in New York City. It comprised eight city blocks of partially or completely burned out buildings. This "urban renewal" area was the scene of almost daily fires in Portland for about six to eight years. At times, we would have multiple fires going at the same time in this area. All of it with a silent nod of approval from the city administration.

As I mentioned earlier, we were losing between two and three people a year in fires in Portland. The cold weather season seemed to be the worst. Heating systems would fail, like at the Pearl Street Apartment fire, when the building boiler blew up and the debris went up through the roof of a three-story apartment building, killing three children. Or the three Christmases in a row when we had fatal fires, one of them with the loss of a woman and her three children in one fire and a single fatal in a second fire, and the Massachusetts Avenue fire/murder in the last one. These fires contributed to my resentment of Christmas and of the whole month of December, for twenty years afterward. Today, I recognize that this was a part of my PTSD, but it still took me years of work on myself to get through it.

Over that period of time, I noticed that fatal fires with anyone over the age of twenty didn't seem to bother me as much as those involving children. The dead kids really hit me hard. They never had a chance to really live a life. I remember one fire where a three-year-old child died from the smoke from a cigarette ash that had dropped into her toy box next to her bed. The smoke from the smoldering fire killed her. That was a tough one to look at.

Or the thirty-year-old man in his reclining chair in the living room of his home. He died while watching TV. He had gone downstairs to the basement to feed the wood stove. He too had a cigarette in his mouth. The ash from the cigarette fell into the wood chips beside his wood box. He didn't notice it. He returned to his living room to watch TV. The smoldering fire slowly filled the house with heavy smoke, and he died sitting in his reclining chair.

Or the number of mattress fires that we had where the person smoking in bed ignited the mattress and died right there. I don't remember exactly, but I was at maybe twenty-five fatal fires and another one hundred fatal accidents. The result is always the same: someone dies. And the pictures in my head and the memories of the smells and the scenes, they never go away.

One of the accident scenes was a single-car rollover. I was one of the first on the scene. It was a young couple. He was the driver and sitting behind the steering wheel very badly injured. She was sitting in the front seat on the passenger side. Both were wearing seat belts. Her body was in the front seat, but her head was sitting on the backseat. As I was trying to cover the body (for privacy reasons), a man kept removing the covering and trying to photograph the body. I asked him if he was with the media. He replied, "No." I took his camera away from him, smashed it into the pavement, and told the police officer to arrest him if he comes near the car. The officer was smiling when he put him in the backseat of his patrol car. I don't like the "vampires."

CHAPTER FORTY

Wakes and funerals

I have just returned home from the wake for another fireman who has made his transition to a better place. This is number five in the last three months. It provokes a lot of introspection. This is from the notes that I made in my daily journal:

Boy, there was a bunch of guys there. I saw maybe forty to forty-five guys. It was good to talk to them again. I know that I had to walk the path that I walked to get to where I am today, but I do miss interacting with each one of the guys.

When we were on the job, at the same time, we were all in our own worlds. We still are not "lone warriors, but not far from that." It's interesting. Each of us has had a couple of friends near us, but as a group, none of us hangs around together. And when we do meet (at wakes or funerals), that love that we have for each other is still very much there. We shared so much. Maybe that's part of what I miss—the brotherhood. And these times that we do see each other, we don't seem to be able to verbalize those feelings. That's an interesting conundrum for you. That very powerful but unspoken love. The love that exists among warriors who have spent time in battle together and faced death together. So strong and yet so silent.

Oh Great Spirit, I thank you so much for letting me be a part of that. Thank you.

Chapter Forty-One

Arsonists I have known and loved
Franklin Street and burning out Bayside.

Over the years in Portland, we have had our share of torches. Some of these problem people were rude and crude. We also had numerous others who were smart and thought it out.

D. was a man who had been in an institution for the developmentally challenged since he was a young man. When the State of Maine Administration, in one of its less-than-brilliant

Moments. Closed the facility and just threw the patients out on the street, with no backup programs to help them, D. was left to wander the streets of Portland. He did have a family in the area, but there was nothing in place to help him adjust to living in the everyday world. He eventually gravitated to Central Fire Station in Portland and used to just hang out near us. Every few days, someone at the station would say something that D. didn't like. He would turn and walk away. Within twenty to thirty minutes, we would be out the door and on our way to the Hampshire Street area or the Franklin Street area for a working fire. On arrival at the fire scene, D. would be standing on the sidewalk across the street watching us arrive. He was arrested on a number of occasions, but the justice system would not send him to jail because of his mental disabilities.

On one occasion, we were having a dull, boring day at Central Station. It was a sunny, beautiful Sunday, in the summertime. And we really wanted a little action. D. showed up, and as he was standing in front of the station talking to a few of us, two other firemen went upstairs, filled a balloon with water, and dropped it out the window onto D. About twenty minutes later, sure enough, we headed out the door and onto Hampshire Street and found two rooms, on the second floor, fully involved with fire. I happened to encounter D. years later after I had retired. He didn't recognize me, but I saw that he was picking up bottles and cans on the sidewalks to get a few dollars. I had about fifteen or twenty in the back of my pickup truck, so I just handed them to him. He was really just one of those lost souls that wander around the cities.

C.'s story was a little different. He was one of those torches who seemed to get a deep satisfaction from burning something, anything. He caused us a lot of problems. He was one of those who just like to watch buildings burn. He did move to Westbrook, and he became their problem for a long time. But they had learned from us, and they kept a close watch on him.

T. was an interesting story. He had some business connections in southern New England. He torched places for money. He also had a couple of businesses in Portland. He was one of the smart torches. But at some point, he must have really pissed off someone out of state because his house burned (a Two-Alarm Fire). At that time, we used an Arson Investigator who worked for the Maine State Fire Marshal's Office; he was living near Portland. He did the investigation on this fire. He name was Lawrence Dolby. He was a legend. His books on fire investigation were used at the National Fire Academy as textbooks. I found out some years later that he and I were third cousins. Maybe we shared something that runs in the genes.

When the judge asked T., the property owner, what caused this fire, he said, "Spontaneous combustion of pigeon droppings in the attic." The judge turned to Lawrence Dolby and said, "Now, sir, please tell me what really caused this fire." For the rest of his life, Lawrence Dolby was referred to as "Pigeon Droppings Dolby." Lawrence informed the judge of the arson cause of the fire. On another occasion, he was able to prove that a particular fire was caused by mice running through a kitchen cabinet and causing some of those famous old wooden kitchen matches known as "strike anywhere matches" to ignite and start a kitchen fire. Old "rats and matches" Dolby.

Most torches don't think things out. I learned very early on to spot the splash patterns from the accelerant and to look for the ignition point. Origin and cause.

Once in a great while, the torch would be burned by the fire that they were starting. It always upset us that these people were treated as tragic accidents. And people raised money through contributions to help them pay for their medical expenses. These people, regardless of their age, intentionally started the fire to cause destruction, usually of someone else's property. They should be required to take responsibility for their actions. They don't need pity. They need accountability.

We went through a period of time, like all city departments do, when we encountered deliberate traps set in the buildings to disable or kill firefighters. We went into buildings in the Bayside area that had had large holes cut in the floors, just inside the front door. These were covered over with a piece of carpet or a flattened-out cardboard sheet. These were created to make incoming firefighters fall through into the basements of the buildings. We also encountered the "gasoline shower" setup: a plastic trash bag filled with about one gallon of gasoline and left hanging at head height from the ceiling, just inside the front door of the building. When the first fireman entered the front door, his helmet would puncture the bag, and he would receive a gasoline shower. This, while he was going into a burning building.

On one particular occasion, the arsonists used dynamite set in a building to explode from the fire. I was on Ladder Three, out of Engine Eight Station in the Allen's Corner area of North Deering. The arsonist had set up two buildings to burn. One building was a barn on Eleanor Street, a side street in the Morrill's Corner area of Portland. The second building was a biker bar, the Brass Rail, on Forest Avenue, also near Morrill's Corner. The intent was for the barn fire to be spotted first, and the Fire Department would respond to it first. And then, while we were fighting the barn fire, the biker bar would ignite. The dynamite would explode, and the bar would be history. But the arsonists got their signals crossed. The bar fire was spotted first, and as the crews were making entry into that location, the barn fire was seen. Ladder Three, because of the height of the barn building, was assigned to the barn fire. The crews making entry into the bar fire quickly made headway and knocked the fire down. As they were checking for extension and doing overhaul, they found a piece of the flooring behind the bar cut open. Inside the opening were five sticks of dynamite set to explode.

We have also had bottles, cans, and rocks thrown at us, especially in the projects: Front Street, Riverton, Sagamore Village, Kennedy Park. For a five-year period, we refused to enter the Riverton housing project without a Portland Police escort. We just got really tired of people stealing things off the trucks while we were there on emergency runs. We had an inside joke that this project should be fenced off with a twelve-foot chain-link fence topped with razor wire and no gate. And we had a series of bad fires in this project, and a few of them were fatal ones.

CHAPTER FORTY-TWO

Unions

Over the years, the various labor unions have done some great work. My Paternal Grandfather was a Union Organizer in Portland in the 1920s at a time when people who promoted unions were killed or jailed. The unions have done some good things, *but* there have been a lot of bad things done by and for the unions.

My personal experience with the IAFF is not a good story. When I was injured, in 1974, at the Wilson School fire, the union did absolutely nothing to help. This when I had saved the lives of three other firefighters. Then the Fire Administration tried to fire me to cover up their actions. The union turned a blind eye and did absolutely nothing. I was left on my own, to fight my battle over what had happened to me. I couldn't even get a response from the union reps. Part of the reason was that the union reps were drinking at night with members of the Fire Administration. If you're swapping beers at night with a person, you are not going to want to fight with that person during the day. Later on, in 1989, when I had my heart attack in the fire station and I was told that I could no longer be a fireman, the union representatives again decided not only to *not* help me, but when the city broke a half-dozen Federal Labor laws in my case, the union never even spoke up as well. The Union President was witnessed to lie to the city representative when he was asked if I wanted to do some other kind of work for the city in another capacity. He told the city administration that I was refusing to do any other type of work. In my attempts to speak up for myself, I called the New England IAFF union representative in Cambridge, Massachusetts, looking for help. He screamed at me over the telephone and told me to never call him again. Twenty-two years of paying my dues and it all went to nothing.

Eight years later, when I was forced to resign from the Maine State Fire Marshal's Office, because I was a whistleblower on some corruption that I had encountered there, again the Union Representative for the State Workers Union told me, "You have a great case to take to court." But if I wanted to take the case to court, the union would have to represent the person who was causing me to leave and to fight against me even knowing the particulars of my complaints.

Even the ACLU office in Boston told me that if I were a woman or a minority, I would have a textbook case, but because I was a white male, there was nothing that they would do for me. It would later take a letter and a phone call to my congressperson to get the ACLU to stop hounding me for donations. This for fifteen years afterward. So much for some people's protestations of working for a noble cause.

Yes, the unions have done some good things, but they also have a lot of amends to make to people like me. And until that happens, they won't get my support.

And with this subject on the page, I would like to write about my opinions on politics in the fire service.

My observations have been that in every single instance that politics has been allowed into any organization, it has destroyed that organization. I have worked for or belonged to a number of organizations, and in each and every single instance, politics has distorted the purpose of and/or destroyed the best intentions of those organizations. I have known a half-dozen people who have entered politics. All of them started out with the best of intentions. In a very short time, they were corrupted by those same politics. A few years ago, I was asked by an acquaintance who had just joined the Tea Party what I thought of a certain politician. I told him that I thought that politicians were on the same level as hookers, except that hookers tended to be in their business because they had to, and politicians were there because they wanted to. But both sold themselves for money, and politicians just charged a lot more. Politics is a field of endeavor for those who are too deficient in moral values to be able work anywhere else. Those personal values of honesty, integrity, honor, compassion, ethics, these values are the very first things cast away (and, in most cases, never to be picked up again) by the person who enters politics.

That said, there have been a few people I have known of within my lifetime who entered politics to try to make a positive difference. These people maintained their personal values against the temptation to cast them aside. They are all dead now. Dr. Martin Luther King, Nelson Mandela, John F. Kennedy, Gandhi. There is one more man from Maine who tried to make a positive difference: George Mitchell. But it's almost like the old comment: "You're trying to shovel shit against the tide. And you have a very small shovel."

In the Fire Department, many promotions were awarded not on the basis of qualifications and education but on the system of "It's not what you know, but who you know." Those who drank with the chief at a certain bar at night were placed high on promotion lists and made ahead of others who were much more qualified.

During some particular periods of time, certain property owners were given a lot of leeway in the conditions of their property because they contributed to certain special "fireman retirement funds," these funds that never really existed. A series of fire chiefs were hired not because of their qualifications, not because of their education with fire service degrees, but because of membership in certain city organizations and clubs. And once they were in place, they became an embarrassment to those very city administrations that had put them into the positions. The many problems caused by this were overlooked regardless of how much damage was being done.

Those of us who went to school to learn more about firefighting and how to do our jobs better were scorned and targeted for harassment by these political appointees. I watched one of these appointees be given the job of Fire Investigator for the fire department. This man had never taken a class in fire investigation in his life. He went on to prove that by maintaining a record of never, ever encountering a set fire in his career. Even when the rest of us on the fire scenes saw the obvious signs of arson, he determined that the fires were accidental or caused by a malfunction in the electrical system. At one particular fire, on a Saturday morning, in the fall, a fire occurred in the first-floor apartment on Washington Avenue in the North Deering section of the city. This apartment was the home of a prostitute who had recently broken off with her pimp. She had a client with her in bed when the fire occurred. The classic signs of splash patterns were on the floor around the end of the bed. What saved two lives that night was the type of bed that she and her john were lying in. The fire was hot enough that the plastic waterbed mattress melted through, and the water gushing from that mattress put the fire out. No one was injured. This self-described fire investigator determined that the fire had been started by a candle being knocked down from a windowsill by the curtains blowing in the wind. As it lay on the floor, it ignited a carpet on the floor. Those of us on the scene who had fought the fire noticed that the window was closed at the time that the fire started. But this Fire Investigator was being groomed for the Fire Chief position, so his actions were ignored. Politics again.

I did learn one thing about politics during all my experiences: never trust a politician. They are experts in lying, cheating, and stealing to meet their own private agendas and to satisfy their greed for power and wealth.

And back to the original topic for this segment. The unions have become just another political organization. Their original purpose and good intentions have long since become lost to the mechanizations of politics and personal greed.

CHAPTER FORTY-THREE

Whorehouses and hooker stories

Speaking of the working girls in Portland, we have our share of them. And some of the stories are interesting.

Working the street, the way firemen, policemen, and emergency medical services workers do, we get to mingle with all kinds of people. There have been a number of brothels in Portland over the years. Some of these were famous, and they later became landmarks. One particular building was in operation for the duration of World War II, on the waterfront in Portland. They have been a part of the city ever since the city was created. All waterfront cities have some form of them. Portland had some that were famous during the boomtown years of the Second World War, with the shipyards and the North Atlantic Fleet staging out of Portland. Some of the hotels were noted for giving an hourly rate for their rooms. In the years that I worked on the fire department, there were three houses for working girls. The one that I remember the most was located in Longfellow Square, on Congress Street. It was advertised as a massage parlor, with extras. We had a fire in the building one afternoon. The fire itself was not very large, just a lot of smoke. But the excitement came from evacuating the building. There were a few prominent faces that were escorted from the building by way of the rear entrance, and we even had two couples that had to be ordered to leave the building; they were "busy and didn't want to be interrupted."

In another series of memories of the "working girls," it was summertime, and I was driving Engine Four, on an alarm, when we passed through Congress Square, on our way to a reported smoke in the building, at an office building further down Congress Street. As we passed through Congress Square, there is a small park, adjacent to the Eastland Hotel. This park was a hangout area for the working girls. One of the men on Engine Four was a young fireman who was single. He was a quiet guy, a real nice guy. As we passed this park, one of the girls started jumping up and down, waving her hands, and shouting out this fireman's name. When we returned from the alarm, we all had a good time asking him, "Hey, man. Just what kind of girls are you dating?"

When I was working at Munjoy Hill Station, on Engine One, we regularly watched the "working girls" working. One in particular used to wear short shorts—very, very short shorts. These shorts were covered in department patches: Portland Police, Portland Fire, Cumberland County Sheriff, Maine State Police. Her nickname was Patches. I was there one day when her pimp started to beat her up, on the street corner. Four of us ran across the street and beat up on him and told him to "keep the violence off the street."

And some of the hooker stories are just so sad, because these women just don't have any way to get out of their lifestyle. They are locked into this, and it's a downhill street with no turns to take to get out of it. There is no good retirement program for them.

CHAPTER FORTY-FOUR

Hydrants

I have mentioned the weather that we experience here in Portland, and I have mentioned the age of the city. Portland's municipal water system is the envy of all the cities east of the Mississippi River. The static water pressure in this system varies from twenty pounds psi at its highest point to 140 pounds psi at its lowest point. This system is gravity-fed with very large mains that come directly from Sebago Lake. I have mentioned that it has more than one thousand miles of piping. About two years after I started on the Fire Department, the Portland Water District began a major renovation project of the city's water system. It was interesting because they found themselves removing wooden water mains from some sections of the city. I had a piece of that wooden water pipe for a long time. These wooden water pipes were left over from the eighteenth century.

Portland has approximately three thousand fire hydrants. When I was on the department, it was part of our responsibility to keep these hydrants clear, tested (for leakage and residual water levels), and pumped dry to prevent freezing during the cold-weather months (October through April). These hydrants were assigned to each fire company. Each truck had a certain area of the city and the hydrants in that area. For some years, this testing and pumping was done by a fireman walking the designated area carrying a plumb-bob testing line, a hydrant wrench, and a hand pump. The fireman would leave the fire station at 8:30 a.m. and return around noontime. Another fireman would go out at 1:00 p.m. and return around 5:00 p.m. Later, that policy would change, and two men would go out in a pickup truck and stay out all day. Hydrants with residual water in the bases would frequently be found to be frozen solid. These needed to be flushed out or cleared with a hot steam water line.

We have had, occasionally, arsonists who would open a hydrant, let it fill with water, and then let it set overnight to freeze solid. Usually this hydrant would be the one closest to the building that was going to be burned. Or they would open a hydrant port, fill it with stones or even a tennis ball, and close it back up. When the first due pumper tried to use the hydrant, the ball or the rocks would clog the intake pipe screen on the pumps. This would slow down the effort to put the wet-on-the-red process. We had on a few occasions that had someone driving around the Munjoy Hill area in the winter and just opening hydrants and letting them freeze. One morning, we found more than thirty frozen hydrants on Munjoy Hill alone. Fortunately, we did not get a fire call during the time it took us to thaw and clear these hydrants. But we were waiting for something to happen.

We also had to shovel these hydrants. This chore was sometimes done by two firemen in a pickup truck or by the entire truck and crew together. We had a Deputy Fire Chief who had a drinking problem. He used to sit in a bar drinking. He would then drive around the city in his official car. He would stop and use a tape measure to measure the shoveled opening to the hydrants. If he found one that he didn't like, he would call the Fire Alarm Dispatcher and tell him to order that truck back out to shovel the hydrants in their area again. We have had to go out and shovel the same hydrants up to three times for each snowstorm.

This same Deputy Fire Chief would order us out in the summer months to cut the grass around the hydrants because "there could be Japs hiding in the grass around those hydrants." As a passing note, this man was not a military vet.

Another incident involved a hydrant in the corner of the parking lot at a commercial business on West Commercial Street. The business owner would have his parking lot plowed by a large front loader machine, and the snow would be mounded up to twenty feet high over the hydrant. Two of us were walking and shoveling hydrants one evening when we found this hydrant like this; this was the third time that this had happened. My friend Hoss just went to a phone and called the on-duty Deputy Fire Chief (Red). He came right down in his chief's car, and boy, didn't he chew that property owner's ass. He told him that if it happened again, then he would be arrested for intentionally obstructing the fire department response.

On two occasions that I was involved in, we had the classic occasion of motor vehicles parked in front of hydrants at fire scenes. There have been some great videos taken of the aftermath of these situations in other cities. One scene was in the summer, and one was in the winter. The summer scene was in front of Mercy Hospital on State Street, in Portland's West End. We had a fire in an apartment building across the street from the hospital. The hydrant was at the front entrance to the hospital. I was told to hook up the feeder line and open the hydrant to supply the engine company. A car was parked in front of the hydrant. The fire hose line was a two-and-a-half-inch, double-cotton-jacketed hose line with brass couplings. Each coupling weighed sixteen pounds. I bounced that coupling across the hood and windshield of the car, leaving a cracked windshield and numerous dents in the hood. I then left the charged hose line in place across the hood of the car. I heard later that the car's owner came out, saw the car, and never said a word.

The winter incident was a fire in a large building on Middle Street, just off Monument Square in Downtown Portland. I didn't do this one, but I was there. This was a major fire. The building was a four-story, multiple-use building. It was completely destroyed in the fire. When we arrived, we had fire showing on two floors. The fire hydrant closest to the building was just across the street. A car was parked in front of the hydrant. The fireman tried the driver's door. It was unlocked. He opened the driver's door, opened the passenger door, stretched a hose line across the front seat, hooked the line up to the hydrant, and charged the hose line. The hose coupling leaked a little water. They almost always do, and it came out as a fine spray that soaked the front seat of the car. At one point, the car's owner came out, and he was furious. He started getting very belligerent to us firemen. The police officer who was standing there just told him that, yes, he could tell the firemen to remove the hose, but then he would have to write a ticket for the car's owner. The owner just stomped off. We were on scene at this fire for two days and nights. When we finally picked up and returned to the stations, the ice inside the front seat of this guy's car was about four to six inches thick all across the inside of the front of the car. Don't park in front of hydrants.

I had one disturbing incident at a fire hydrant. I was walking the hydrant area alone testing the hydrants in the late fall. I was confronted by a dog as it came charging out of the driveway from the house across the street. The dog's owner was standing there watching this happen, with a smile on his face. I was about one hundred feet away from the owner's house across an intersection and on the opposite side of the street. I didn't really think about much except to protect myself from being bitten. I yelled, and the dog kept coming. When the dog got really close, I dropped the hydrant pump, and I swung the steel hydrant wrench and hit the dog. The dog went down. I thought that I had killed it. The owner started to yell at me. There was a witness who said that the dog attacked me. The owner picked up the dog and walked off to his house. I never heard anything more about this incident. But whenever I was in that area again, doing hydrants, I had no trouble from that house.

CHAPTER FORTY-FIVE

Memories of fires

I have not lived in the city itself for twelve years now; I live about twenty miles outside it. But over the last few months, I have found myself driving through the peninsula area of the city on appointments or on errands or perhaps just taking my wife to dinner. I can't help but to remember the fires and the buildings. I think that, this is common with us old guys. The City has changed a lot with time. They all do. But when I'm standing outside a restaurant in downtown Portland and waiting to go in and I look around me and see the buildings, I remember the incidents. Sometimes my wife will just say, "Are you all right?" Yes. I'm just crawling around inside the memories that are within my head for a few minutes.

There is not a street, neighborhood, or area of the city that I don't remember as "this fire or that fire." I believe that these memories are a special gift to me from my spirit guides. It's a way of them telling me that this is what you did with this lifetime, and we are proud of what you've done. I attended a Wake recently for an old friend, and the photos brought up memories. For me, the memories are both good and bad and frequently humorous.

Doing things that most people would run away from in fear and doing those things not just once but time after time after time.

Clark Street with the kids and the gas leak;

Upper State Street, being in a building with hidden fire and stepping out onto the front steps, and passing out, and then waking up in the hospital and finding out what high amounts of carbon monoxide can do to you;

Free Street and the Elks Club;

All the fatal fires on "the Hill";

The fires and the rescues on the waterfront;

East Deering and Engine Eleven, with both Ed M. and later with Joe T.;

The old station buildings;

Engine Nine at Morrill's Corner;

Engine One on "the Hill";

The first airport crash truck, in an open shed, with a door that only came down partway, and an old military crash truck that had to be jump-started once every two weeks to make sure that it would run;

The long cold runs from Bramhall Fire Station to the airport (about seven miles), on a first-response alarm.

All firemen have these kinds of memories. These memories are what makes us who we are. That's why whenever I meet another fireman from another city, I recognize them almost immediately by that look in the backs of their eyes. That thousand-yard stare that marks those of us who have been there, who have seen it, who have done it. We share that stare, and we have faced the "Demon" and walked away.

CHAPTER FORTY-SIX

The battle with the city

Before I began work with the Portland Fire Department, it was considered a place of pride. This is because of the work that the firefighters did and had done for decades. There had been no lives lost in a fire in Portland for twelve years. The only firefighters lost on the job were in a fire truck accident six years earlier. This at a time when firefighters were still getting in and doing their job with a less than minimum of safety equipment: rubber hip wader–style fishing boots with no steel toes or steel shanks, plastic helmets, rubber coats, gloves that were just heavy work gloves and were not fire retardant and no fire-retardant pants, no SCBAs. These would not come onto our trucks for almost three more years, about 1970. Not bad, considering that they were invented in 1890, by the Drager company in Germany.

About eight months later, the union won a major contract with the city. This contract included a significant reduction in work hours (from sixty-two down to forty-six), a change from two shifts to three shifts, a pay increase, and a reduction in the time that a firefighter needed on the job to retire (age sixty-five down to twenty years' service time or age fifty-five). These concessions had taken two years to argue out. This event also started a war between the city and the fire department. For the next twenty years, the city fought against the fire department on every level.

Even the media got caught up in it. For my entire career, there was never any fire story in the media that did not start off with "the Portland Police Department responded to a fire at ______, and the Portland Fire Department was also on the scene." The city carefully selected a series of political appointees for fire chief. Most of them had no close affiliation with the firefighters themselves. They were selected to make all Fire Department Administration decisions in favor the city and to make the work environment for the firefighters as difficult as possible. In my career, there was never a time that we did not have some fight going on with the city. We were unofficially designated the proverbial bastard child. We were there, but we were not welcome. We were needed, but we were disliked intensely.

During this same time, our union leadership, with the exception of two men, developed into a series of men who were more focused on their own political aspirations and their own private agendas. Their interests were in making themselves look more important.

All this began to gradually erode that sense of pride that we had in ourselves. On some deep level, we began to accept that the city's description of us, that we were that "unwanted child," was true.

As the Fire Prevention Bureau was decimated by the loss of manpower and support from both the city and fire administrations, property loss and deaths began to increase, and the city pointed this out by saying, "You're not doing your job." At the same time, the city took the stance that for every man who retired or left the department, there would be no one hired to replace that position. We lost 43 percent of our manpower in six years. When, in the mid-1970s, the city very publicly hired an outside consulting firm to do an efficiency study on the fire department (this would be done three times over fifteen years), at a cost of about $50,000 each time, each study showed that we were severely understaffed. Each study was circular-filed and forgotten. We also experienced a series of bad fires where firefighters were injured and they were given zero amount of long-term help. This culminated in the Phoenix Restaurant fire when we had our first firefighter death on the line of duty in more than twenty years. Again, the city did absolutely nothing to resolve the conditions within the department. I recall standing in the funeral procession for this downed firefighter and watching the new city manager and a certain city counselor (who was also a retired Deputy Fire Chief) standing at one side and trading jokes and laughing. It was at this time that the heart of the Portland Fire Department was eviscerated.

Today, although the firefighters are still there and the trucks are still there and the runs are still there, the heart is gone. That brotherhood is some tiny little thing that is struggling to stay alive, but it is just barely there. Today, that city mind-set is still there. There has been a series of political "yes men" who have been appointed fire chief, interspersed with one man who tried to do a good job, but he just got tired.

My personal experience with the city administration's treatment of injured firefighters is very typical of an attitude that borders on gross negligence. Politics should be outlawed in public safety. Everything that allows politics to enter becomes corrupted. And all good intentions are cast away to be replaced by greed, avarice, lies, and the quest for personal gain. This never fails. It is always what happens when politics is allowed into any situation or organization. *Always.*

I have recently spoken to another retired Portland fireman. During the course of a one-and-a-half-hour conversation, I came to understand some of what happened to the Portland Fire Department and to its spirit. There was an environment of fear that was intentionally created and kept in place by the combined efforts of the Fire Administration and the city administration. This fear was that "if you say or do anything to draw attention to yourself, then the chief will come down on you hard and make your life miserable." So keep your mouth shut, and whatever happens, don't say a word.

This environment of fear permeated the entire firefighting staff. There were a number of fireground decisions that were made where men were injured or almost killed. In each and every instance, the Fire Administration let everyone know, "You just shut up. Or else." Three of these firefighters were almost killed, myself included. This environment of fear allowed us to be harassed, and in three cases, one man was fired, and two more were almost fired, and no one said a word, for fear of becoming the next target of the Fire Administration.

In one instance, the firefighter was electrocuted by a high-capacity electric wire on a street pole. The aerial ladder at the fire scene came into contact with the wire because the "ladder boom spotlights were broken," and the operator could not see the wire. That electric current, in excess of seventy thousand volts, grounded itself out through the aerial, down through the tires on the truck (these tires were burned off the truck), forty feet down the street (in the water stream that was leaking from the ladder truck pump panel), to the next truck down the street, an engine company. The tires on this engine company truck also burned off. The firefighter was walking up the street between the trucks. He was in the process of just taking a step so that one foot was raised slightly and the other one was in the water stream. He was knocked unconscious and awoke in the hospital ER. It was later determined that the electrical current had partially boiled his spinal fluid. He was left with a lifetime of Epilepsy and nerve damage. The Fire Administration and the City Administration tried to fire him over the next five to ten years. Eventually, he was given a severance package and told to just go away.

I have already written about my experience. This repeated mind-set of the fear of saying anything, coupled with the union representative's having more interest in playing politics instead of working to protect the firefighters, led to this prolonged environment of "shut up and don't draw attention to yourself." This environment lasted for more than thirty years. It was, like any life-threatening disease that is allowed to flourish, able to effectively kill the heart of the Portland Fire Department. So much so that even today, the adverse effects from this are still evident in the way these retired firefighters still interact with one another. There is still an inner sense of guilt, from spending so much time with this fear, seeing what they saw, and then not being able to say anything.

I attended a seminar on cancer, in Augusta, Maine, a few years ago. The keynote speaker was the chairman of one the most powerful committees on cancer in the United States. To become just a member on this committee, one has to be the CEO of a top-rated fundraising or research organization for cancer. This just to be on the committee. This speaker was the chairman of that committee. He told us that each time that this committee meets, he has a sign posted on the door leading into the meeting room that reads "Leave your hat, coat, and ego outside the door." What a great idea. He further mentioned that he has ejected people from the committee meetings, people who brought their egos into the meeting. They tried to force their personal agendas on other people at the meetings. It would be nice if this man's integrity were a mandatory requirement for everyone in any of the public safety organizations. Integrity, ethics, honesty, honor. What an interesting requirement. Too bad about all those fucking politicians; they would just be out of work and standing in line at some food kitchen, perhaps learning how to say "Welcome to Walmart." Imagine that for a dream scene.

CHAPTER FORTY-SEVEN

Central Fire Station—the building

Central Fire Station, Portland, Maine, is a unique building for Portland. It is built of gray granite and yellow brick with a flat parapet roof. It houses Engine Five, Ladder One, the heavy rescue, and fire headquarters. The building was designed as a firebreak location for the city following the 1867 Great Portland Fire. It is almost midpoint for the inner city areas. Central is sited almost directly across Congress Street from Portland City Hall. Almost all of the history of the Portland Fire Department is connected to this building. Following the Great Portland Fire, the Portland Fire Department, as a full-time fire department, was created, and this building was a part of that. During the early 1980s, the building began to fall into disrepair, and no effort was made to correct this. Eventually the Fire Administration decided (at the strong prompting of the city administration) to close the building. The building was vacant for almost a year, when a judge in the Portland District Court made the announcement that he was going to occupy the building as his new office. We firefighters had already voiced our resentment over the closing of the building, and now this judge was going to use it as his private office. This also told us why the city had not made any attempt to repair the building and instead had let it go. When the judge found out how much it was going to cost him to repair the building, he backed out on the proposal. The building stayed vacant for two more years. We firefighters with all our combined skills and contacts within the building industry came together. We offered to donate our labor time if the city would provide us with the money for materials to repair the building. A deal was struck. We worked on duty and off duty. We insulated the building. We repaired the damaged areas. We refinished the floors and poured new concrete floors for the second-floor hallways. We rebuilt the roof. We repaired the plumbing and the electrical systems. We installed a new kitchen. All as volunteers. The result was that we reoccupied Central Fire Station. The Fire Administration gave us all many promises of what they would do for those of us who did the work. No promises were kept except to a very few select individuals. But we have the personal knowledge that it was our effort that brought that building back to us. Today, Central is again one of the anchor points for the fire department on Congress Street.

CHAPTER FORTY-EIGHT

Car accidents and drunks

That old saying that "God watches out for kids and drunks." There are so many stories about car accidents that turned out funny. I was driving Engine Three, out of the Stevens Avenue Station when we received this call. About 11:00 p.m., we were dispatched to the end of Capisic Street near Frost Street for a funny smell in the area and an intermittent squeaking noise. When we arrived and looked around the area, we saw a trail of broken brush, small trees, and muddy tire tracks leading in a straight line out into the woods at the sharp corner in the street. This was located on Capisic Street. As we followed the trail into the brush, we heard a small screeching/squealing noise and the smell of burning rubber. About fifty feet off the road, we found a car stuck in the woods. The driver was so drunk that when he went off the road, he destroyed the undercarriage of the car, but he didn't know it. When the car stopped moving. He jammed it into reverse and floored the accelerator and just sat there in the woods with his foot on the gas pedal, thinking that he was backing out. The smell was from the burning rubber from the tires, and so was the sound. We stood quietly beside the car and knocked on the window until he finally noticed us. We told him to shut it off. We determined that he was uninjured. We turned him over to the police. He had no injuries at all, but the car was destroyed.

Another incident was on Johnson Road near the end of the runways for the Portland Airport. We received a call for a car/tractor-trailer truck accident. When we arrived, we found a car, one of my dream cars—a 1975 Jaguar XKE—embedded under the trailer of a tractor-trailer truck. It seems that the traffic light turned green, and the truck started to proceed out across the intersection. Well, the driver of the car thought that he could drive the XKE under the trailer and get away with it. Almost a smart idea except for the dolly wheels on the trailer. He hit them right in the middle of the car's hood. He pushed the car's engine back into the front seat. He had no injuries, but after we got him freed up and he was waiting for a tow truck, he told us that he was in big trouble. It seems that that beautiful car didn't belong to him. It belonged to his girlfriend.

At another accident scene, on Washington Avenue near the intersection with Ocean Avenue, about 2:00 a.m., a young man had been drinking all evening in the Old Port area and was headed outbound on Washington Avenue. He left the road and struck a very large oak tree exactly head on. His car was a small compact car, and it collapsed like an accordion. The engine block was in the front seat. The right front tire was in the passenger seat. The left front tire was jammed into and through the firewall into the driver's seat area. It was exactly between the driver's legs. We could only see some of the driver. But it was enough to see that he was alive. I got creative and ran out some steel winch cable and threaded it through the door columns of the car behind the driver's head. I then attached it to the front hooks on the heavy rescue truck and just gently backed the truck up. This action pulled the car apart in two pieces. The driver fell out onto the pavement on his face. The Police Officers rushed in to see how badly he was injured. Then we all had a pleasant surprise. He stood up and drunkenly checked himself out. His only injuries were some cuts and bruises. He was arrested and taken to jail.

So many accidents. Some funny and some tragic.

Chapter Forty-Nine

People from a whole different generation

This call was for Jackson Street off Auburn Street in the North Deering area of Portland, just a short distance from the Falmouth town line, in Engine Eight's territory. It was a summer day. One of those beautiful days with a blue sky, and it wasn't too hot. We received the call for smoke coming from the window of a single-family residence. We responded, and on arrival, we saw a two-and-a-half-story, single-family home, in very good condition. We saw light gray smoke coming from a first-floor window. We saw that the smoke was being pushed out the window by an electric fan. When we knocked on the front door, the owner met us at the door. He was an older man in his nineties. He promptly told us that we weren't needed there and that if he let us in, we would just break all his windows. His face was all covered with smoke stains. There were tears running down his cheeks. There also was smoke flowing past his head and out the door toward us. He then slammed the door in our faces. Captain R. knocked on the door again and when the very elderly man opened the door again, the captain told one fireman, "Hoss, move him out of our way." Hoss gently picked the man up by his arms and set him off to one side, and we all entered the home. We found a modest home with two elderly people living there. As we entered the kitchen, we found the source of the smoke. The home had an old cast-iron, wood-fired kitchen stove. The couple had been cooking lunch on the stove. The problem occurred when the owners forgot to remove a large pile of newspapers sitting on top of the stove. These papers were smoldering and were just starting to ignite. We put out the fire in the stove, removed the papers, and cleared the smoke from the house, and we didn't break one window. That whole generation of people, the people who had lived through the Great Depression and afterward, they were so self-reliant and so used to taking care of themselves that in their later years it became a challenge to try to help them. We were told hundreds of times, "I can take care of this myself. Just let me alone."

I recall a chimney fire with a similar situation. We were on the roof putting the fire out, and we were puzzled that each time that we put the fire out, it would start right back up again in just a moment. We would knock it down, and a few moments later, it would start again. Finally, the Fire Chief went into the house and found out the problem. The woman who lived there was very angry with us. She was cooking a meal on the old cast-iron, wood-fired kitchen stove in her kitchen, and each time that we put the fire out, she would swear at us and start the fire in the stove again, so that she could finish cooking the meal.

Watch the crowds around the fires

We frequently encountered multiple-alarm fires at the same time. On one occasion, I learned a valuable lesson about people. We responded to Oxford Street and Pearl Street, in the Bayside area of Portland, one summer day. We had been on scene at the warehouse fire, for about ten minutes, when a man standing on the street called out to me. He said, "Hey, there's a fire." I replied, "No shit." The man then said, "There's a fire up that way," as he was pointing up the street behind us to a building about one and one-half blocks away. I looked, and sure enough, we had another fire in an apartment building, two blocks up the street from where we were. I yelled to the Deputy Chief and started running up the street toward this second fire. When we reached the building, this man told me that he lived on the second floor and that his wife was home asleep in his apartment. I followed him up the outside stairs, and when we reached the apartment door, he told me that he had forgotten his key. I kicked in the door and entered the apartment. As I searched the rooms, he ran into the living room, grabbed the television, and ran out the door. I finished searching the apartment and found no one there. I realized too late that the whole story that he had given me was an excuse to get me to kick the door in so that he could steal the television set. Live and learn especially in ghetto firefighting.

It was summertime and nighttime. It was a cool evening when we had an interesting evening shift. I was on Engine Four, out of Bramhall. The fire alarm came in for a multiple-alarm fire on Danforth Street near the corner of May Street, in Portland's lower West End, as we were making entry into a three-story apartment building, we saw fire on the first and second floors. At the same time, we heard another fire alarm go out for a working fire at a lumber company, located six blocks away. The fire that we were at became a two-alarm fire, and the fire at the lumber company became a second two-alarm fire. We had the fire knocked down at Danforth Street, and we were making up. As two of us were dragging hose out of the alleyway between the buildings and feeling a little cock-sure of ourselves, a spectator walking past the alleyway asked us, "Hey, you guys! Dragging that hose out must be hard!." My partner shouted back, "It's easier than trying to push it out." A few minutes later, a woman with a small child stopped and watched us work. She was just being nice when she said, "My son wants to be a fireman." My partner answered her by saying, "Hey! Have you taken him to a head doctor about that?"

Sometimes, when you're really tired, you just let your mouth run away with it for a bit.

CHAPTER FIFTY

Fire Chiefs

In my lifetime, I have known and known of a number of fire chiefs. Some of them are like minor gods to me: Stapleton from Boston (I read his books); Brunicini from Phoenix (I attended a seminar that he taught on municipal fire administration); Coombs from Oklahoma City; and a handful from FDNY including Vincent Dunn, that great Deputy Fire Chief who wrote textbooks on structural collapse and building construction for the fire service. I attended a workshop where he taught tactics and strategy. Some of these men were from volunteer fire departments, and some were from career fire departments. One of the volunteer fire chiefs gave me a piece of advice that stays with me today concerning public speaking before a class. Denny said, "Remember the definition of an expert. An expert is the stranger from out of town with a briefcase in his hand. When you are stepping up onto a stage to speak before an audience, you are the expert that they have come to hear."

One or two of these fire chiefs should have been in a different line of work. One career fire chief was scared of going into burning buildings, and he took his fears out on the men of the department. A number of them were pure political appointees, and on firegrounds, they were worth just about as much. One fire chief spent almost every day drinking in one of two bars in the city. His drinking buddy was a Deputy Fire Chief. The Fire Dispatchers had unwritten instructions that if these two could not be reached on the radio, then the dispatcher was to make telephone calls to these two bars to try to pass on the information to them. This particular fire chief's daily activities were well-known to the city administration, and a blind eye was given to this for more than ten years. This despite numerous car accidents, until one night when it got out of hand, and this Fire Chief was involved in a fistfight in the union bar, and a firefighter was badly injured and later forced to resign from the department. This particular fire chief was a good firefighter; he just could not get a handle on his drinking problem. He asked me to go drinking with him one evening after I had received a commendation from the Portland City

Council for a rescue, and when I declined, I was yelled at. He and the deputy called me "that asshole. We'll get you."

The fire chiefs I know today are by and large a dedicated group of people who are under a tremendous stress load because of the requirements that are made of them in today's culture. Even the small volunteer fire departments are now required to be trained in terrorist activities, hazardous materials, explosives, fire investigation, and so much more. These people are a dedicated group, willing to commit themselves to what needs to be done, and they are a mostly under-recognized group of individuals. They have to work very hard, just in order to stay up-to-date with the requirements and changes in the fire service. I have met and chatted with many of them. I am honored to have known them.

It has been said that for the fire service, there are three kinds of people. There are the used-to-bes. Those like myself who were in it and are now retired. There are the people who are in it now. And there are the wannabes. Some of these wannabes will never have what it takes to be one.

I have also known a few people who were wannabes. And they are a bunch of people that usually pull every underhanded, dirty political trick imaginable to try to become a Fire Chief, and they usually just end up becoming very, very dangerous on firegrounds and emergency scenes, because they do not know what they are doing, and they usually manage to get good firefighters injured or killed. It's too bad that there isn't some federal law to make people like these, made to be held responsible and accountable for their actions.

CHAPTER FIFTY-ONE

Slum landlords I have known

I have no sympathy for slumlords—those people who buy properties in low-income areas of cities and just collect the income from the properties and refuse to put anything back into the upkeep of the property. Over the years, I have dealt with many of them, and like the old saying reads, "I am not on their Christmas card list, and they aren't on mine." On one period, there were two firemen who were slum landlords in Portland. That made me ashamed to work with these men.

We fought one slum landlord for more than fifteen years in and out of court battles, to try to get him to clean up his properties. This man had an estimated $30 million in assets. I fought him for years. Later, after I retired and started to work for the Maine State Fire Marshal's Office, I found myself fighting him again. His favorite trick was to wait until the court-ordered time was up, do a little bit of work on the property, and then go back to court and claim that he was getting work done on the property. The only winners in his game were the lawyers. The city administration would rarely support the Fire Prevention Bureau on these cases, and over the long time frames, fires in these properties would cost untold millions of dollars. On an interesting note, in some cases the insurance companies would not pay claims on fires that occurred at some of these properties because of their condition at the time the fire started. Sometimes, I felt like cheering for this version of street justice.

In some cases, the slumlords were just people who became overwhelmed by the problems of taking care of the properties, and they just could not keep up with the necessary repairs. In other cases, it was a case of pure greed. A person would buy the property and just milk it for all the money that they could get and with no effort at taking responsibility for the conditions of the building. I have heard of cases where the tenants were threatened by armed men who were working for the slumlords because they complained about the buildings' conditions. Some of these slumlords were allowed to continue doing their thing by the city administration.

Chapter Fifty-Two

Terminology that we used

It seems like in the different areas of the United States or the world, firefighters tend to develop nicknames and terms for the same tools or actions that are different from those of other areas. In my travels around to fire departments while taking classes and/or on vacations, I was interested in all these different names for the same thing. Later, while teaching classes in firefighting, I would make a special point of passing on this information to my students. Sometimes, this terminology would create some funny situations.

In one class that I was teaching, one of my students was a carpenter who was also building his own house. This class culminated in the burning of a mobile home trailer, located at the transfer station for the town that we were training in. At an adjacent trailer was a very large, intact "bow window." This carpenter asked if he could remove the window and take it home for his house. I asked the manager of the transfer station, and he replied, "Sure. Just take it." As this carpenter was working hard to salvage the bow window, I knew that it would be very heavy for one person to handle. I told one of the other students, whose nickname really was Bubba, "Hey, Bubba, go take out that window."

And he did. He picked up a Halligan Tool, walked over to the window, and took it out with one good swing. I thought that the carpenter was going to cry at the destruction. I should have been more careful with how I worded my orders to Bubba.

In Portland, we gradually came to use phrases like "drop the ladder," meaning to take it down; to "set the ladder" meant to raise it; large water nozzles on trucks or ladders were "guns"; the driver was a "wheel man" or maybe a "chauffeur"; a "line" was a fire hose; "laying a line" was using an engine to connect a hose line from a hydrant to another truck; a "Jake" is a good fireman; "gimme da tool" meant "give me that tool"; the pipe was the hose nozzle or the tip or the knob; a "Siamese" was a hose fitting where two hose lines came into one hose line; and a "Y" was just the opposite. It was one hose line going into two hose lines. Every department everywhere has their own versions of terminologies.

CHAPTER FIFTY-THREE

Structural collapse

In my studies in firefighting, I was introduced to the books by Vincent Dunn, Deputy Fire Chief, Fire Department of New York (FDNY). I was also privileged to attend a seminar that he taught in Portland. He studied and wrote about building construction for the fire service and about structural collapse. One of the leading causes of firefighter deaths and injuries is from structural collapse. My worst physical injury during my career was from such an incident. I learned about this, and I later taught this subject in classes. I experienced this on other fire scenes. Anytime a building comes under impingement from fire, where the fire burns away the structural elements that hold the building together, this building will collapse, and if there are victims or firefighters inside the building at the time of the collapse, someone is going to be hurt or killed. Of the dozens of instances that I witnessed, I am going to write about just a few, each one different, but with similar lessons.

The first incident occurred on Irving Street in the Woodfords Corner area of Portland. This was a nighttime fire, and it was in very cold weather. The building was a two-and-one-half-story apartment house, one of those homes that had started its life as a single-family house but was later converted to a multiple-family building. It was wood-framed, with a pitched roof with asphalt shingles. The siding was painted clapboards. We responded on the Second Alarm with Engine Eleven. I was driving for Lieutenant H. When we arrived on scene, the lieutenant and I were ordered into the building with a 1¾-inch attack hose line. We made entry into the first floor and made good headway against the fire until we reached the rooms at the rear of the apartment. We encountered a stubborn fire in the walls. As we were working at this, we began to think that we were making good headway against the fire. Suddenly another firefighter ran into the room behind us and hollered out, "Drop that line and get out of the building right now." We were puzzled by that, but we did what he said. Outside we found out just how close to the danger from collapse that we had been in. From the outside of the building (the area of the fire that those of us inside cannot see), we found out that the roof and second floor had collapsed onto the rear of the building, and the whole place was coming down. We neither felt anything nor heard anything because of the noise from the fire inside the space where we were. It's just that close sometimes.

The second incident was on Sherman Street at Deering Avenue Hill. It was warm weather and I was driving Ladder Three out of Stevens Avenue Station. We responded on the second alarm to this fire. I had made a mental note of the time that the alarm was struck. When we arrived on scene, the Ladder Three crew was ordered in for manpower. I was left with the truck in case the ladder would be needed. There was no policy in place within the Portland Fire Department, but because of my studies, I knew the value of a rehab point on fire scenes, so I set up one in front of my truck, a place where I changed air tanks on SCBAs and when some fluids (water) were brought in. I had it all set up at that same place where I was changing the air tanks. The Deputy Fire Chief in command was the same one who had only been in burning building once. He had no personal reference for what was going on inside the building. This building was a three-story wood-framed apartment building with four small apartments on each floor. It had a flat roof with tar-and-gravel roofing. The fire was located in the top floor and the roof structure. Again, because of my studies, I was tracking the time from the alarm to present. My concern was that this was a very stubborn fire, and it was taking a lot of time to make headway against it. I knew that fifteen to twenty minutes of fire impingement was dangerous to the structure. When we hit the twenty-five-minute mark and this Deputy Chief was doing nothing to start bringing the firefighters outside, I voiced my concerns to the Fire Chief from a neighboring city, who was standing with me on the fireground. He and I agreed that the situation was growing hair by the minute. He went to the Deputy Fire Chief in command of the fire. He told him of the concerns. The Deputy Fire Chief refused to change what he was doing and continued to send firefighters into the building. I was surprised that the roof did not collapse onto the third-floor flooring. Later, I would talk to one of the fire captains who had been inside the building. He told me that the roof support structure had burned away, and the entire roof was resting on the interior partitions for the third-floor apartments. These partitions are not load-bearing, and it was just luck that it all didn't come crashing down at any time. As a side note, at this time the Portland Fire Department also did not have an evacuation alarm system in place to call firefighters out of collapsing buildings. "We don't need that kind of shit!"

Bridgeton, Maine. Training burn. The value of evacuation alarm policies for fire scenes. I had been teaching a Firefighter One Academy in Bridgeton for three months, and this was the final class and the hands-on test. This building was a donated building for the fire department to burn. It had been a single-family house in disrepair. Interestingly, the roof was a pitched roof with five layers of asphalt shingles over a single layer of cedar shingles. The building was a wood-framed, two-story building, with asphalt siding (gasoline siding). I had included six other firefighters as coinstructors. I had a well-earned reputation for never having had an injury on any fire training scene that I was in command of. I also took pride in being able to get twenty to twenty-five good working fires out of a burn building before I let it go up in smoke. This day was one of those really good days. We had had our twenty-five fires, and the students learned a lot. There is one additional benefit to being an instructor on fire training grounds. You can take the opportunity to go inside and watch the fire and learn a little bit more about how it acts and moves. This day in the late afternoon, there were six of us instructors gathered around when I decided to let it go. We chatted and decided to go inside the building and watch the "Demon" moving around and maybe learn something new. We crowded into the downstairs hallway and watched the fire moving back and forth at the top of the stairwell. We all were geared up. Suddenly, we heard the Evacuation Alarm going off; on this training ground we had chosen the repeated air horns from the trucks as our Evac Alarm type. When the alarm sounded, we instructors were looking at each other and wondering why the alarm was being sounded. We could see no problem from where we were. But we exited the building according to the evacuation plan. Once outside, I looked at the outside safety instructor, and he was just pointing toward the roof. We had a surprise. The roof had collapsed onto the second floor, and the rear of the building was collapsing onto itself as we were watching. Those of us inside the building had been in great danger, and we didn't even know it. It's really a good policy to have another set of eyes watching the outside of that burning building.

When it comes to masonry construction, the safety rules get stronger. I have taken many brick showers, and it's scary to look back and think of these large buildings collapsing especially if you were inside them at the time. In Vincent Dunn's books, he teaches about collapse zones and the dangers of these even when you are outside the building. A classic example of this is the incident in Boston with Leo Stapleton's chief's aid. The masonry wall of the burning building collapsed outward, hitting a tree, knocking the tree down and across a street, where the chief's aid was standing. He was dead on the scene. I was at the National Fire Academy taking a class at the time. Chief Stapleton was scheduled to be a guest speaker that evening. When the call came in about his chief's aid, he left to return to Boston immediately.

In Portland, we had numerous examples of masonry wall collapses. The one that I remember the clearest was a summertime fire in a warehouse on

Middle Street near the intersection of Franklin Arterial. It was early evening. When we arrived on scene, it was immediately determined that we had an extensive fire. I was driving Engine Four out of Bramhall Station. I took the hydrant at Franklin Arterial and Commercial Street. We hand-laid feeder lines to the ladder trucks that were operating near the building, and I started pumping. Maybe one of the lessons of this could be that pump operators could be given the additional task of being that extra set of eyes on firegrounds. And be taught what to look for and how to look for the classic signs of impending Structural Collapse. I was watching the sides of this warehouse, and I suddenly saw smoke and water coming straight out through the walls. I noticed that the wall of the building was starting to show cracks running through it. I went to Deputy Chief R. and pointed these out to him. He immediately recognized the problem and started pulling the crews out of the building. As we were regrouping about twenty minutes later, these walls collapsed suddenly. This was a tragedy averted. Deputy Chief R. was another one of the very few of us progressive thinkers on the Portland Fire Department at that time. He and I worked on a few projects together.

There can be no notations about structural collapse without mentioning 9/11 and the Twin Towers. No firefighter anywhere can forget exactly what they were doing and where they were at about 8:30 a.m. EST on that date. This writer was working at Unum Insurance Company's office building in Portland, Maine, as an electrician. I was walking past the Unum Internal Security office at the time. I watched as the second aircraft hit the towers, and it all collapsed. My very first thought as I watched it all come crashing down was, *Oh my god! What about all the emergency people on the ground? All that stuff is crashing down on top of them.* Three hundred and forty-three dead on scene, and in the following months and years, another five thousand would die from the effects of the concrete dust and debris. *You are all in our memories and our hearts forever. We will never forget you.*

CHAPTER FIFTY-FOUR

False alarms

Every fire department has them, some more than others. We would go through cycles when there weren't many and at other times when, well, they didn't seem to stop. The worst night that I remember with false alarms was a summer night when two guys were driving through the Woodford's Corner area of Portland and pulling every single street box that they could see. We responded to seventeen false alarms in one hour that evening. The police caught these clowns.

Sometimes we would get really tired of these nights. One evening, in a snowstorm, I was driving the Portland Fire Rescue. We responded to the Oxford Street area street box. We arrived right behind Ladder One. I saw one of Ladder One's crew jump off the truck and start running up the street ahead of the truck. They had arrived on scene and found a false alarm. Paul, the crewmember, had seen the perp's footprints in the snow, and he was chasing them up the street while he was waving a Halligan tool. We thought that he was going to use it on them.

Sometimes we would get a little blasé about false alarms. We had one lieutenant on an engine company who was notorious for calling out false alarms from two or three blocks away from the street box as they were still responding to it, long before he could really see if there was a problem.

One false-alarm response that will always stay in my memories occurred when I was on Ladder Six at Bramhall Station. It was a summer evening, about 2:00 a.m. We had been chasing falses all night, and we were tired. This box came in for Tyng Street and York Street, in the lower West End of Portland. This was close to home for me. I had been raised as a small child on that corner. When we arrived, we found a five-year-old boy standing at the alarm box. We checked his hands, and, yes, he had the dye from the Alarm Box on his hands. But the alarm box was about three feet higher than his head. He physically could not have reached it himself. We questioned him and found out that some older boys had picked him up so that he could reach the pull handle on the fire alarm box. He pulled it, and the older kids ran off and left him to take the blame. We sent him home to his parents with a stern warning. What bothered us the most about this call was that this five-year-old boy was on the streets at 2:00 a.m., and his parents just didn't care. They should have been arrested for that.

We even had the occasional false alarm for a cat in the tree. But most of them were just a pain in the butt.

CHAPTER FIFTY-FIVE

The cold weather

I have mentioned the cold weather before. Sometimes the memories about all that are a little humorous. It was midwinter, and we received a call for a kitchen fire on Riverside Street in the Riverton area of Portland. This fire was confined to the kitchen and living room areas of the house. The house was a single-family, one-and-one-half-story cottage-style home with a pitched roof, clapboard siding, and asphalt shingles on the roof. It was so cold that night the air temps were below zero degrees Fahrenheit. We were the last engine company to stay on the scene. We were still putting the wet on the red in the kitchen, and the Deputy Chief (Red), went out to his car to start his reports while we finished up. He waited and waited for us to exit the building, and we hadn't yet. Finally, he grew impatient, and he came back into the building. He was not happy with what he found. There were four of us huddled in the corner of the kitchen around the last pile of burning debris, and we were keeping the fire going by feeding it small pieces of wood material. The Deputy Chief, "The Big Red Machine," exploded with frustration at us. He hollered out, "What the fuck are you guys doing here?"

We answered, "But Chief. We're just trying to stay warm."

He responded, "You're here to put the fire out. Now put it out, and get out of here."

Boy! He had no sense of humor that night.

This same Deputy Chief was forced to chew us out again, on another long cold evening at the old Portland dump on outer Ocean Avenue. We were there for another extended period. Some of these long sessions there at the Portland dump were for as long as thirty days and nights straight. These dump fires would get started under the surface and just burn away everything underneath, and huge cavities would be formed similar to the problems with the sinkholes in Florida. One of these cavities at a scene one day swallowed a Caterpillar D-8 bulldozer and the driver. On one particular long-term fire scene, we had just started, and there were two fire crews on site. We were bored silly with nothing to do but watch the rats and cockroaches run around. We decided to make things interesting. The following night, we all brought twenty-two rifles with us. We would turn all the truck lights off, wait for ten minutes or so, turn the lights back on, and shoot the rats. By six-thirty the next morning, when the Deputy Chief came out to see how we were doing, there was a pile of about forty dead rats near the front of the trucks. Once again, he was not happy with us. Firemen can get very creative when they are bored.

CHAPTER FIFTY-SIX

On the subject of Haz Mat fires

On a less-than-humorous note about dump fires, you don't know what is burning in these fires, and the smokes and steams from these fires can have long-term hazardous effects on your health. This may be one of many, many causes of cancers in firemen. It's something to think about. Dumps. Dumpsters. Trash bins. Rubbish compactors.

On the same note, dumpsters, car fires, these were also locations where all bets were off on what might be burning. A National Fire Administration report came out around 1981 about the PVC in plastic products and what it would do to human beings if it burned. This is what killed so many of the victims at the MGM Grand Hotel in Las Vegas. And we were walking around in this stuff from motor vehicle fires and/or dumpster fires. In the classes that I taught, I warned my students about what might be in motor vehicles, trucks, railcars, even motorcycles, anything from Hazardous Materials; to radioactive materials; to guns and ammunition; and anything in between. Aerosol cans are like bombs when they heat up and explode. As firemen we just have to be aware of what might be there.

The scariest Hazardous Materials fire that I ever saw was a railroad tank car that was burning. The closest that we could approach it was from one quarter mile away. The tank bottom valve had been broken, and the product ignited. This railcar contained thirty thousand gallons of ethyl alcohol. Alcohol burns almost 100 percent pure, so it burns with no visible flame. This fire was so hot, and there was no visible flame at all. The only indicator of the fire was a column of heat shimmers in the air above the railcar. These shimmers extended upward for hundreds of feet in the air. The only way that we could combat this fire was to protect the exposures and to let it burn itself out. Whew. Alcohol is used frequently as a fuel in many applications and is shipped in tank cars and tank trailers. At the time that I am writing this, we in Maine are still going through the process of recovery from the Lac Megantic railroad fire that killed forty-seven people and destroyed the town. Lac Megantic is 150 miles from here. I have visited there three or four times.

The thought-provoking video that was used in Hazardous Materials training classes was the one showing a Fire Department Officer walking up to a reported rail tank car leaking some unknown product in a rail yard in Chicago. He can see this product leaking from the railcar, and he reaches out and touches it with his fingers and brings it to his nose and mouth. We just do not know what some of these products will do to us if our bodies come in contact with it. Fortunately for this man, the product leaking from this railcar was heating oil. He is lucky to be alive.

We also experienced a motor vehicle accident involving a small truck that was carrying radioactive materials from dentists' X-ray machines. And in one very interesting incident involving radioactive-materials signs on a storage trailer at a car tire dealership on St. John Street in the West End of Portland near Park Avenue, the owner of the dealership thought that he could outwit the local thieves by labeling the storage trailer with radioactive-materials signs. He was given a warning by the police to stop.

During this same time, we encountered a tractor-trailer driver who left his trailer in the parking lot of a fast-food restaurant, in the Morrill's Corner area of Portland, while he visited his girlfriend's apartment. The trouble arose because of what he was hauling in the trailer. The trailer was full of sixty tons of radioactive waste material from the dismantling of the Maine Yankee Nuclear Power Plant. He left it in that parking lot for two days. This driver got more than a warning.

What you can't see can and may kill you. At the time, we had two large cold storage plants in Portland, one located in the Morrill's Corner area of the city and another located on Fore Street in the waterfront area.

The plant in the waterfront area had an incident that stays in my memories. It was in warm weather and in the morning. A workman was operating a forklift inside the building, moving pallets of material around. He hit one of the overhead pipes that contained ammonia coolant. This pipe was three inches in diameter. This ammonia was in a 90 percent concentration and was used as a cooling agent in the plant. The broken pipe sprayed liquid ammonia onto the workman, and he died on the spot within a few moments. Ammonia in this concentration is fatal on contact with the skin. We responded to the rescue call, and within moments, we had six firemen on their way to the hospital. It took over an hour to vent the building so that this body retrieval could be done. Anytime Hazardous Materials are involved in the scene, it pays to stop, to take the time, and to carefully plan out just what you are going to do. According to the textbooks on hazmat, there are more than fifty thousand kinds of materials being shipped around, over, or through this country every day; any one of which can kill you on contact.

CHAPTER FIFTY-SEVEN

Ladder One and David

David D. was a good fireman. He became the driver for Ladder One when it was the Snorkel, and stationed at Central Fire Station. Dave was a good guy, and he was great with that truck. He could put that articulated boom almost anywhere that it was needed including in between the wires of power lines, at a few fire scenes. I spent a few long nights in that bucket.

There are two instances that remain in my memories of Ladder One. On Oxford Street one night at a Two-Alarm fire, we had six trucks on scene and maybe thirty firefighters. We had two ladder trucks in operation. When these aerial ladders are in operation, they require outrigger jacks to stabilize the truck. These outriggers usually extend out from the truck by more than five feet on each side. They also have flashing lights on them for warnings. This particular night, Ladder One was set, and the outriggers were extended. A woman in a car drove up the street past some firefighters and crashed into one of these outriggers. The police officer asked her, "What the hell happened?" She told him that she hadn't seen the flashing lights on the outriggers.

We were always concerned about bystanders at scenes; they tend to focus on the fire itself, and they just don't even see everything else that's going on around them at the time. Ladder One, as the Snorkel, was another truck that is unique to the fire service, with its ability to carry three firefighters and their gear, with the piped-in compressed air and a master hose stream piped to the bucket. With its articulating boom, the maneuverability of this combination makes this a unique truck.

Another long night in Ladder One was at the Cumberland Cold Storage Plant on Fore Street, in the Waterfront area of Portland. This fire call came in during the early afternoon of a summer day. This building was three stories tall, masonry construction, with a flat tar-and-gravel roof. This fire became a Third-Alarm fire very quickly. There are a number of scenes from this fire that stay with me. I was driving the old fire rescue; it was a reconditioned, donated bread truck, and that's what we nicknamed it ("the bread truck"). When I arrived on scene, I started to work with the crews making entry into the building. We had to use circular saws to cut through the overhead doors to make entry. We saw heavy smoke coming from the roof area, but no visible fire. As soon as we got the doors opened, six of us dragged a two-and-a-half-inch attack hose line into the building and started to move up the stairwell toward the third floor. When we reached the third-floor hallway, we faced a strange scene. There was medium smoke. But we were encountering a lot of heat, but no visible fire. We were crawling around on the floor trying to figure out what to do next when I happened to look behind me down the hallway from the direction that we had just come from. The smoke was getting heavier by the minute, and we still could not see a source. The smoke was now banked down to just above waist level. As I looked behind me, I saw a figure standing in the hallway just behind all of us. I began to slowly look upward at this figure. I first saw a pair of uniform dress shoes, then uniform dress pants, a white dress shirt with a Gold Deputy Fire Chief's Badge, a black tie, and a man's florid face. He was wearing a crumpled white uniform dress hat, and he was puffing on a large cigar. This picture of "The Big Red Machine" will stay with me always. He just looked around and said, "We better get the fuck out of here. This place is getting bad."

He told us to drop the fire hose and just get out now. We did. Later, we would find out that because the building was a cold storage plant, the roof was insulated with cork insulation to a depth of eight feet. This was where the fire was burning. We were on scene at this fire for three days and nights before we got it put out.

A second scene from this same fire stays with me. Lloyd C. was a captain, and he was one of the old guys. In the hustle of the initial scene, Engine Six had dismounted its water cannon and was setting it up on the street aimed at the building. Captain Lloyd was helping set it in place when a member of another city fire department, who was trying to help us, walked by the scene, reached out, and pulled the valve handles on the Engine Six Pump Panel to wide open. This sudden surge of water, under 120 pounds of pressure, lifted that water cannon up off the street and threw it backward into Captain Lloyd's chest, knocking him backward onto the sidewalk. We thought that he had been killed. He did spend some time in the hospital with broken ribs. But eventually he returned to work. Sometimes bystanders can be helpful, but sometimes they create more problems than they are worth. There have been many instances of hydrants being turned on prematurely by a helpful passing onlooker.

CHAPTER FIFTY-EIGHT

Reggie W. the cartoonist

The years 1968–1975 we called the manpower reduction years. That time, when the city pushed on us, our manpower was reduced from 320 men down to 180 men, a 43 percent loss. This created lots of problems and some creative ideas—futile, but creative. One solution that we tried was a system of calling up more fire companies as they were needed at fire scenes and calling up these companies one at a time. For example, the officer-in-charge on the fire scene could radio in and say, "Give me another engine" or "Give me another ladder." All this effort was just for additional manpower. On the reports, the fire call would still show just a First Alarm or just a Second Alarm and nothing more. This was also the time that our manpower on the trucks was reduced to much less than the recommended numbers. We were operating with two men on ladder companies and two or three men on engine companies. The only ladder company in the city that ran consistently with three men was Ladder Six, because it was the Seagrave tractor-trailer aerial, and it required a tillerman. I have mentioned that the city contracted out during these years for efficiency studies, on multiple occasions. Each and every time, these studies recommended that our manpower be increased for safety reasons. Each and every time that these studies were completed, the city administration with the cooperation of the Fire Administration circular-filed the studies. And we still kept doing our job; we still kept getting in and facing the "Demon." It was during this time that we firefighters sustained a lot of injuries.

One our firefighters, Reggie W., had a great sense of humor, and he was a good cartoonist. On the truck that he was assigned to, Engine Three, out of Stevens Avenue Station, Reggie drew a side-view outline of a firefighter, and he attached it to the windows of the jump seats on the truck. People could see this and know where we were getting our additional manpower from. This action raised some eyebrows, rattled some cages, caused some chuckles, and created some caustic remarks about "those damn firemen." But unfortunately, it did not change our manpower situation. But, oh, Reggie! Thanks for trying, man!

CHAPTER FIFTY-NINE

Random observations
Changes in truck colors

Over the years, I have seen a wide variety of colors for fire trucks. And at one time, I witnessed a parade in New Jersey that included fire trucks in a wide assortment of colors, every color from black to white, from various shades of green, even to pink and purple. I tend to be a traditionalist when it comes to some parts of the fire service, and for me, fire trucks should be red. My personal favorite is Seagrave red, that deep red that's almost a candy apple red, with gold leaf trim. But that's because of the first truck that I was assigned to: a 1961 Seagrave, a one-hundred-foot tractor-trailer aerial ladder.

Today, well, if the color makes the truck stand out and draws your attention, this makes the person seeing it know that it's a fire truck and not a delivery truck. Well, that's okay. But I still shake my head when I see lime-green trucks; they remind me of some public works vehicles or some truck that you might see doing maintenance on the turnpikes. There are a few things that I am a traditionalist about, and a fire truck's color is one of them.

House explosions

In our culture today, building explosions are getting to be an almost common occurrence. But when I was on the job, these were rare incidents. Two in particular that I remember were both in single-family residences.

The first was another very cold weather fire. The building was a wood-framed older-style building with a pitched roof. The building was located on Presumpscot Street in the East Deering section of Portland. The building's heating system was an oil-fired boiler for steam heat. The incident occurred about 7:30 a.m. The housewife had just stepped out of the home to walk her child to the sidewalk to catch the school bus. The bus picked up the child, and the housewife turned to walk back toward the house when it blew up. The explosion was a smoke explosion that took out the windows and the doors. The investigation was interesting because it showed that over the course of many years the iron pipes carrying the steam throughout the building had created a pyrolysis effect in the surrounding wood of the floors, until it reached a point where the fiber material of the severely dried wood literally exploded. I have tried this out in classes, and it happens. This particular incident happened during an intense cold period in Portland, and the heating system in the building had been running strongly for three or four days. This family was very fortunate. Had this incident happened two hours earlier in the day, then they all could have been killed.

The second home explosion was caused by a faulty natural gas line feeding a single-family home. A small leak had developed at a pipe fitting, and the home's cellar filled with gas vapors. At last the gas vapors found an ignition source, and the house literally exploded. The building was lifted off from the foundation. Fortunately, the occupants were all away from the house when this happened, so there were no injuries. Portland has a very large natural-gas piping system within the city streets. This system has been in place for decades.

In a related note on natural-gas systems: Natural gas is very different from propane gas. Natural gas is a cryogenic gas. It is lighter than air, so it rises if it is vented to the outside and when it is pumped through piping systems. It is at very cold temperatures and at low pressure (about three pounds per inch).

I encountered an incident one day on Oxford Street, in the Bayside area of Portland. A backhoe operator had been digging on the sidewalk in front of an older house. He broke the gas line that led into the house. Engine Five and Ladder One were dispatched to the scene. I was in charge of Engine One, responding as the second due engine. When I arrived on scene, I saw eight firemen standing around an open hole in the sidewalk and trying to decide what to do about this leaking gas line that was still venting into the air. It seems that out of the whole crew of firefighters there, I was the only one who read the books. No one was even close to resolving the hazard. I stepped over to Engine Five's pump panel, reached into my pocket for a cloth handkerchief, opened a valve on the pump panel, and got the cloth soaking wet. I then jumped down into the hole in the ground beside the leaking pipe. Making sure that I had my gloves on, I slapped the wet cloth over the leaking hole in the gas line. It immediately froze itself into place from the cryogenic temp, and the leak stopped. This stopped the leak until the utility company responded later that day and shut off the pipe valve at the street connection. Yeah. I was one of the few guys who read the books.

Some house explosions are really bizarre. In one instance, in a neighboring community, the house explosion was caused by a leaking valve from a twenty-pound LP gas cylinder from a barbecue grill tank that had been taken into the cellar for storage. The vapors found an ignition source with the house furnace. Tragically this was a double fatal fire, with one body being found twenty feet up in a tree near the backdoor of the building.

The climate as a factor in Portland

I have sat down, during the class breaks, at Emmitsburg and chatted with firefighters from all over North America and, in one instance, with a Fire Marshal from the country of Greece. My statement has been that half of what you learn at the academy is learned in the classroom the other half is learned in the social settings. I have chatted with firefighters from Alaska, and the conversation became very interesting when we began comparing climate conditions. We share harsh winters. They have the deep cold. We have heavy snow levels. We share the effects of the sea on the weather. One fireman from the Kenai Peninsula was telling me that they keep multiple hose loads for their trucks because at any prolonged fire scene, they just leave the hose there and return in the spring to pick it up.

One of the very first things that I did not miss after I retired from firefighting was shoveling hydrants or testing hydrants, although it is essential that firefighters know exactly where those hydrants are. And sometimes, in the middle of a snowstorm, after the streets have been plowed a few times, having that intimate knowledge of exactly where that hydrant is, i.e., twenty-five feet between that driveway and just to the left of that utility pole. This knowledge can make a major difference in being able to get the wet on the red.

Portland's annual snowfall can be between sixty and one hundred inches. I have had to probe snowbanks with a ceiling hook to try to find the hydrant while the engine driver was waiting to lay the line on toward the fire scene. There have been some recent news about fire scenes in areas where the cold was well below zero degrees Fahrenheit. The scenes of massive frozen landscapes are familiar to me. Been there, done that. It doesn't make it any easier, but at least the firefighters can know that they aren't alone in having to deal with it.

Ice buildup around the trucks can create some interesting experiences. At one particular fire scene on a bitter cold January afternoon, we responded to a two-alarm fire that burned the top floor of a three-story, six-apartment building on Grant Street in Portland's West End. This area is now known as Parkside. When we set Ladder Six to the front of the building, we set the outriggers for the aerial. As Hoss climbed the ladder to the roof, the tension under the outriggers increased exponentially. Suddenly, the six-inch-thick layer of ice under the ladder outrigger collapsed; this caused the truck to tip sideways. The aerial tip fell about four feet to the edge of the roof (with Hoss on it). Later, Hoss would say that he "thought it was all over for himself."

We had burned a lot of top floors off from these three-story and four-story apartment buildings and changed them into two-story buildings. This was an area where I first encountered the slumlord mentality. It was also my introduction to city firefighting, in my OJT on Ladder Six. I experienced being one of two men, myself and Hoss, who set a fifty-five-foot Bangor wall ladder in a narrow alleyway between two buildings and up to the forty-foot roof edge above us. Just the two of us. Yes, it can be done. It takes a heck of an adrenaline rush to do it. Today, I think about the aches and pains in my body and how many ways that I hurt it. And as I drive through that area again, I am reminded that "this building was four and now it's two," or "that building was three and now it's two," or "that vacant lot used to be a building and now it's no longer there."

One story that stays in my memory was a winter fire on Cumberland Avenue near Deering Avenue, just one block from Congress Street in the West End. Again, this area is now known as Parkside. It had been a deep cold day with temps near zero degrees Fahrenheit. The call came in during the early afternoon. When we arrived on scene, we found heavy fire and smoke showing from the entire top floor. We would later find out that the landlord had emptied the rubbish barrels and apartment wastebaskets down into the dumbwaiter shaft, and there had been cigarette butts in it. The dumbwaiter shaft was in the center of the building and connected the fourth floor with the first floor. This fire had a good start before we were even called. We lost the roof and most of the fourth floor. That night, the temps dropped to below zero degrees Fahrenheit. Everything was frozen hard. We came back on duty the next morning, and at 10:00 a.m., a man came into the station and asked for the Deputy Fire Chief. The deputy was John M., a good friend. A few minutes later, he called me into his office with the man, and he asked me to do him a favor. I said, "Sure. What do you need, Chief?" The man wanted one of us to go back to the burned building and accompany him to his apartment on the third floor to look for his pet cat.

This man lived alone. His only companion was his pet cat. During the confusion at the fire scene, he could not find his cat when he had to evacuate the building. I was in dread of what we would find. His apartment was one floor down from the burned-out top floor of the building. Added to that problem was the subzero temps from that night, in a building that was all water and fire damage. I took the man back to the building, and we entered the hallway and climbed up the third floor. We climbed to the door to his apartment. He used his key to enter the apartment. All that I could envision was finding the body of that cat. When we fought fires, we had an aggressive policy about salvage and overhaul. This was something that I had learned from the old guys. We were always trying to save people's belongings by gathering them into the center of the rooms and covering them up quickly with salvage covers (treated canvas tarps). This fire scene was no exception. As the man and I were searching throughout his apartment, we came to his bedroom, and I pulled back the salvage cover and there was the cat, all curled up into a ball, trying to stay warm and dry. The cat looked up and stood up; the man grabbed the cat with a yell of happy delight. This story had a happy ending.

CHAPTER SIXTY

Paying attention to the scene when you arrive

One of the lessons that I learned early on was from a District Fire Chief from Keene, New Hampshire. I attended his seminar on "sizing up." He commented that the first on-scene fire officer should be a cigarette smoker. My thought was, *You're crazy.* He then went on to explain, "The first Fire Officer on scene should stop what he's doing, light up a cigarette, and, as he slowly smokes it, he should walk completely around the building and look at everything there that he can see. By doing this slowly, he can size up the scene effectively."

He can tell where the fire is, i.e., cellar, attic, kitchen, second-floor bedroom, and how advanced it is, which direction it seems to be moving toward, and what the extra hazards are (LP gas tanks, heating oil tanks, motor vehicles, invalid window stickers, victims inside trying to get out windows, power lines to the building). So much can be learned with an effective size-up. I learned a lot that day. Size-up can also prevent a lot of unpleasant surprises to the oncoming firefighters.

It was a summertime fire on Munjoy Hill. Morning Street is a compact residential area. Most of the buildings are in good repair. This area faces Portland Harbor and its entrance channel. Over the years, it has gone through numerous changes: from a mostly Italian community to housing for workers during World War II, to a rundown area, and now it is in resurgence again as an upscale residential area.

It was about 10:00 a.m. I was in charge of Engine Eleven. We were responding on a Second Alarm to this fire. A four-mile run for us. When we arrived on scene, the Engine Five crew had already entered the building. The fire location was on the first floor. The Engine Five crew entered the stairway for the second-floor apartment and climbed the stairs. What they did not do was determine just how fast the fire on the first floor was moving. As they reached the second-floor stairway landing, the fire broke through the door of the first-floor apartment and pushed out into the stairway, forcing them to retreat into the second-floor apartment. Fortunately, they were able to enter the second-floor apartment, close the door, and make their way to the front of the building, where they jumped from the front porch to the street. A distance of about ten feet. A close call. The fire was held to the first-floor apartment. We were back at the station within two hours. Size-up is important!

In another similar situation, again on a summertime fire call to a condo development, Princeton Pines, on outer Forest Avenue, near the Morrill's Corner area of Portland, a lieutenant from Engine Nine took a young rookie fireman with him into a building that was showing smoke and heat coming from a second-floor apartment. Each condo had its own balcony facing a central landscaped area and the parking lots. I was driving Engine Eight, the Quint. The firefighters entered the second-floor apartment to do a search. Without doing a size-up and checking for an escape route for themselves, they started searching through the apartment. As the fire was given its welcome dose of air from the hallway door that had just been opened, suddenly, the fire erupted outward from the kitchen area and into the apartment's center area, and the firemen were cut off from their escape route. They retreated to the balcony area and from the fire that was aggressively pushing them out of the sliding glass balcony doors. I saw what was happening and quickly set the aerial to the balcony to give them a way out. Even as they were climbing down the ladder, the fire was pushing through the balcony doors out onto the balcony itself. Size up!

There is a term used in warfare called "situational awareness": making yourself stay aware of just what is going on around you at any given time. This is a lesson that we should be pushing in the rookie schools. Just stay aware of what's happening around you, especially within an emergency scene. Unpleasant surprises can come at us from anywhere, and they can do us harm (an aerosol can exploding from a car fire, guns and ammo shooting back at us from a room fire, paint cans in a dumpster, frightened animals charging us at fire scenes). Size up!

CHAPTER SIXTY-ONE

Sometimes what we do is just not enough

We become so emergency scene–focused that we are even drawn to emergency scenes that we encounter, even when we are not on the job. I have been at more than a dozen where I stopped what I was doing and stepped in to help. Today, I am finally able to look, and to see, and to judge whether I can really be any help or not. And sometimes I just keep moving along with the traffic. I was the only responder (for the first twenty-five minutes) at an accident scene in a remote campground on a lake in Rangely, Maine, where a drunken man fell off a twenty-foot cliff. That one was interesting. He had been celebrating a good day of fishing with a few drinks. He was very fortunate. When he hit the ground, his head missed a series of recently cut-off tree saplings. The saplings had been cut off about twelve inches above the ground. They were like a bed of sharpened stakes. His body hit the ground surrounded by these stakes without hitting any of them. His head landed less than four inches from the stakes. If his head had hit them, he would have been impaled on them and died on the spot. A lucky man.

Another incident where I was stopped at a traffic light, in front of a major hotel in South Portland, Maine, and a car drove out around my left side and tried to cross the intersection against the light. He broadsided another vehicle. I jumped out of my truck into the middle of that incident, again because I was the only trained person on scene. It got really scary really fast when I climbed into the vehicle's backseat to evaluate the driver and found myself standing in a two-inch-deep puddle of gasoline, from a ruptured five-gallon gas can that he had been transporting in the backseat of his car. I evaluated his injuries, and as the emergency responders arrived on scene, I passed that info on to them. I also had to stop this driver from lighting a cigarette while he was lying down, crumpled up, in the front seat of that car. Even with the smell of the gasoline all around himself, he still wanted to light one up; he almost lit up himself.

There was a humorous note to this story. When I jumped out of my vehicle to assist, I had left my wife sitting in my pickup truck, in the middle of that intersection. My vehicle was equipped with a manual shift transmission. She did not know how to drive it. She asked another bystander for help, and he drove my vehicle out of the intersection and out of the way, for her. Oh well.

I was recently on the Maine Turnpike with my wife, traveling to a meeting in another city. We came upon a traffic accident between a tractor-trailer truck and a motorcycle. I took one quick look at the motorcyclist's body, the radical angle of the head and neck, the position of the body entangled within the motorcycle, and I knew that it was a body and not a victim. I continued on my travels after calling it in to the Maine State Police Emergency Dispatch Center. There was nothing that I could help with. Sometimes we can help, and sometimes we can't.

Leo Stapleton from the Boston Fire Department said, in his book *Thirty-Five Years on the Line*, "Sometimes we win and sometimes we make parking lots." We have to remember that. Sometimes we can make a positive difference, and sometimes we just can't. Those of us who have spent years doing this kind of work and have the experience behind us can look at a scene and very quickly determine: "Can I help or not help? Is this situation a victim, or is it a body?"

Chapter Sixty-Two

Police Patrol Officers

I have mentioned that the police patrol officers are invaluable to the fire service. Many instances of fires are seen early on by these patrolmen and called in before they can become extensive. And these patrol officers are mostly roving the streets even when we are back in our stations. They are an invaluable source of information for us, whether they are someone who sees where the homeless street people are hiding out or where someone is lighting fires. They are our eyes out onto the street. And it pays to remember that, for those of us who work the streets, we are all in this together, whether we were working as Firemen, Policemen, or in EMS. I have friends today who I met when they were on footbeats, and I asked them to come inside the station for a while to warm up and to have a meal with us. They have become lifelong friends. This is a special kind of "we were there together" brotherhood.

That said. There have been a few cases of the police officer seeing something that looked like a fire, when it wasn't. We had a series of fire calls in hot-weather months that point this out. At that time, Commercial Street in Portland had railroad traffic frequently moving along it. In the early mornings, some of these railcars would be parked on the tracks, waiting for the morning crew to unload them. Sometimes, these railcars were refrigerated cars with compressors mounted on them to keep the contents either cooled down (like produce) or frozen (like meat). It sometimes happened that the patrol officer would be finishing up a slow night and struggling to stay awake when he would see the vapor exhaust from these compressors on the railcars, venting into the hot, humid air. It can look like smoke from a fire. So about 5:00 a.m. or so we would be out the door to Commercial Street for a reported smoke from a railcar fire and be back in the fire station, in fifteen minutes, to put on the coffee and wake up for the day.

But they are still a valuable asset for us. And they should still be welcome to the station meals. We had two officers who transferred from PD to Fire. One stayed with us to his retirement. Eddie was a great guy and is still a friend. Jeff stayed with the Fire Department for about eight years and then transferred back to the police department because "this Fire Department stuff is just too slow for me. I want more action." Jeff was on my truck when I was a lieutenant. He was a great Fireman. He was kind of like an albino gorilla. Jeff is still a friend.

Connections that last a lifetime

I am frequently puzzled and sometimes very disturbed by the lack of brotherhood that I have encountered from most of the firemen I had worked with during my career. With the exception of three or four men, we never seem to gather together to just hang out a little while. The (poor) running joke is that the only time that we come together to say "hi" is at someone's funeral. And I find that this is not uncommon for those of us who have been warriors together. I don't know if this is a situation unique to the Portland area or if this is common throughout the fire service in North America. I have visited other cities and have been more than welcomed into the stations and into their lives, but in the Portland area, it's a feeling of "Oh, you're welcome, but don't stay too long." A few of these men and women that I meet in public are friendly, and we chat for a bit, but there is no regular coming together to just be in each other's company.

I have recently become involved with the American Legion Post near my home. And I was immediately welcomed and made to feel at home. The camaraderie was so welcoming. My military service pre-dates my fire service by two years. At the American Legion Post, we just sit and chat and perhaps work on mutual projects for the community. Sometimes, we just sit in each other's company, a group of people who have seen the elephant who are just sitting down together, enjoying each other's company, having dinner together, joking, laughing, and just being there for each other. No booze, no drunks, just enjoying each other. I have offered my help and my home to other firemen from Portland on numerous occasions, and it has been consistently rejected. I finally reached the point where I told the Retired Fireman's Association to take me off their mailing list. I no longer will offer anything to them.

Perhaps someone, at some time, can do the research and come up with a master's thesis on this subject, and it would make a good subject for one. Why do these old warriors, who no longer have to go into battle together, tend to shy away from contact with each other? It's something to think over.

Chapter Sixty-Three

Joey

In my observations, this was the incident that took the heart out of
the Portland Fire Department. This was that crux point in that timeline of
the Portland Fire Department. That time when the future path of the fire
department could take one of two very different paths. The date was March 24,
1980. The incident took place at 83 Oak Street in Portland's peninsular area,
in town, just a few steps from Congress Street. The name of the business, at the
time, was the Phoenix Restaurant. The time was 2:31 a.m.

In the previous twenty years, the Portland Fire Department had incurred
three on-duty firefighter deaths, one from an accident involving two fire trucks
and two from heart attacks following fire calls or emergency calls. This incident
would be the first firefighter death within a burning building, since February
24, 1945 (an explosion and wall collapse).

I have written about that old guy, Lou, who took me under his wing when
I first went on the job. He was one of those World War II vets (navy, Pacific
theater combat). I would frequently have breakfast in his kitchen, with his
children playing around us as we ate—Lou's wife Babe, the two girls Mary and
Janey, and the boys, moving around the house. I remember Mary as a three-
year-old girl. This family slowly became family to me. Lou would be like a father
to me. He guided me. He taught me. He chewed on me, once in a while, if I
did something really stupid. Sometimes, that happened frequently. He and I
ended up working at different ends of the city and on different shifts. We tried
to keep in touch. The years would pass quickly, and suddenly, it was March of
1980. Mary had been married for some time to a young man named Joey C.
They were so much in love. They had two children. Joey had followed in Lou's
footsteps and became a Portland fireman. I didn't have a lot of contact with
them. We worked on different shifts, and it could be months at a time between
chats. Lou retired. He had been on the job for over thirty years. Lou would
later die of a heart attack, while at his own home. It was the following year after

Joey's death. Lou's wife told me, "He died from a broken heart." The tragedy would continue for years later.

There is very little information that has circulated around about what happened. Parts of it have been handed to me, unasked for, and in piecemeal form for over many years. Some of it come from witnesses' personal experiences. Some of it come from comments made by close friends.

Back to that old basic: Origin and Cause! That basic foundation element of fire investigation. Where did it start and how did it start?

There have been two names mentioned as doing the investigation into this fire. All records have long since been destroyed. It's been thirty-seven years now. There are two separate names mentioned as the fire investigator for this incident. One man is now deceased. This man was an Investigator with the Maine State Fire Marshal's Office at the time. This man had also been a Deputy Fire Chief with the Portland Fire Department. He had retired and gone to work with the State Fire Marshal's Office. The second name mentioned is of a man within the Portland Fire Department who had had no prior training as an investigator and a reputation to never ever determine that a fire was arson. He always determined that the fires were always caused by an electrical problem or, in one case, wind blowing through a closed window and overturning a candle that ignited a carpet.

The determination on the Phoenix Restaurant fire was that it was caused by an electrical problem. Two years later, a man working part time as a guard at the Cumberland County Jail reported to have overheard a conversation by a man who was in the prison for multiple arson charges from other fires in Portland. This man was bragging to another inmate that he had started this particular fire. No investigation was ever done. One retired Portland Fire Department captain, who has since died, told me that he eye-witnessed a conversation between two fire chiefs that the fire incident reports for this fire were rewritten multiple times and worded as such to protect themselves.

In addition, for two decades prior to this fire, elements within the city had been fiercely working behind the scenes to prevent members of the gay community from moving to Portland and establishing themselves here. The owners of the restaurant at the time of the fire were a gay couple.

The bottom line is that this is firefighter LODD. On-duty death was the straw that broke the camel's back when it came to the heart of the department. In the aftermath of this death of a firefighter, the heart of the Portland Fire Department stopped beating. The tragedy is that no one was there who was willing to do CPR for this victim.

On a final note, in 1892, the British author Rudyard Kipling published the poem "Gunga Din." It was about a man who was beaten and abused by British soldiers in India. This man rises above all abuse and becomes a hero by saving the lives of some of his abusers. In the last stanza of Kipling's heroic poem, he wrote this description:

Din. Din. Din.
You lazarushian leathererd, Gunga Din.
Tho I've flogged you and I've flayed you.
By the God that made you.
You're a better man than I am Gunga Din.

When I think of the abuse that I experience while working as a firefighter in Portland, I have endured, I have learned, I have survived, I have evolved to come out of it all as a "Gunga Din" to those who did the abuse.

A quote given by a good friend of mine, as I struggled through those first two years after my forced retirement, stays with me today. He said,

"Just remember, Bob, that the strongest steel comes from the hottest fires."

I am that strong man who survived all that was thrown at me during those years. I am so much a better man than those who tried to push me down into the mud and to keep me there. I have risen from all that abuse to become a man who spends his time reaching out to help other people who are hurting, those who are looking for someone to help them. A man with the reputation for being a healer. I am highly respected for what I do. I am a product of my life experiences. I have become that piece of strongest steel. I am a Reiki practitioner and a shamanic practitioner.

"What determines us is not the hand that life deals us. What determines us is how we play the damned hand."

EPILOGUE

Some of my thoughts come from a place of residual bitterness. But as I have written, my footsteps have brought me along a strange path to where I am today. Today I am a healer. I am an author. I am a writer. I am an inspirational speaker. I speak to other people who are starting on this path of recovery from trauma.

This story is my gift to firefighters everywhere. And this poem is my hope to all of us who chose to face the "red demon" to save others:

When that firefighter stands before Heaven's gates.
He will shuffle his feet and mumble his words,
perhaps with a little embarrassment,
as he hears these words spoken to him.
By those who wait at those gates.
Welcome, friend. You have earned your place here.
Come in. Sit down. And rest.
Ya done good, kid.

Lightning Source UK Ltd.
Milton Keynes UK
UKHW011452110920
369746UK00001B/25